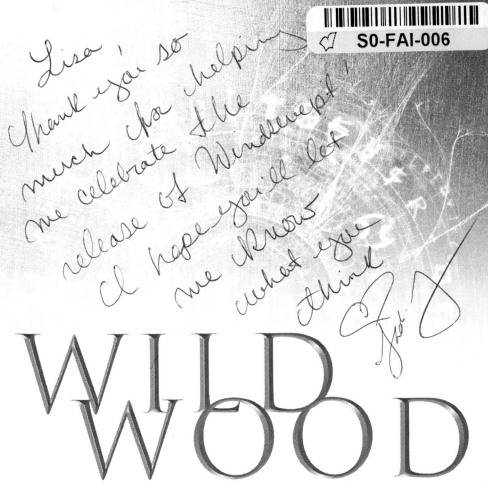

WILD WOOD

-THE HIGHTOWER TRILOGY-

BOOK ONE

JADIE JONES

The Parliament House Press Edition, September 2017

WILDWOOD

ISBN: 978-1976389122

Cover & Interior Design by
Shayne Leighton | Parliament House Book Design
machoviprods@gmail.com

Edited by
Chantal Gadoury

Published by The Parliament House
www.parliamenthousepress.com

Printed in the United States of America.

WILD WOOD

PROLOGUE

Virginia's trees look like they're burning. Most of them blaze crimson or gold, but some still have a chokehold on their green. I wish they'd give it up already.

Leaves are more beautiful when they're dying . . .

PART I

TRADITIONS

The sweet scent of coconut pancakes draws me from the edge of sleep. I smile, knowing my mother is standing in the kitchen downstairs mixing batter, no doubt wearing a few clumps of it in her coal black hair. I toss my denim quilt aside, cool air whisking across my skin, and blink against the warm light of dawn that filters through the old lace curtain panel covering my window and sets the worn wood floor of my room aglow. The constant autumn rain must have finally offered a reprieve. My mother will be happy to see it. She's convinced a clear sunrise on a person's birthday is a sign of good things to come.

As I pull on jeans and a shirt, Dad's laughter rumbles up the stairs, and then the fire alarm chirps. Mom has probably burned a pancake on the griddle.

In the kitchen, Dad is opening the window behind the sink, and Mom is perched on one foot in a wooden chair with her back to me, stretching to fan the smoke away from the alarm.

"I swear this thing is too sensitive," she mutters. There's a streak of flour on her hip and a glob of batter on the sleeve of her T-shirt. My mother can forecast rain better than any meteorologist. She can predict the approach of a gust of wind a few minutes before it roars across the Shenandoah Valley, but she can't cook to save her life.

There are three plates on the table. Two of them are still empty. Mine has a short stack of blobby pancakes and a streak of runaway butter. A couple charred pancakes are tossed on the counter, and one more is on the floor at the foot of the trash can.

My dad grins at her over his shoulder and catches sight of me standing in the door.

"Happy birthday, Tanzy!" he says. "It's the big eighteen. You know, Hope, Tanzy's an adult now. You should make her do the cooking," he teases, and snaps a washcloth in my direction. His smile is all teeth, and his amber eyes glitter. It's the one physical trait we share. Otherwise, I don't look much like either of my parents.

"I've made her coconut pancakes for her birthday every birthday since she was six. She may not be home for her birthday next year." Mom's chin quivers. She presses her lips together.

"I'll come home for my birthday, Mom." I slide into my seat and shovel in a bite. It isn't cooked all the way through, but it's warm, and sweet enough to chew and swallow without making too much of a face.

"Thank you, Tanzy," she says, casting a mock glare at my dad. He winks at me before disappearing through the door that leads to the back porch. He reappears less than a minute later with two mason jars full of wild flowers.

"For my girls," he says, and places one on the window sill and the other in the middle of the kitchen table. "Birthdays are big days for moms, too."

"Travis, when did you pick these? Did you leave any flowers in the garden?" Mom arranges the blossoms with her nimble fingers, and then leans into them, breathing deep.

"Why do you think I got up early this morning? It's freezing out there," he says, watching her. "Weatherman said the temp is going to drop overnight and the whole valley will be covered in frost tomorrow morning. They'll all be dead in twenty-four hours anyway."

"Weatherman is wrong," she replies, one corner of her mouth curling up.

Dad snorts. "We'll see." He rolls his eyes, but I know he believes her. "Eat up, Tanzy. We have a lot to do today."

"Tanzy has school today," Mom replies.

"You cook her coconut pancakes, and then she comes with me to the farm. You have your tradition, we have ours." He winks at me. "Besides, she's a senior. Isn't the rest of this school year just for show? And who says she's going to college? What if she decides to ride professionally?"

"Travis Hightower," Mom scolds. "We'll argue about this tomorrow. As for today, stick to tradition." She wipes her hands on the front of her pants. "But make sure you pick up any homework assignments while you're out. And please get home before dark. I made a dinner reservation for six p.m."

Dad makes a face. "Isn't that a little early?"

"I'm pretty sure that's when normal people eat dinner," I say, and then choke down a sticky clump of semi-cooked batter.

"We are as normal as normal gets," Dad replies. "We'll do our best, honey. Let's get a move on, Tee. I'll take my breakfast to go." Dad kisses mom on the cheek, scoops a fresh stack of pancakes onto a paper towel with one hand and picks up his metal coffee mug with the other, and then heads through the back door toward the truck.

"Have fun," Mom concedes, "and please be careful." She glances out the window at the streaked sky and gnaws on her bottom lip. Her fingernails tap a quick rhythm on the countertop. I take my plate to the kitchen sink and follow her gaze to the glowing dawn. I wonder what she sees in it, and why she seems to hunt it for answers every morning.

"We'll be fine, Mom," I offer.

"I know."

"Thanks for breakfast," I say. "I really will come back every year, no matter where I go after graduation. Nobody does coconut pancakes like you do."

"Thank you, sweetheart." She looks at me, blinking rapidly. "Now go, the day's wasting," she says, and then turns back to the sun. I steal one more glimpse of her, and follow Dad to the truck.

We ride in silence for the first few minutes. Dad rolls up the pancakes with one hand so he can eat them like a burrito while he drives. Once he finishes, he wipes his mouth with the paper towel and then tucks it into the pocket of his flannel shirt.

"I don't know why you like those," he says, and sucks at his teeth.

"I haven't liked them since I was about ten," I admit.

Dad lets out a honk of a laugh. "You're a good girl, Tanzy," he says. He turns up the volume on his favorite radio station to listen to the morning show. The voices fade in and out for the first few minutes as we make our way to the main road. The radio host's voice becomes audible, announcing the beginning of the routine Science Fact or Fiction Friday segment.

"With us today is Dr. Andrews, who has a rather extraordinary theory about light and lightning, and some compelling studies to back up her claims. Dr. Andrews, thank you for joining us."

"Thank you for having me," she answers.

"So Dr. Andrews, give us your science fact."

"Did you know that the human eye sees less than one percent of the color spectrum, and our ears hear less than one percent of the sound spectrum?"

"No, I did not."

"What do you think is in all that clear, all that quiet?"

Dad glances at the radio dial as if checking the station.

"I don't know. I haven't thought about it," the host answers.

"What if I was to tell you that there's an entirely separate world in the clear, undetectable by human senses."

"A world?" the host repeats. I shift in my seat.

"Yes, a world," the woman continues. "A world happening around us all the time. It has been operating alongside ours like two plays on one stage."

"Do you have proof of this world?"

"None that you'd believe," she replies. A chill of interest conjures goose bumps from my elbows to my wrist. I pull the sleeves on my jacket down to cover my knuckles.

"Well it's pretty safe to invent something that you claim you can't prove."

"There's nothing safe about it," she answers.

"I'm not sure what this has to do with light or lightning." The host's voice raises an octave, and his question sounds more like an accusation. I lean toward the dash.

"Lightning and other weather events aren't random. They're tools of—"

"Okay, that's all the nonsense I can take for one morning," Dad interjects, his voice filling the cab, and turns the knob on the radio until a country song comes in clear enough to recognize. "Ruined my morning show and my drive," he grumbles. "Let's hope your mom didn't hear that woman spreading her paranoid crap. She'll stuff our house with furniture from floor to ceiling just to take up all the empty space. A world in the clear." He huffs. "What's wrong with these radio shows and news reports anymore? All they do is try to stir people up. They'll give any nut a microphone and air time so long as it'll get a reaction out of somebody."

My gaze drifts out of my window, and to the clear air whistling by the car as we wind down a tree lined road, soaring skyward until it fades to black thousands of miles above us. Maybe it's just the sound of the tires grinding against the asphalt vibrating through the bottom of the old Ford truck, or the whine of air curling around the hood, but the silence seems fuller than it did a moment ago.

"You are your mother's daughter," Dad says softly. "Don't give wild hares prime real estate in your head. Your mom thinks her fears keep her safe, that they prepare her. All fear does is build walls, Tanzy—walls she can't break because she's convinced herself they're useful."

"I can cook. And I would rather be outside than inside," I say, listing off the first two differences I can think of between my mother and me. I can't imagine islanding myself at home the way she does. We only have one vehicle because she doesn't like to drive and won't go anywhere alone. In the last year, the walls of my room, of every room in our house, have felt a little closer in than they did before, the ceilings lower, too. Still, my heart sinks. I have felt the rabbit of nervousness race through me with nothing prompting the chase. What if, one day, I need walls the way she does?

"Before you came along, your mom couldn't stand to spend a whole day inside. Hell, even a single lazy morning would make her agitated, and she'd need to go for a ride. Then she had that bad fall, and she didn't want to have another one. Taking a risk has a higher price tag attached to it when you have someone depending on you. And it's not just that. Being a parent changes things—changes everything. You see the world through the eyes of someone whose sole purpose becomes keeping a tiny, helpless baby safe. This world we're in has more sharp edges and teeth than you realize."

"Now who's paranoid?" I smile at him.

"You'll see one day, if you decide to have a kid of your own," he says, his gaze following the nose of the truck as he makes a turn.

"That's a big if," I say.

"It's also a long ways off. It better be, anyway." He winks.

"Dad, seriously." I fold my arms across my front. "But is Mom . . . is she okay? I know me leaving next year is hard on her. But she wants me to go, doesn't she?"

"Of course she does. She'll feel better once you know what you want to do and where you're going. It's the unknown that bothers her most. But you don't need to worry about her. She's stronger than you could ever imagine. I think when you have to raise yourself like she did, well, it shapes your perspective."

"What really happened to her parents? I know you guys have said no one knows, but I always thought maybe it was some secret you were keeping until I was an adult or something. I am eighteen now." I raise an eyebrow, and try to keep my tone light.

"It's just something your mom isn't willing to talk about. It took me a long time to accept it, and it's natural for you to be curious. That's a piece of your family and your history, too. But whatever it is, your mom keeps it from us for her own reasons, and I have learned to respect that."

"I know." I bite at the inside of my cheek, my mind still digging at the dark place in my mother's past. I'm not as curious about who the people were in her life as I am interested in who she was during it.

I stare at the eastern horizon. Dad has watched the sunrise through the windshield of his truck on this drive to Wildwood Horse Farm six days a week for as long as I can remember. Nested against the west side of Virginia's Shenandoah Valley, the sunrises are long and spectacular. Mostly, so are the days. The sun comes up. The horses eat. Some of them are worked through training exercises, some are shown to potential buyers, and the rest are turned loose to run in the pasture. Stalls are cleaned. Water buckets are filled. Aisles are swept. Students are taught. The horses eat again. The sun goes down. He drives home. Aside from the sun, Dad controls everything at Wildwood. He is the head trainer there, and the biggest gear in the proverbial clock, making the other parts turn.

Next year will be different. Where will I be? Mornings will either find me in a saddle, working to climb the rungs of the international show jumping circuit, or sitting in a desk with a college text book propped open in front of me. Either way, it won't be here in this truck. It's hard to imagine my world changing so unequivocally while theirs remains the same, save my absence.

We pull into the parking lot at Wildwood Farm. We are the first car here. Dad could turn over the first daily chores to the staff, but he likes to be the one to start each day, to see how each horse has come through the night, and wants to be the one to discover anything out of the ordinary, not be told about it secondhand.

Today, the morning runs like clockwork. I am allowed to come to the farm for my birthday, but I'm certainly not allowed to throw off the farm's routine. I wouldn't want it to. The routine is a heartbeat, a living thing, breathing life into the cracked concrete aisles and faded barn walls. A horse farm isn't wood and sand and grass and steel. It's the movement that happens around and in and on the wood and sand and grass and steel.

After a quick lunch, we unload a tractor trailer's worth of alfalfa into the hay shed. My dad throws a bale of hay like most people toss laundry into a hamper—easy and mindless. I grit my teeth to keep from grunting with the effort it takes to try to keep up with him. By the time we're halfway through, sweat beads along my scalp and trickles into my ears. The radio show from this morning resurfaces in my mind. Dad's right, that woman was a loon. She's probably never worked a day on a farm, never felt the ache of real labor, the release of exhaustion. If she'd just look around at her own world, maybe she wouldn't need to invent something invisible, and impossible to prove or disprove.

My thoughts drift to my mother. I don't know how different I would be if I grew up without parents or any family to speak of. Who would she be if she'd had the security of walls and home-cooked meals, no matter how badly they were burned? I wish she'd tell me about her life growing up, and I wish she would want to be here with us on days like this. Maybe a hard day of farm work is exactly what she needs to remember that life doesn't always have a twist lurking around every corner.

Dad waves at the driver as the empty rig pulls up the driveway.

"Do you want to take Teague and Harbor for a ride in the woods, Tanzy?" he asks. "It's the first pretty day we've had in a while. It's not going to last, though. The radar looks busy again in about an hour."

I pause, studying his face for any sign he's kidding. I still have stalls to clean, and he has three client horses on the schedule for training sessions. Dana McDaniel, his assistant manager, has the day off. Not to mention my mother expects us home at a decent hour. There's no time for a leisure ride on our own horses.

"Your mom was right. This might be your last birthday at home for a while, depending on where you are next year. We should make the most of it," he continues.

"Okay," I answer slowly, waiting for him to change his mind or list off what we need to take care of before we tack our horses. Instead, he retrieves his helmet from his office and heads to his horse's stall. I hustle to Harbor's stall, buckle her halter, and jog down the aisle to where Dad has tied Teague for tacking.

"We haven't done this in too long, Tanzy," he says on an exhale as we finish fitting the bridles to our horses. "Life is short. Too short. Sometimes you have to slow down and take in the view. I don't care what that whack job said on the radio this morning. A big clear sky is one of my favorite things on earth, and I think we should go enjoy a little piece of it. Let's ride up the ridge. I bet the river is up high with all this rain we've had."

"Are you sure we have time? Mom did say to stick to tradition. Leaving work behind . . ." I trail off and glance back at his office door, imagining the to-do list printed on the whiteboard. It's only half-done. "Well, it's not tradition," I finish. My middle stirs and twists. Is this just one of the wild hares dad was talking about before? Is this how it all starts, and then one day I'm staring out my window at the sun, reading its color and clarity for omens of the day to come? My entire life is going to change in a matter of months. Change is a good thing.

"Maybe it's time we start a new tradition. A birthday trail ride sounds like a good one. Are you coming?" Dad asks.

I steel myself with a quick breath in. Harbor peers at me, black eyes round and soft. "Yep, here we come," I say, and lead her down the hall.

For Every Action

The trail to the ridge is narrow and overgrown, and runs along the top of a ravine. Dad and Teague take the lead. Our horses pick their way carefully down the path, trees encroaching from the left, and the ground giving way to a growing drop on the right. The river roars and spits at us from the chasm floor. Teague spooks as a fallen branch sweeps downstream, spinning in the frothy current.

"Easy, boy," Dad calls out, his voice low and gravelly. Teague settles beneath my dad, but his tail still arches with awareness.

Harbor's head swivels from her neck, and her ears are pricked so hard they nearly touch. I step deeper into my stirrups and stretch taller in the saddle, preparing to slow or steady Harbor if she bolts.

"We should've worked them in the arena first; ridden some steam off," I shout over the noise of the river.

"We'll be fine," he answers. "They'll be worn out by the time we get to the top."

We continue the ride in silence, each of us focused on our horses. The climb steepens, and the terrain becomes rocky. The roar of the river fades with the increasing distance to the bottom. The trees begin to thin out. The few that remain are tall and spindly. The lookout point becomes visible ahead, and already we can see where the tips of far off mountains cut into the cloudy horizon like the teeth of a saw.

With miles around us visible and the sound of the river faded to a whisper, Harbor finally relaxes, stretching her neck out low in front of her. I pat her sweaty shoulder and glance ahead at Teague. His back legs and flanks are covered in white lather. Rivets of sweat dribble down his cheeks.

"Teague still seems pretty keyed up," I say.

"We'll both sleep good tonight," Dad says with a grunt as he blocks Teague's sudden sideways movement with his leg. Teague bows away from the pressure and nearly crab-steps into a tree.

"You're being ridiculous," Dad says to his horse. "I don't know that you'd survive a single day in the wild." Teague snorts and shakes his head.

I smile at the two of them. "You treat that horse like he's the son you never had."

"Who says he's not?" Dad takes the reins in one hand and strokes Teague's dripping neck with the other.

Dad reaches the summit first, and moves Teague over so I can stand Harbor beside him. The green of the valley spills out below us. Overhead, heavy clouds skirt across the sky. Sunlight and shadows play tag on the emerald floor. I watch a shadow race to the end of the green, and then grow as it climbs the wooded foothills bordering the other side. Teague drops his head and searches the ground for something to nibble on, finally relaxed enough to be interested in potential food.

"See, there can't be a world in the clear. The rays of sun pass right through." Dad points to a beam of light that pierces through the cloud cover and turns a column of clear to gold. "There's not nothing there. Or there's already enough there. Whichever way you want to look at it."

"That lady really got you worked up, huh?" I peer at him.

An acknowledging smile pulls at the corners of Dad's mouth. "It's not that." He stares out across the valley. "It's your mom, and how people like that woman pray on sensitive, innocent souls like her."

"But you said—"

"I know what I said." He pauses. "Sometimes, this world finds innocence, and does whatever it can to save it, grow it, and help it last. But other times, it tracks the innocent like a wolf tracks a lamb, and when people target the innocent at heart . . ." He pauses and shakes his head. "It just upsets me, is all."

"Dad—"

"Hold on, now Tanzy. I'm not finished."

"Okay."

"That's why I want you to go chase down whatever dream you have. Whatever it is that makes you happy to get out of bed in the morning, you go after it, and don't you let anyone or anything stop you. Distance, time, stepping stones, setbacks—they're all a part of it. You can make mistakes. You can take wrong turns and the long way. But if you get your sights set on something, something that really, truly moves you, don't you dare quit. You promise me?"

I stare at him. My eyes and throat burn. "I promise."

"Good. Now let's get off this damn ridge before the storm rolls in." He pulls his helmet off and rakes his fingers through his auburn hair. "Lord have mercy I haven't sweated like this in a minute."

I stare past him and out across the clear, wondering if there's a dream he gave up on, or if this is his dream and he has everything he's ever wanted. I nearly ask him, but hesitate when a gap in the clouds allows the sunlight to beam through. Between the moisture in the air and the position of the sun, a rainbow blankets the valley. The colors intensify, becoming iridescent. I lean forward, my breath in my throat. Something big and dark passes across the face of it. I glance up at the sun, but it's still in plain view.

"Dad, look." I point. "What is that?" I whisper.

"What is what?" He drops his helmet back on his head and follows my gaze.

"That." I look from the rainbow to my dad and back again. The colors have begun to fade, but they're still plain to be seen.

"What do you see?" He frowns.

The dark thing circles, then swoops upward.

"Dad, that! Look at that!"

"Tanzy, I don't see anything," he says, frustration punctuating his words. Teague whirls, excited by the sudden shift in energy. "Whoa, boy. Easy." Dad clamps down on the reins and then eyeballs the ledge, which is precariously close. Beyond it, the rest of the rainbow vanishes, and the moving shadow fades into the dark places on the valley floor.

"I thought you knew better than to startle a green horse, much less on the edge of a cliff," he grumbles.

"Sorry," I murmur, flushing. What had I just seen? Why hadn't he seen it too? Or was he not as impressed with the rainbow effect as I was? That shadow though . . . it moved differently than the dark places cast on the ground by the passing clouds.

"No, no. I'm the one who's sorry." He heaves an exhale. "A horse has to get used to unexpected things happening around it. I just like a little more wiggle room than this when they do."

Cold wind sails across the ridge. A spritz of early rain patters the ground, and the valley is swallowed up in the shadow of thick storm clouds. Lavender lightning forks across the sky.

"Come on. It's about to get ugly." Dad wheels Teague to face down the path. Teague bounces sideways, eager to have turned toward home. "Don't tell your mom I let us get caught in the rain. I'll never hear the end of it," he calls over his shoulder.

I snort, imagining the face she'd make. If she'd been here, she would've known exactly how long we had before we needed to start back down the trail. It'd be really nice if we were all here together. Maybe if she saw the valley and how beautiful it is, she'd start riding again.

"Hey Dad, do you think we could convince Mom to ride up here with us for your birthday? I think this is a pretty great new tradition." I shield my face from the sting of rain.

"What was that, Tanzy?"

"I said . . ." A flash of blue light draws my eye to the right, at the same time Harbor jumps left. Is lightning already that close? No thunder comes. The only sounds are the rain drumming the earth, and the growing hum of the river. The clear place above a tree branch distorts and ripples, outlined in a sapphire glow. The blue fades to deep purple and then inky black, and begins to spread inward, vibrating and grainy like static on a television screen as it fills in the space. I don't know what it is, but Teague won't like it.

"You said what?" Dad prompts.

"Dad, stop," I call out.

"What's wrong?" Dad twists in the saddle to look back at me, so he doesn't see the crackling black not ten feet away from his horse, or that Teague is lifting his head, pricking his ears. Teague's haunches tense, and he coils deep into his hocks like the compression of a metal spring. I suck in a breath, and the brisk air pricks my chest from the inside, when the darkness tumbles from the tree and fills the narrow trail.

Dad rights himself, trying to stay center as Teague shifts beneath him, but he's too late. Teague rears to full height, striking the air, and rips the reins out of Dad's hands. Dad throws his weight forward, encouraging his horse to land, and claws for the reins, but they've sailed over the top of Teague's head, and dangle out of reach. My heart pounds in my chest. The trail is narrow, the rocky footing slick as wet glass. If Teague takes off, Dad will have no way to stop him, and the horse will almost certainly fall.

"Dad, jump off!" I scream. "Jump off!"

Teague lands, and bounds straight upward, his nose on the ground, his spine curled in a wave. Dad wraps his legs around Teague's barrel, his empty stirrups swinging with Teague's explosion. Teague's hooves touch down again, and his steel shoes slide on a stretch of flat, wet rock at the same instant that the stirrup irons strike his sides. He scrambles and leaps forward.

"Dad!" My scream floods my ears and echoes in my brain. I know it's my voice, but it sounds foreign and far off. The world slows down. My heart pounds on the base of my throat. He leans back, ripping at Teague's mane. The lip of the ravine is two strides away. One stride.

"Jump off!" I shriek. Harbor peddles backward, and I realize I'm squeezing her reins. I kick her sides, urging her forward, desperate to catch any piece of Teague in hopes of slowing him down.

Teague leaps into the air, and disappears over the side. I blink once, disbelieving that the trail is empty, that Teague and Dad are not on it, that Teague just jumped off the edge of a cliff with my father on his back.

They're gone . . . *They're gone.*

"Dad!" I fling myself from Harbor, straining to hear them hit the water. "Dad!" My pulse hammers against my palms. My legs wobble beneath me as I sprint to the spot they went over. Below, the swollen river is brown with silt and frothy with turbulence. There's no sign of them. Could he have landed on the bank somehow?

"Dad! Dad! Can you hear me?" A rumble of thunder drowns out my voice. The sky opens, and sheets of rain pour down. I steal a glimpse down the path, but whatever I'd seen is gone. Had it been real? What if it hadn't been there, and hadn't been what spooked Teague? What if . . . what if I did?

I grab hold of a sapling and throw my legs over the side, preparing to slide to the bottom. A dark place coasts under the surface of the water. I squeeze the skinny tree trunk as new fear washes over me, when Teague's head and neck emerge from the water. I nearly call out for him. Then Teague glances off of a jut in the bank, spins around, and slides back under the brown water. My stomach lurches, and the air leaves my lungs.

"Dad!" I lean forward, searching the water for any sign of him. My heart hammers against my ribs. I lean farther out, searching for the best way down. The heel of my boot slips in the mud. I clutch at the tree, but my fingers lose their hold of the skinny, slick trunk, and I tumble into the ravine.

Roots and rock tear at my skin as I try to slow myself down. The water rushes toward me, and I pummel through the churning surface. The chill of the river nearly makes me inhale. I twist around, but I can't tell which way is up. The current slams into my back, sending me into a barrel roll. I curl myself in a ball so my feet are pointed downstream, but the force of the river pushes my helmet over my eyes and nose, and the chin strap digs into my throat. I fumble with the buckle, burning precious seconds of the oxygen I have left. Finally, the helmet releases, and I peel it off my face and let it go.

Starbursts bloom in front of my eyes. I push my arms straight down, forcing my body up. My chest constricts, demanding fresh air. I push up again, and my face breaks through the surface. I gulp in a breath, and am slammed sideways by another wall of water.

"Dad!" I can barely hear myself over the rapids. Water pours into my mouth faster than I can spit it out. I descend a rapid and am sucked back under. I keep my face trained toward the surface so I don't lose my position. I kick out for anything to push off of. The water is too deep. A new current slams me from the side, and catapults me above the surface. I cough and sputter. My teeth clatter together. "Dad," I try to shout, but I'm barely taking in enough air to breathe.

Ahead, the river doubles in width until it disappears around a curve. On the right bank is a sliver of a beach. I spin myself around, and swim hard for the patch of dry ground. If I miss it, I won't have enough energy to find another way out. My legs flail behind me, and I paddle as fast as I can, but the current is still too strong. I've barely shifted my position, and I'm nearly even with the bank. I'd have to swim straight across to reach it in time.

My boots and jacket have filled with water. The added weight drags me further down with every movement. Another wave smacks me in the face. I gasp and wipe at my face, trying not to lose sight of the bank. The river carries me down a short drop, and pushes me back below the surface before I can draw a new breath. An icy current tosses me sideways, and I lose my position. Under water, I search for a hint of day light, but the water is cloudy and I'm moving too fast. The second I see a bright spot, I'm swept out of reach.

My lungs throb. Thick cold permeates my core. My arms flail along with the current, and my legs barely kick out behind me. I stretch my fingers above me, hunting for air, and find none. Even though everything in my mind screams not to, my mouth opens, and my lungs release the stale air. I close my eyes. The heaviness turns into the sensation of weightlessness, and I feel like I'm flying.

As darkness closes in around me, something solid slides around my waist and jerks me upright. *Dad's here.* The thought sets my nerve endings on fire, and ignites one last ounce of fight inside me. I open my eyes and give one last kick. The water turns from murky brown to tan, and then I burst through the surface. I gasp in a breath, and then another, the world around me spinning. Two strong hands take hold of my shoulders and steer me forward. Grit and water speckle my eyes and make it hard to focus. I blink clear for half a second. Directly ahead of us is a short, flat bank. My feet contact the river bed, and a sob of relief escapes me.

"We made it," I mumble through tears. Dad releases me. I stumble forward on shaking legs for three steps until they give out beneath me, and I plunge into the river up to my shoulders. I jab my fingers into the riverbed, anchoring myself in place. I heave for several seconds, emotion and exhaustion coming out of me in choked cries. We're okay. We're going to be okay.

I drag myself forward. The bank is slimy and covered in rotting leaves and debris, and the wind and rain batter my trembling body. I crawl to the high side of the beach, shielded from the driving rain by a fallen tree. I scoot to the side to leave a place for Dad in the meager shelter, and then turn back to look at him. The bank is empty,

"Dad?" I swing my gaze up stream and rub my eyes, certain he'll appear. "Dad!" The word is a razor in my throat. I lurch to my feet and stumble to the edge of the water. He was just with me, wasn't he? He saved me. He pulled me out of the water. So where is he?

I shrug out of my soaked jacket and step ankle deep in the water. This placid spot in the river lasts all of about twenty feet before the rapids begin again. My heart accelerates and cool dread snakes through me. I can't go back out there. My knees give out and I catch myself with my hands.

My head swims with possibilities. Dad is the strongest man I know. He could raft this whole river on his back if he had to. Couldn't he? Maybe he went for help . . . he got me to a safe bank and he went for help.

But what if he's not fine? What if . . .? Even the idea of it digs a hole inside of me.

I stare through the rain at the river, and then look behind me at the wall of earth. I might be able to climb the fallen tree to a better vantage point. I move to the tree, and try to pull myself up. My muscles tremble with exhaustion. There's no strength left. There's no way I will be able to climb out on my own.

What if we both die today, and leave Mom alone? Tears spill from me at the thought of her pacing from wall to wall, staring out the window at the sun every morning, wondering what's left to be taken away. Had she seen this in the sun, or some hue of caution? Is that why she told us to stick to tradition?

"Help," I call out, pressing my cheek into the grimy, wet tree. It's barely loud enough to reach my own ears. "Mom. Mom. Help."

"Tanzy!" a voice shouts. "Travis! Tanzy!" The sound of it strikes me like an electrocution. I whirl around, grab a branch, and wave it.

"I'm here!" I use everything I have left to yell.

Movement at the top of the opposite bank draws my gaze. A dark horse appears with a rider on its back, holding a trailing Harbor by the reins. I can't see a face, but the rider's short limbs and jockey-style position is a dead giveaway. It's Dana, my father's assistant who shouldn't be here. I have never been so glad to see my father's assistant in all my life. I should've known she'd be riding, even on her day off.

"Help! Dana!" I wave my arms, flinging the branch. Harbor turns in my direction and freezes, pulling back on her reins. Dana stops her horse, and follows Harbor's focus across the river.

She brackets her mouth with her hands to make a little megaphone before shouting: "Tanzy! What happened? Are you okay?"

"I . . . I'm okay. Dad's here, too. Do you see him?" I try to answer, but my voice is swallowed up by the roar of the river. My breathing comes fast, and a tremble runs the length of me as I stare at the water, and then peer up the hill.

"I can't hear you. Stay there. I'm going to get help! Stay right there!"

I drop to the sand, exhausted, and watch the river. If it wasn't Dad who pulled me out, was it just the current spitting me into the bend? Wouldn't it have done the same for Dad if he came this far? I check the length of the bank again, but it's still empty.

If it was neither my dad nor the current, what was it? And why did it push me out of the water and not him? I force the thought aside. It didn't save Dad because he didn't need it. He must've found a way up and out, and is headed back to the barn for help, or he thinks I rode back for help and he's going to find me. He got out of this river somehow. I know he did.

We're going to be okay. I hug my knees to my chest, pushing against the tiny hole this thought can't quite fill all the way up.

THE RIVER

The world around me is thick and black. Roaring fills my ears. My heart races. I can't breathe, can't swallow. There's too much sand in my eyes. I can't open them. My chest burns. In the dark, a sliver of pinkish light becomes visible. My mind races for the light. The pressure in my chest swells to bursting, and all at once I jolt awake. Still the trapped feeling lingers. I throw the heavy quilt to the floor, and clutch at my chest, gasping until my breathing becomes normal.

"Tanzy," my mother says from beside me, and touches my arm. "It's okay, honey. I think you were having a bad dream."

"Have they found Dad yet?" I ask. The roof of my mouth is hot and sticky.

"Not yet," Dana answers from the chair in the corner of my room.

"How long was I asleep?" I pull myself up to sitting. My limbs are sore, and my skin a kaleidoscope of scrapes and bruises.

"Just through the night. It's early," Mom says.

"We haven't found Teague, either," Dana continues. "We searched the river and the woods until it was too dark to see. There's a team of divers at the farm now . . ." she trails off, her eyes flitting in my mom's direction. "They're going to search the river, just to be sure he isn't there."

"You are absolutely sure he went into the river, too?" Mom clasps my forearm with both hands.

"He went in first. Teague got spooked and took off. There was this . . . this thing in front of Teague. He was scared, and he didn't have anywhere to go . . . he just, he just went over." My voice cracks.

"What thing?" Dana leans forward in her chair.

"It . . . I don't know what it was. It was like a flash of light that turned into something pitch black. At first I thought it was part of the storm, but it was . . . it's almost like it was alive." I shake my head at myself. "I know how crazy it sounds, but it seemed like it blocked the path on purpose. Teague was going too fast to stop, and Dad . . ." I stop, biting back how Dad should've jumped off, should've never tried to stay on a horse bolting along a ledge. I look from Dana, who's watching me with concern on her face, to my mom, whose expression has hardened, and my heart sinks. "It's what I saw. I don't know how else to explain it."

"You went through a lot yesterday, Tee." Dana stands. "I have heard that our minds sometimes skew or block memories to protect us from reliving the moment. Give it time. It'll come back. You focus on feeling better. Hope, I will call you with any news. There's no need for you guys to be out there right now."

"Thank you, Dana." My mother's voice is strangled. She puts a hand on her throat and steals a glimpse of the sun through my window. Dana gives me a tight smile, and then shows herself out.

In the quiet, I watch my mom watch the sky. A tear rolls down her cheek. She swallows, blinking.

"What do you see out there, Mom?" I ask before I can stop myself.

She turns to me, her bright eyes wide. "I just, I think better when I look out."

"What are you thinking about?" I whisper, not believing her, but not willing to push her for the truth.

"Where your dad is."

"I thought . . . I thought I felt him in the river. He saved me. I felt him."

Mom studies me through her tears. "He would do anything to save you. Anything."

"But if he was there, if he saved me . . . where did he go?"

A cry escapes my mother. I scoot closer, and take her hands in mine. Together, we stare out into the clear morning.

"Did you . . ." I start, unsure of how to finish. Did she know something bad would happen if we broke tradition? Did she see it in the dawn? Does she see anything in the clear? Would she believe the woman on the radio?

"Do you believe in things we can't see?" I finally ask.

My mother stiffens. "Do you mean like an afterlife?"

"No. I mean . . . the air we see, and accept that it's clear, that there's nothing there but, well, air. Do you think there's something in it?"

"Like atoms or molecules or . . ." She trails off, her expression a question mark.

"No." I work my lower lip between my teeth, trying to decide how to explain what I mean.

"Where is this coming from?" she asks, softening.

"There was a woman on the radio yesterday morning. She said there's a world in the clear. And when Dad and I were on the ridge, I saw something."

"What did you see?" She narrows her eyes.

"A huge rainbow. It covered the whole valley. There was something dark under it, moving fast. And then everything just disappeared."

Mom's expression hardens, as does her grip on my arm. "Does that have anything to do with what happened?"

"I . . . I'm not sure." I glance at my arm, startled by the pressure she's applying.

"You said Teague was spooked by something, and then a shadow blocked his path." She pushes, her grip unyielding.

"He hadn't been right the whole ride." I pause, blinking back tears. Teague had most likely been spooked by the sound of my voice. If I hadn't yelled . . . if I had kept my mouth shut about the shadow, Dad would've had more time to react.

Downstairs, the phone rings. Mom's whole body tenses. Anticipation and dread are two corsets, squeezing tight around my middle.

"Stay in bed. I will be right back." She jumps out of the seat and bolts from my room. I listen to her descend the stairs, and then slip out of bed and paint myself against the door frame, straining to hear her end of the conversation.

"Hightower residence, this is Hope speaking," my mother says, her voice unnaturally high. In my mind, I can see her strangling the phone with one hand and chewing her nails on the other. "Hi, Dana," she continues. I tiptoe to the banister. "That's . . . that's terrible. No, no go ahead and take care of it. There's no reason for Tanzy to see that." Her voice drops an octave, and I can tell she's turned her back to the doorway that leads to the stairs and where I stand. They must have found Teague.

"I need to go out there. I want to see the river," she says.

I freeze. Mom hasn't been to Wildwood in months, maybe longer.

"Dana, my husband is still out there somewhere. I need to be there." She pauses. I hear her feet pace the tile floor. "There's just something I need to see." After another pause she adds, "I want to see my husband's horse. It's important to me."

I blink, questioning what I've just heard. My mother hasn't touched a horse in a year, and I'm not sure she could pick Teague out of a pasture. Then again, Teague was Dad's pride and joy. She can't take care of my father. Maybe seeing to his horse's body is the closest thing she has for now.

"No, Tanzy needs to rest. I can't ask her to drive me. Will you come pick me up? I'll have a neighbor sit with her."

I rush down the stairs, clinging to the banister to keep from stumbling. When she hangs up the phone, I'm standing behind her.

"You're not coming, Tanzy," she says without turning around.

"Yes, I am."

"No. It's too soon. You need to rest. They found Teague, and they're going to bury him. You don't need to see that. You're not ready to see that."

"Yes, I am!"

"Tanzy, please. I am begging you. This is going to be hard enough." She deflates. Her arms hang at her sides. "I need to know you're home, safe in your bed. That's the only way I'll be strong enough to look into the river and . . ."

"And what, Mom?"

"I'll know, Tanzy. One way or the other, I'll know."

"You'll know . . ." I trail off. She turns around, and we lock stares. "You'll know if Dad is gone," I whisper.

She doesn't respond.

"Then I need to be there," I state.

"I'm not strong enough to keep us both together," she whispers.

"I'm not asking you to be," I plead. "Let me go with you. Let me be there for you."

Mom nods, and bursts into tears. I wrap my arms around her shuddering frame, and we sink to the tile floor.

"What if he's gone, Tanzy?" She lets out a sob. I squeeze my fist around a lock of her hair. "I don't know how to do this without him."

"We don't know, yet. We don't know," I murmur. Inside, the little hole I felt open inside me yesterday grows wider and deeper. It's black as night and ice cold, and I know. *I know.* But I can't say it.

We're waiting in the driveway when Dana's truck rumbles to a stop in front of our house. She does little more than raise an eyebrow at me when I climb in the back seat. Mom sits in the front passenger seat. Dana turns off the radio, and we ride to the farm in silence.

I watch the sun paint the sky through Dana's windshield, and my breathing quickens. Yesterday's drive roars to life in my mind—the pancakes, the radio show, the smell of alfalfa. I pull the sleeves of my hoodie over my knuckles and press my hands against my mouth, forcing myself to slow how fast I'm inhaling. My eyes and nose burn with the threat of new tears. I close my eyes and recall my mother and her need for me to be strong enough for us both.

We pull into the parking lot. A flatbed trailer is already there, and two men are off loading a skid steer with a front bucket attachment. I look away, unable to stop myself from envisioning how they'll use the bucket to move Teague's body. I wonder why Mom wants to see him. Will it be the proof she needs that Dad went into the river?

"Take me to the river," Mom whispers.

Dana opens her mouth and then closes it, a rebuttal probably stalled in her mouth. She glances at me, as if asking for permission, and I nod.

"We can take the Gator," Dana says, breaking the silence, and we follow Dana to the front of the barn, where the UTV is parked. Mom waits for me to slide in first, but I step aside and motion her ahead of me so she'll be in the middle.

Dana drives the Gator carefully out across the pasture and into the woods. I train my eyes straight ahead, but I can't help noticing the shadows that lean out from behind every tree and shift along the forest floor. The moment we turn onto the ridge path, my pulse skyrockets and my hands turn clammy.

"We won't be able to drive much farther," Dana says. "The path gets pretty steep and narrow."

"That's okay. We can stop here." Mom points to a grassy shoulder. Dana pulls off and kills the engine. The river isn't as swollen today, the rapids less angry. Still, my legs are shaking so hard I can barely stand. I support myself on the hood of the Gator, and clamor out so Mom can step down. She shields her eyes and scans the path.

"What's the best way to the water?" Mom asks.

"Hope, you can't go down there," Dana says gently.

"That's why I'm here," Mom replies. "Now show me the way down."

"I'm going with you," I say. She lifts her gaze and focuses on me, the word "no" rounding her mouth. Instead, she presses her lips in a line, and turns to the river. I fall in step behind her, and we follow Dana down the trail.

Once we reach the river, Dana points to an easy drop to the bank below, and then steps aside to let us go down without her. Mom toes out of her shoes, and walks out onto the shore with her feet bare. I fumble my way to her side, slipping more than once on the slick rocks. At the water's edge, she closes her eyes and tilts up her chin. Her black hair blows loose behind her. Sunlight catches in it, revealing mahogany undertones that I can't recall ever noticing before. She opens her hands and lets them hang at her sides. I stare at her, mystified. She's not a religious person, and I have only ever set foot in a church when Dad's parents made us during their only visit south, but in this moment, she looks like she's praying. Her pale skin is marble smooth, and her frame barely stirs with breath. She could be a statue on this riverbank. Bathed in sunlight, she is aglow, and it's as if I am seeing her for the first time.

Without opening her eyes, she crouches down and reaches for the water. Even though the river is calmer and transparent here, I have to stop myself from grabbing her shirt and hauling her backward. I step closer to her side, ready to catch her if she loses her balance. She reaches through the surface and allows the current to play with her fingers. She shudders, and a jagged breath parts her lips. Her eyes open briefly, then she squeezes them shut, and new tears roll out.

"Mom?" I bend down and touch the center of her back.

"Take me home," she says, gasping, and staggers away from the edge of the water. I hurry to her side and wrap an arm around her waist. She covers her face with her hands, and leans into me. She's head and shoulders taller than me, but the weight of her barely sways me, and I wonder if the emptiness I feel inside has hollowed her out, too.

Dana retrieves her shoes before starting the Gator, and we ride back to the barn without speaking. The dive team has assembled in the main corridor. Bile paints the back of my tongue, and my throat swells with dread.

I hug my mom to my chest, stroking her hair, and exchange a glance with Dana over the top of her head. Dana nods, acknowledging the presence of the team, what they're here to do, and the need to avoid it all. We drive around the far side of the barn, past the empty flatbed, and pull up at the passenger side door of her truck. I open the door and help Mom step up, and then climb into the back as Dana parks the Gator and returns to her truck.

The engine cranks to life, and we turn up the driveway. Once the barn and all traces of the team are behind us, I slump against my seat and close my eyes. Every inch of me aches. My mind is a storm of images from yesterday and today. I wonder what Teague looked like when they found him. The hope that he died quickly and painlessly whispers through me. I sit up right. We never saw Teague's body.

I reach toward the console, where my mother's elbow rests, when I catch sight of the reflection of her left eye in the rearview mirror. She stares ahead, pupils blown wide, and tears pour from the corner. I slowly ease back, unable to tear my gaze from the mirror. She would've asked about Teague when we first arrived if she'd really wanted to see him, wouldn't she? But why did she ask about seeing him at all?

I look to Dana. The side of her face is tense. The underside of her visible eye is puffy from either crying or lack of sleep or both. Dana can understand a person needing to see a horse's body for closure, but would she have been willing to drive us to the barn for the sole purpose of Mom seeing the river? From Mom's side of the conversation, it sounded like Dana wasn't willing to have Mom come to the farm until she mentioned Teague. I recount my mother's actions on the shore, how much a part of the woods she'd seemed. What if she hadn't wanted to see Teague at all? What if it's not the sunrise she's watching every morning? What if all this time, she's been studying the clear?

I try to recall how she responded when I asked her about the radio show earlier, but all I can remember is the phone ringing, and the tornado of fear and hope that twisted inside at the sound of it.

At home, Dana walks in the middle of Mom and me, offering us both her support.

"What can I do?" Dana asks once we're inside. Mom walks away as if she doesn't hear her, and slips through the doorway to the kitchen.

I raise my chin, even though my head feels like it weighs a hundred pounds, and my heart is barely pumping in my chest. "When you call to tell us that the dive team found Dad's body, ask for me. Don't tell Mom first," I say.

The corners of her mouth turn down, and she nods, drawing a hard breath through her nose.

"I'm going straight back to Wildwood now. I won't leave again until the dive team is finished."

"Good." I open the door for her with a trembling hand.

"I'll talk to you soon." She steps out onto the front steps.

"Yes."

She turns and heads for her truck without looking back. I pull the door shut behind me, and watch her car until it disappears up the road. Then I sink to the concrete landing, bury my face in my knees, and weep until I am empty.

The muted sound of the phone ringing reaches me through the door. I wipe my face on my sleeve and blink my eyes clear. I have to get inside and answer it before Mom does. Even if Dana asks for me, there's a good chance Mom won't acquiesce.

The phone is on the third ring when I step inside. Four. I hurry to the kitchen, expecting to see her staring out of her window. The kitchen is empty. Five. The answering machine triggers, and the line goes dead. I check the caller ID. The number is not one I recognize. To be sure, I pick up the phone and dial Dana's number. It goes straight to voicemail. I don't leave a message. I take the phone cord and pull the jack out of the wall so no more calls can come through, and walk down the narrow hall toward her room. The door is closed. I press my ear against the wood, listening for proof she's inside, and hear her muffled cries, as if she has her face buried in a pillow.

"Mom?" I turn the handle, but it's locked. I tap on the door. "Can I come in?"

"I . . . I just need a minute," she says. "Unless . . . are you okay? Do you need me?"

Yes. I swallow down the truth. "No, I'm okay. I'm going to go upstairs."

"I'll come check on you in just a minute."

"Okay." I rest my forehead and palm against the door. How will I tell her Dad's gone? How will I be the one to break her in two? Judging by her reaction on the riverbank, she's already come to that conclusion, but there's a difference between feeling something and knowing something. No matter how prepared we are, no matter how many times I tell myself he's gone, having proof will be a bomb inside. I will not be the same. Nothing will be the same.

I exhale, trying to release the pressure building under my ribs, and return to the kitchen. I retrieve the phone, and carry it to my room, for the first time thankful we only have one phone in the house. I plug it into the wall and stow it under my bed. I only have to keep it a secret long enough for Dana to call.

I curl up in my bed, draw my covers to my chin, and watch scattered clouds pass by. As the light passes through them, an iridescent sheen shimmers on their borders. I roll over and stare at my wall. My gaze drifts to my bedside table, where there's a picture of Dad and me from Harbor's first horse show. I touch his face with my finger. I've heard knowing is better. Closure can happen. Acceptance. The stages of grief. So why am I sure that knowing is going to be the worst thing on earth?

I reach under my bed and check the phone to make sure the line is working. A dial tone sounds in my ear. I replace the phone on the cradle and roll onto my back, staring at the ceiling. I can't just lie here. I sit up. But what if I am downstairs and the phone rings? What if I leave to go to Wildwood, and Mom needs me?

I can't stop picturing what she must be doing in her bed, sobbing into a pillow or staring at their wedding pictures. She wore a gauzy, full length sun dress, and he wore jeans and a button-down shirt, and they exchanged vows in a forest in Vermont. There's a picture she hates, where a beam of sunlight seems to pass right through her, and casts a platinum glow all around her. But it's Dad's favorite, and he keeps it propped on his bedside table, no matter how often she protests.

That same glow happened on the riverbank. I look at the evening light filtering in through my window. I slip from my bed and approach it, what I have seen with my own eyes a contrast to what Dad said on the ridge yesterday. Mom and I don't share many physical traits. She's tall and willowy, with ivory skin and straight, black hair. Her blue eyes are so pale most people call them gray. I'm compact and sturdy. My face and arms are tan from spending every day outside. My hair is thick, defiant, and brown, tamed only with a rubber band and a ball cap. And my eyes are my father's eyes, wide set and hazel. Is there any chance sunlight affect me the same way it does her? I've been in the sun thousands upon thousands of times. How could I have never noticed?

I pass my hand through the rectangle of light. The air is warmer, and dust particles glitter as they wander aimlessly from ceiling to floor. Nothing happens to me, neither inside nor out, save being drawn closer to the window. I peer out to our front yard below. Mom had been right. There was no frost last night, and the few flowers Dad left in the garden are still alive and bright.

"What are you doing, Tanzy?" Mom's voice spins me around. She stands in my doorway. Dark circles rim her eyes.

"You... you glow in the sun," I stammer, unable to stop the truth from tumbling out. "I wanted to see if I do, too."

"I don't glow," she says, stepping into the light. "The light glows, and I reflect it because I'm pale as a sheet." She attempts a smile, takes me by the hand, and guides us to my bed. We sit side by side. "I can't imagine how hard this must be for you." She squeezes her eyes shut and turns away briefly. "You've been asking some strange questions today. With everything that happened, I'm sure your mind is trying to process some parts and block others."

"Mom, it's more than that."

"Maybe it is." She touches my hair. "Or maybe you're creating things that don't make sense, because the truth, the real, concrete, awful truth is too much to bear."

"No. I heard the radio show before the accident. I saw the rainbow before the accident. And then the shadow . . ."

"What did that woman say on the radio?" she interjects.

"She said there's a world in the clear, like two plays on one stage, and that we have something the other world wants." I squirm, hearing it as if for the first time. It sounds utterly ridiculous.

My mom frowns, and then covers her mouth with her hand. With a start, I realize she's trying not to laugh.

"Dad said . . . Dad said not to tell you because you'd believe it for sure," I say, somehow relieved and sad all at once.

"Oh Travis." Mom's eyes glisten again. "Always so protective." She clears her throat. "I'm protective, too, Tanzy. This world has enough risks in it without inventing an entirely second world to fear. That's why I need to ask . . . I need to ask you to consider not riding again for a while."

"But I'm fine. Banged up, but I'll be good as new in just a few days. Harbor isn't as reactive as Teague."

"It's not about that. It could be you they're looking for in the river. I could've lost you both. Horses . . . there are just too many ways you could be hurt. Promise me you'll think about it."

"I . . . I can think about it," I say, bewildered. "What happened at the river, Mom? Maybe you didn't glow, but something happened. I saw it."

She visibly swallows, and then twists her wedding band. "When you love someone like I love your dad, sometimes, sometimes you can feel things. I thought if I went to the river, I'd know if he was still alive somehow, or maybe I would know where he is."

"Did you feel anything?" I whisper.

"No." Tears spill out of her eyes. "No, not a thing. I have no idea where he is, and it's the worst pain I have ever felt." She trembles, and presses her knuckles into her mouth. I pull her into my lap, run my fingers through her hair the way she used to do to me whenever I was upset, and let her cry. How could I have pushed her so hard? How could I have let a woman on the radio have so much of my mind in a minute flat? Dad was right. People like her feed on the reaction of people like me, and what all has my reaction cost me and the people I love inside of a single day?

"Please, please don't ride again," Mom whispers against my leg. "You can go to any college in the country, as far away as you want to go, but please don't ride anymore."

Grief blooms anew inside, the worst kind of spring. It's cold and hot at the same time, and growing so fast it chokes me. If Dad is really gone, riding will be the closest thing I have to his presence—his voice will be in my ear every time I get on. But then again, will I ever be able to climb in a saddle without seeing a flashback of Teague leaping into the river . . . without remembering how Teague's body reacted to my voice? Dad is dead. She might not feel it, but I do, and I'm the one to blame. If agreeing to not ride for a while brings her any kind of peace, I want to give it to her.

"Okay, Mom," I say, barely believing that I'm saying it. "Okay."

Ghost

I stare at the clock on the cafeteria wall, my lunch sitting untouched in front of me. I have been away from home for three hours and forty minutes. What if Dana has called? What if they finally found Dad?

I shouldn't be here. The thought grows bigger and bigger. I couldn't concentrate in my morning classes. Teachers ignored me, or gave me sympathetic gazes when they caught me staring. Other students don't seem sure whether to speak to me for the first time or avoid me completely. The school counselor I had to meet with this morning advised me to lean on my friends. My friends aren't here. My friends are at Wildwood.

The bell rings, announcing the end of the block, and I startle with a jerk. Everyone surges into movement, and the volume doubles in the big, rectangular room. The voices blend into a roar, the torrent of feet on polished floor becomes akin to pounding, driving rain, and all of the sudden I can't breathe.

I leap to my feet, leaving my full tray on the table, and run for the parking lot. I climb into the driver's seat of Dad's truck and slam the door, panting. Once my hands stop shaking, I turn on the ignition, and pull out of the lot. Everything inside of me wants to go to Wildwood—where I am a piece of a puzzle that I know how to put together. Even though Dad's absence has left a hole there, it's still a place that makes sense to me. Home ... home has become a puzzle with half the pieces missing. What has Mom done while I've been gone? Has she left her room yet? Worry for her chases me down every street. She'd been the one to suggest I return to school. Maybe she figured if I left, Dana would finally call.

I pull into our driveway. There's a blue cooler propped in front of our door. Someone must've dropped off another meal for us—someone who knows Mom well enough to be prepared for her to not answer the door. With Mom refusing to leave the house, and me refusing to leave Mom prior to today, these meals are the only way we eat. Rather, the only way I eat. Mom has done little more than pick at a plate. In the last few days, she's stopped bothering to set herself a place at all.

I climb out of the truck. On a hunch, I backtrack to the mailbox. It's completely full. Neither of us has checked it since the day of the accident. I stuff the mail in my backpack, retrieve the cooler, and step inside.

The house is quiet and still. I shoulder off my bag and then thumb through the mail, automatically beginning separate stacks for Mom, Dad, and me. I drop the mail and grip the countertop, besieged by a wave of sadness. Envelopes scatter all over the floor. I bend down and gather them.

I don't know what to do with the letters for Dad. A few of them are obviously junk. I tear them across the middle, the way he does every evening, before I toss them in the trash. A letter with my name on it catches my eye. It's from the University of Kentucky, where I'd submitted an early admission application. It's probably just a form letter acknowledging they'd received it.

I haven't thought once about where I'll be next year since Dad went missing. I peer down the dark hall to my parents' room. What if she still won't leave the house alone come next fall? I can't imagine packing all my things and moving away, knowing the farthest she'll go from her bed is to stare out the window behind the kitchen sink.

I take her stack to the windowsill and prop it against the glass pane, knowing she'll see it there. I thumb through what's left of Dad's mail. A couple pieces are definitely bills.

"What are you doing home so early?" Mom asks from behind me. I whirl around. She's barefoot, and still in her nightgown. Dad calls her "lightfoot" for the way she can move around the house like wind through a window.

Called. Dad called. I press my fist against the sudden ache in my middle.

"I . . . I just wanted to be home. Someone brought us food." I point to the cooler, which I left in front of the refrigerator.

"We should go to the store," she mumbles.

"I can go, Mom. I should've gone while I was out."

"No. I should go. I should go," she repeats.

I stare at her. Her hair is matted and dull. She picks through the knotted ends with her fingers. Her transformation has been so slow and slippery over the past three weeks that I didn't catch how far she's sunk until I stepped away.

Neither of us should go. She can't leave the house like this and I can't leave her again.

"Tomorrow. Tomorrow you can go. We'll go together," I say.

"Tomorrow." She turns back toward her room.

"Mom, why don't I draw you a hot bath? Don't you have some lavender bath oil that you like?" I call to her. She keeps walking as if she doesn't hear me. I follow her to her room, which is dark. Dad's clothes are strewn across the bed. She curls up on top of them, and brings a shirt to her face. I stifle a sob and move past her into her bathroom. I start the water, for once grateful for the sound of it. The silence emanating from the bedroom is almost more than I can take.

The bath oil is in a basket on the bathroom counter. I put in two drops, watching them fizz for a few seconds, and then grab a towel from the linen closet. Once the tub is full, I turn off the water, and tiptoe back into the bedroom. Mom lies there, stone still, her ribcage barely stirring with breath. Her eyes are open, and she's staring at the wall. Her knuckles are clenched tight around Dad's shirt.

"Come on, Mom," I say, and rest a hand on her shoulder. She jerks from beneath my touch, and anger flickers across her face. She blinks, and it's gone.

"I'm sorry, Tanzy," she murmurs.

"It's okay. Let's get you in the bath." I want to take her hand, but I won't be the one to pry Dad's shirt from her fingers.

"I don't want a bath."

"You need one. Come on, it's nice and hot."

"No, Tanzy." She rolls over.

"Mom, yes." I sit on the bed and try to help her sit up. Now that I am this close, I can smell her, a sickly sweet, syrupy smell. "When's the last time you took a shower?" I ask softly.

She starts to cry. "I was about to get in the shower when Dana called and said they'd found you in the river, and that Travis was missing. She came and picked me up, and brought me to the hospital to see you, and it wasn't until we got home that night that I realized I'd never turned the shower off."

I wrap my arms around her. "It's okay, Mom. It's okay. I'll sit with you in the bathroom, okay? I can read to you from whatever book you're reading now."

"Okay," she says. She leans on me, and we walk to the tub. She's probably lost ten pounds, maybe more. She steps out of her nightgown, and I hold her hand as she settles into the tub. A long breath leaves her mouth, and she closes her eyes, easing back against the round rim. I roll up a towel and tuck it under her head.

"I'm going to get your book." I hurry to her nightstand and grab the top book from the pile. When I return, she's staring blankly ahead.

"Do you still want me to read?"

She doesn't answer.

I back to the counter for something to lean against while I watch her. She doesn't move. I glance at my reflection in the mirror, and gasp. The circles under Mom's eyes belong to me, too. My face is all bone and angles, just like hers. My father's voice enters my mind: *you are your mother's daughter.* The thoughts in my head begin to brew to a storm. Needing to drown them out, I open to the folded page, and start reading.

I read to her until her water turns cold. Once she's clean and dressed, I head to the kitchen and heat up the casserole. I set out two plates and two forks, and serve a small portion on each plate. I sit down, mashing the casserole with my fork, and peek down the hall. She isn't coming yet, but I can hear her moving around her room. I take a bite, barely tasting it. Her shadow appears in the rectangle of light coming from her room. I straighten in my seat. Then the light vanishes, and her door clicks shut.

The bite of food in my mouth swells, and I have to spit it out. Exhaustion creeps in from all sides. We can't keep going like this.

I leave her plate on the table, and retreat to my room. I sit on the floor, resting my back against my bed, and call Dana.

"Dana, we need help," I whisper.

"I'm leaving now," she says.

I hang up the phone, and press the heels of my hands into my eyes. Once I hear her truck rumble into our driveway, I stand up and head downstairs. Mom is standing at the foot of the stairway, watching me. Her hair is pulled on top of her head in messy bun, and her eyes are more alert than they've seemed in days. Still, the bath seems to have washed away another ten pounds, and her clothes hang off her frame.

"You can visit outside for a little bit, but then Dana needs to leave," Mom says.

"She's here to help."

"With what?"

"With . . . with us."

"We are fine." Her expression hardens.

"We are not fine."

"Your father is gone," she barks. "This is what fine looks like when someone . . . when someone is gone who shouldn't be," her voice breaks. "I don't want her in my house, Tanzy," she whispers.

"She's a friend!"

"She's not family," she counters.

We don't have any family. I clamp my mouth shut, trapping the thought. "Eat something. Eat something right now, and I will tell Dana that we're fine," I counter.

"Okay." She squeezes her hands to fists, her knuckles blanching.

"Promise me," I insist, knowing I won't be able to see her.

"I promise."

I watch her spoon out a chunk of the casserole, take her plate to the counter, and nibble at a first bite, her gaze already locked on to something on the other side of the window pane.

I slip through the front door. Dana is standing at the bottom of the steps.

"Do you want to go inside?" Dana asks, pointing at the door. "It's cold out."

"The fresh air is nice."

"If you say so." She moves forward and sits on the second stair. "What's going on?"

"It's like . . . it's like we are a ship, and Dad steered the ship," I start, trying to explain how lost we are, how motionless. "We don't know how anything works without him." There's no map, no compass, no destination, which didn't previously point somehow, someway to him.

"Wildwood is falling apart, too," Dana says. "I'm doing the best I can, but I'm not your dad. It seems like everything that could go wrong has gone wrong since he . . ." She wipes her face. "Enough about me, though. What can I do to help?"

"You're helping." I muster a smile.

"I just . . . I just wish we could find him," she says.

"Me too. It would help Mom a lot."

"If we don't find him soon . . ." Dana pauses, and drops her gaze to the bricks. She clears her throat. "I lost my mother when I was a little older than you. I remember the blur, mostly. But I also remember her funeral service. It was horrible, honestly. The hardest thing I've ever sat through. But it helped. And it seemed to really help my dad. He saw how many people she touched, how her life wouldn't be forgotten, and that he didn't have to carry the torch of her memory alone."

"I didn't know about your mom." Tears burn in my eyes. I haven't even considered this additional pressure my mom must be facing. I remember my father's warning about the walls she built, how she thinks they help. She just refused to let Dana in our house, when Dana has been here hundreds of times.

"How could you have known? I never told you." She pulls at the brim of her ball cap. Between her elven features and her wiry stature, she appears much younger than most thirty-somethings I know, too young to be without a mom. Is there such a thing as old enough?

"When does it get easier?" I ask.

"I don't know that 'easier' is the right word." She blinks rapidly and looks away for a second. "Have you two talked about maybe doing a memorial service?" she asks gently.

"I don't know if she's come to terms with . . ." my voice fades.

"Say no more." Dana holds up a hand. "Why don't you come out to the farm? Harbor came in from the pasture today covered in mud. You can't even tell she's supposed to be gray."

I snort at the mental image. The laughter, however short, fills me with relief even as tears spill from my eyes. "I'd like that. I'd like that a lot."

"I could use your help, too. We need a pair of good hands in the afternoons to help with evening feedings and lesson prep. You can come straight from school. I'd pay you."

I glance back at the house. "I'd have to ask Mom."

"Of course."

"She's not ready to be alone yet."

"How could she be?" Dana asks softly.

"She . . . she asked me to stop riding."

Dana's face shifts with a kaleidoscope of reactions before going completely blank. "She'll come around. But you don't have to ride, Tee. Especially if you don't want to. Anyone would understand you needing to take a break. I do think some time out there would do you good."

"I think so." In my mind, I wander the barn aisle. Before I can stop it, my mental view races ahead, out of the door, across the pasture, and into the woods. I can hear the roar of the river, and in these trees, the shadows move and flash. "Maybe not yet though." I stand.

"Let me know when you're ready," Dana says, rising. "We'll take care of Harbor in the meantime, so don't worry about her. We could all use you out there. It would do everyone good to see you. We've been trying to give your mom space." She steals a glimpse of the front door. "But everyone misses you."

"Thank you for coming. It helped more than you know." I steal a glimpse of Mom's favorite window. Her eyes are on Dana, and her hands look like they're in the sink. The phone rings, and she disappears.

"I . . . I have to go." I back up the stairs, my heartrate escalating. The ringing stops. Mom has answered the phone.

"Call me if you need anything again, okay? Even if it's just fresh air."

"Okay." I turn and open the door, then I pause. Whoever is calling can't be Dana with news. Still, a sense of urgency rushes me into the house, and I close the door without telling Dana good-bye.

My mom's footsteps sound through the ceiling above the foyer. She's in my room. I take the stairs two at a time. My door is open. Mom sits on my bed with her back to the door, pressing the phone against her face with one hand, and smoothing wrinkles only she can see on my bed spread.

"Are you sure?" she asks, and then waits. "You checked the entire river?"

I hold my breath, wondering who she's talking to, and the burst of energy animating her body.

"I don't know, as far as it goes." She squeezes the quilt, and the smooths it flat again. "Well, thank you for checking. I'll be in touch." She hangs up the phone, and then presses both hands into her face. Tension ripples across her shoulders, and she turns to spy over her shoulder.

"You seem like you're feeling better," I start, keeping my voice soft.

"Food helped."

"Who were you talking to?" I take a few steps forward, and even though it's my room, I feel like I'm trespassing.

"Just someone about your dad." She stands. "I hired a private team to search the river. They didn't find him."

"When did you do that?" I ask. I haven't let her out of my sight with the exception of this morning, and the phone hasn't left my room since the day after the accident.

"I took the phone out of your room while you were sleeping one morning last week, and put it back under your bed before you woke up. We should return it to the kitchen."

I stare at her, knowing she's lying. I just don't know which part she's lying about, or why. But I do know it's the first bold-faced lie she's ever told me—the first one I've caught her in, anyway. I never sleep late, and in the last three weeks, I've barely slept at all, while sleep is all she's seemed to do. Dana's right. We need a way to move on. We need to face that this is our reality now, a family of two people and a man—a ghost—of a million memories.

"Do we . . . do we need to think about planning a memorial service?" I ask.

Mom turns toward me with her whole body, and then goes completely still. "How could you ask me that? Why would we do that when we don't know where he is?"

"I don't think we ever will, Mom," I say quietly. "And even if we do, if we find him . . . it's . . . it's. He's gone, Mom. He's gone."

"You don't know that," she says through her teeth.

"No, I don't know that for a fact. But Mom, if he's not gone, where is he?"

"I don't know! And that's exactly why we shouldn't have some memorial service like he's dead. We don't know!"

"Okay. Okay." I catch myself wishing she'd leave my room. Instead, she turns away from me, and lies down. The temperature in my room feels like it's dropped ten degrees in a matter of seconds. A shiver passes across Mom's back, as if she feels the chill, too. I start forward, ready to cover her up with the blanket folded at the foot of my bed, but stop after two steps. I wait for her to peer back at me, or roll over. She does neither.

I back out of my room, and walk down the stairs to the kitchen. I pour a glass of water, and my mind drifts back to the morning of my birthday, the smell of burning pancakes, the batter in her hair. How could that only have been three weeks ago? How far will we fall before we hit bottom? I choke on the overwhelming sense of helplessness. How am I going to help my mother when I can't even make it through a whole day of school? Where do we go from here?

I snap out of my head, and, with a start, realize I'm staring out of Mom's favorite window, projecting my fears to the eastern horizon. Rage and grief course through me. My heart throbs in my chest, and my hands tingle. A growl escapes me as I heave the empty water glass at the wall. It explodes on contact, and tiny shards rain down all over the tile floor.

Flushing with shame, I retrieve the dustpan and broom from the closet. The clear glass glitters on the floor in the evening glow. A few pieces have scattered into a shadowy corner. Multi-colored light shimmers on the surfaces. I freeze, staring at the dark place, waiting for it to become more, for the edges to glow. But the dark is only dark. Relief and longing pass through me by turns. If the shadow moved for me, would I have stood still? Let it swallow me whole? I cast a gaze through the doorway and up the empty stairwell. Then I let out a breath, and begin to sweep.

REMEMBER ME

The sunrise is blood red today. I swirl my black coffee in Dad's travel mug, and watch the sky go through the spectrum of pinks and oranges before yielding to a clear, cloudless morning. It's the first day of spring, and Mom isn't watching it begin. Her bedroom windows face west and south. There's no way she can see it from inside her room. If the spring sunrise can't draw her from her room, I'm not sure what will.

While my mother has yet to agree to a memorial, Dana has arranged one for the equestrian community, to be held at Wildwood this afternoon. I have tried to drive to Wildwood on my own more times than I can count, and have reached the turn for the driveway, but each time, I turn around.

Today, I will drive down the driveway.

I will park my car.

I will turn off the engine.

I will open the door.

I will get out.

I will.

I walk down the hall to my mother's room. "Mom? Are you up?"

She doesn't answer.

"They're honoring Dad's legacy today, remember?" I wait a few seconds. "You need to be there." I tap on her door. "It's going to be a beautiful day, first day of spring. So many people loved Dad. They just want a way to pay their respects. It's not a real memorial. It's a . . . It's something else." I wait a full minute this time. She still doesn't answer. "Mom, I need you to be there." I rest my head against the wood, my mind already heavy, what ifs beginning to pick trails down my spine. "I don't think I can do this alone."

"I can't, Tanzy," she says from the other side of the door. I look down, and can see the shadows of her feet in the sliver of air under her door. "I'm sorry. I can't."

"Why not?" I regret asking the question the second it leaves my mouth. Mom hasn't left the house since the day she knelt at the river. But if the river drew her through her walls once, maybe it could do it again. And if she's in the car with me, I will make it all the way to Wildwood. If I can't finish the drive for myself, I know I can finish it for her.

"I don't believe in it," she whispers.

"Don't believe in what?"

"They're going to sit around and talk about Travis like he's dead. But what if he's not?"

"It's been five months. He's gone, Mom. Dad is dead! He's not coming back!"

The door jerks open. Mother stares at me, her eyes dark and narrow, her lips pulled back in a snarl so feral I almost expect her to bite.

"How dare you." Her black hair spills over her shoulders. "Tanzy Leigh Hightower, you go to that memorial if you want, but don't you ever call your father dead in my presence ever again until I have put my own eyes on his body. Do you understand?"

I step back on trembling legs. "Mom—" I start, but before I can finish, she slams the door. I spin and run down the hall and out of the front door. The service doesn't start for three more hours, but I can't stay here. I hop in the truck, crank the engine, and roar up my street. Before I know it, the turn for Wildwood appears in my windshield. My breath quickens. The edge of the pasture is visible from here. Its trees sway with a gust of wind. I will my foot to press down on the gas pedal. My leg locks at my knee, refusing to release the brake. I strangle the steering wheel, and even though I can hear myself breathing, I feel like I'm suffocating.

A horn blares from behind me. I jump at the sound, and then turn the wheel and let off the brake enough to roll onto the shoulder. I shift the engine into park and sit back against my seat. I won't turn around. I won't drive back home. If I can't make myself drive, I will get out and walk from here. I turn the key, and touch the door handle with my fingertips. I close my eyes. Just open the door, Tanzy.

Someone taps on the window. I gasp, and my eyes fly open. Dana peers at me through the glass.

"Are you okay?" she asks, and opens my door from the outside.

"I don't know." I wipe my eyes with my sleeve.

"Leave your truck and ride with me," she says. "You can park it over there." She points to a level place several yards off the road. "No one will bother it."

I unbuckle my seatbelt and slide out of the car. The wind whistles as it slices a path across the valley. Dana shields her eyes with her hand.

"This wind better not knock down all my decorations," she says.

"You decorated?" The absurdity of decorations is a welcome distraction.

"I mean, decorations fit for your Dad." She rolls her eyes. "You'll see."

I follow Dana to her truck and climb into the passenger seat.

"I'm glad you came," she says, cranking the engine. "I wasn't sure you'd make it."

"I almost didn't," I mutter.

"You made it far enough." She moves to shift the car into drive, and then hesitates. "I need to tell you something. We brought in a new trainer at the beginning of the year. We didn't want to. It didn't feel right, and I haven't known how to tell you. I still don't really know how. But she's going to be there today, so I don't want it to come as any more of a surprise."

"What's her name?" I stare ahead, imagining someone else standing in the middle of Dad's arena, teaching lessons on horses he brought in, arranging the jumps he built.

"Kate. She's nice. She's different, and the way she teaches is different, but she's really nice, and she's doing a good job. We've had to hire a few new people. Your dad could do the work of ten men."

I smile despite the sensation of my face becoming liquid.

"I'd hoped one of those people was going to be you," she continues. "It still could be. You can have any shift you want. I can work around your school schedule."

"The school is letting me complete the year online." I exhale through my nose, wishing I hadn't told her.

"Tanzy, you can't stay in that house forever. The kind of help your mom needs, I'm not sure you can give her that," she says softly. "Is there anyone you can call?"

"You."

Dana looks away from me. "What do you think you'll do after you graduate? What will she do?"

"I don't know."

"It sounds like you two have some things to talk about."

"She doesn't talk. It used to be at least she'd roam the house, but now she barely leaves her room, and if she does it's at night."

Dana lets out a sigh. "I thought you were just refusing to come to the barn because of the accident. Tell you what, I will make a couple calls for you and see if we can get a professional to come talk to your mom. I can't imagine what she's going through, and five months is not a lot of time to adjust to losing your dad, but you also shouldn't have to try to carry her grief on your own. You have enough to handle."

"Thank you," I whisper, already feeling like a traitor. What will Mom do when a stranger rings our doorbell? Do they make house calls, or will I need to drag her to the car? Either way, she will have betrayal in her eyes when she figures out what I've agreed to do.

"Remind me to give you something when we get to the barn," Dana says as she pulls back onto the road.

I nod, and watch the trees blur by, forcing my eyes to not train on the shadows, to not wonder at the clear.

The parking lot is already full. Dana pulls into her customary manager's spot. It's the only empty place left. My chest constricts. Dad was well-known, but I hadn't considered how many people would want to come tell him good-bye. The absurdity washes over me. Mom is right, Dad isn't here. There isn't even a body or ashes. What if there's a big photograph? Is that what we'll talk to? Will people look at it and smile like he can hear what they're saying through the canvas?

"Come on," Dana says, sensing me stalling. "I know a horse who would really like to see you."

My racing heart calms the instant I think of touching my horse. I slip out of the truck and hurry down the barn aisle. I didn't think to bring a treat. Harbor's silvery head and neck appear over the top of the stall door, and her ears prick when she sees me. I break into a run. She snorts and bangs her hoof against her door. I let myself in her stall and slide my arms around her neck, breathing in her salty, warm scent. She nuzzles my pockets, looking for peppermints.

"Not today, girl," I whisper, and scratch her under her chin. She tosses her head and lips at my hair. "I'm so sorry. I should've come out before now. I . . . I . . ." I stop, recognizing in this moment a fraction of how my mother must feel. I couldn't force myself to drive here, just like she can't force herself to leave. What can I use to make Mom remember that life is still going, the world is still turning, and she's still a part of it?

"I don't think she's minded the extended vacation," Dana says from behind me. "I've had the staff treat her like royalty. But don't worry, no one else has tried to ride her. I know how particular she can be."

"Thank you." I run my fingers through her mane. Her coat glows with health and care, evoking a pang of guilt. Dad always said a horse was a reflection of a person's integrity, but I can take no credit for how good Harbor looks today. She counts on me, and I am lucky people were there to care for her when I couldn't.

"I think your dad would want you to have this," Dana continues. I turn around. Dana's fist is outstretched. I hold my hand out, and she puts something cold and metal against my palm. I recognize the feel of them immediately: his dog tags. "I found them in his office when I . . . when I was organizing his drawers."

"It's your office now, isn't it?" I murmur.

"It is."

I slip his dog tags into my pocket. "Well, if it had to be anyone else, I'm glad it's you and not Kate."

Dana gives me a wry smile. "You haven't even met her yet. You might like her. She's not much older than you."

I purse my lips.

"No, no you probably won't." She rolls her eyes. "She's been well received, all in all. It took a little while for everyone to get used to, but I think it helped that she's so different than your dad. Except she brings a chair to sit in when she teaches."

"She what?" I raise an eyebrow. "The only time Dad sat down was to drive or ride, or if we forced him to take care of paperwork at his desk."

"I know, right?" Dana laughs. "I'm sure he's rolling over in his . . ." she stops and clears her throat.

My dad doesn't have a grave. A lump rises in my throat.

"Dana, they need you in the barnyard," someone says from beside her. A man I've never seen before appears in Harbor's doorway.

"Sure." She turns to me. "Do you want to come with me?"

I lean into Harbor, drawn to the warmth of her, and stare across the barn and out of the big double doors on the other end. Silhouettes mill around the opening. From here, they look like moving shadows.

"I don't think so," I say.

"Okay. Well you know where to find me," Dana says, and pushes off the stall door. "It's good to have you back," she adds, before disappearing down the hall.

All of these people have accepted he's gone. They're here to honor who he was and what he meant to them. They are ready to move on in their lives without him. They don't need me to be here to do that.

I pull his dog tags from my pocket. If I can't bring Mom to the service, I'll bring the service to her.

"I'll be back, girl. I promise," I say, and give Harbor another pat before stepping out of her stall. The hallway is clear. I jog out of the barn.

"Tanzy!" Dana's voice calls from behind me.

"I have to go. I'm sorry!" I shout over my shoulder.

"Tanzy, wait!"

I don't stop until I reach the top of the long driveway, panting and sweaty. A breeze pushes at my back, urging me on, and I don't rest again until I reach Dad's truck.

"Mom?" I call out as soon as I open the door. I cradle the tulip I bought on the way home against my side and walk into the kitchen. There's an empty glass on the counter. She must've come out of her room at some point. I head to her room. Her door is open, and her room is empty. "Mom?"

A movement in the window draws my eye. Mom is standing in the yard in one of dad's plaid shirts and the dress she wore for their wedding, and there's a picture frame in her hand. Panic buzzes inside of me. What is she doing out there? I whirl around and race for the back door. I half expect her to be vanished or lying flat in the grass when I get to her. But she's still standing there, eyes closed, bathed in sunlight.

"Hi, Mom," I say quietly, and tiptoe down the wooden porch stairs. "You look really pretty."

"I'm not ready to say good-bye." She doesn't open her eyes.

"We don't have to say good-bye." I walk out onto the grass. "What if we

46

just make some place somewhere in the yard where we can go when we want to talk to him?" I squirm. The idea had sounded better in my head, and when I rehearsed it in the car on the way home.

She opens her eyes, and her focus zeroes in on the tulip. "It will die in the winter."

"I . . . I should've bought a tree," I say, flushing.

"No, no. This is good." She takes the pot from me. "Because it vanishes in winter, but then it always comes back each year even more beautiful than before." She turns the flower around, studying it from all sides. With her this close to me, I smell a faint, warm aroma of Dad's bourbon on her breath, and I wonder if that would explain the empty glass at the sink, and my mother's sudden willingness to walk outside. I stare at her, a storm of emotions brewing in my chest. In this moment, the fact she's out here is more important than whatever it took to make it happen.

"Is the memorial already over?" She furrows her brow.

"No. It's probably just now starting."

"So it was a memorial."

"Maybe."

She regards me from her the corners of her eyes for a few seconds before asking, "Where should we plant it?"

"You're the gardener here," I say.

She moves around the yard. I can't help noticing that the path she walks traces the border between the light and the shadows in our yard, and I tell myself it's because tulips need the sun.

"Here." She points at her feet. She's returned to exactly where she stood before: a random spot off the right-hand corner of the house. As I approach her, I realize she'll be able to see it from her bed, and I'm not sure if that's good or bad.

"Should we get a shovel?"

"No." She drops to her hands and knees, and begins prying at the earth with her fingers. She tears out the grass, and then claws at the dirt. A wet, brown stain creeps up the front of her dress. I want to stop her, but the look on her face makes me reconsider. Instead, I reach my hands in, and scoop out more dirt. Mom squeezes the black plastic pot, loosening the soil. I fiddle with Dad's dog tags behind my back for a few seconds, wondering if I should try to sneak them into the ground or if I should tell her I have them.

"Go ahead," she whispers. "Whatever it is that you have, just go ahead."

I bring my hands to my front. Sunlight flashes on the metal plate.

"If that's what you need to do, go ahead," she repeats.

I drop the tags into the bottom. Mom tosses in a few handfuls of loose dirt before gingerly places the tulip, and then we fill in the rest of the hole.

"I can go get some water," I say, standing.

"No need. The ground is plenty damp, and it's going to rain in about an hour."

I peer at the sky, which is streaked with a few wisps of white clouds.

"You go on in. I want to stay out here a little while longer," she says.

"Do you think we should say anything?" I ask.

"No. This isn't a memorial, remember? This is here so we can come say what we want to say when we want to say it."

"Okay." I stare at her, bewildered. This is probably the most she's spoken in five months. What changed today? What brought her outside? It couldn't have just been a consequence of a glass of bourbon. There was something out here she needed bad enough to walk through the door. But what?

"Go, Tanzy. I want to talk to my husband."

"Okay, Mom." I move up the stairs and into the house, tempted to look back. It takes all my will power to keep my eyes trained straight ahead.

I walk into the kitchen, exhausted and relieved. Dana had been right. This is exactly what we needed, we just needed it here, where Mom can visit it whenever she wants. I smile to myself and pick up a glass and the bourbon bottle off the kitchen table and carry them to the sink. I stop in my tracks, and my gaze travels from the glass in my hand to the glass on the counter.

Why are two glasses out?

I smell both glasses, both scented with bourbon residue. I hold up the glass from the table. A smudge of silver lipstick is imprinted near the top of the glass. Mom hadn't been wearing makeup, and I've never seen anyone wear silver lipstick. Who would have come by that mom actually would've let in?

She's not family. My mother's words from the day Dana visited echo in my mind. I turn and stare through the door way to the screened-in porch, and peer at the sliver of her I can see from where I stand. I've always assumed my mother's past was an island made up of just her and her parents. But what if there's someone else?

I set the bottle on the counter, and arrange the two glasses in front of it, twisting one so the lipstick mark shows. I'm not sure if she'll acknowledge what I found, but she'll know I found it.

I take a backward step, and run into something solid. I whirl around.

"Mom, you scared me." I press my palm to my chest. "I didn't hear you come in. Who was here with you?" I blurt.

"I . . . I'd rather not say."

"Why? Was it . . . was it family?"

"No." Mom hangs her head. "It was a psychic . . . the kind of psychic who talks to the dead."

"Oh, Mom." My heart sinks. I glance at the two cups, seeing them in a completely different light. I never should've left her alone. "Did the psychic suggest a drink?"

"It seemed like a good idea. It helped with everything."

"I'm sure it did."

"I feel better."

"I'm glad."

We stand in silence for several seconds.

"What did the psychic say?"

"That your father is somewhere beautiful." A sad smile pulls her eyes down. Fresh grief, warm and thick, trickles through me. "There's more though. She said she got a message, and it's about you," she continues.

"What is it?" I ask, tensing.

"She said you should never go to Wildwood again."

"That's . . . that's a little extreme, don't you think?" I try to keep my tone light, but my heart begins to race.

"No, not at all. I think she's right. Tanzy, I don't want you to go to Wildwood anymore."

My mouth falls open, and I rock back as if I've been struck. "Mom, no. That's insane. Dana offered me a job. I can still live here after graduation. I can stay with you. I can help pay bills. It's . . . it's where I belong. I could feel it out there today. It's where I'm supposed to be."

"Your dad left plenty behind. We'll be okay for a while. And you, you don't belong there. After you graduate, you need to go somewhere new, go start your life away from all these shadows."

"What did you just say?" I narrow my eyes.

"Go start your life." She frowns.

"No, about the shadows. You said to start my life away from all these shadows. What shadows, Mom?"

She sighs. "Not this again. I mean the shadow of your father and his accident. Start your life free from all that weight and darkness. I don't want

49

you to turn into me. I don't want you to be a prisoner of what you think might happen if you step left or right. I want you to leap, Tanzy. To run. And I want you to do that somewhere brand new, where none of this will follow you."

I study her. "It's inside of me. How can it not follow?"

She rests her hands on my shoulders. "So take him with you wherever you go, but don't let the end of his path be the end of yours, too."

"You got all this clarity from a glass of bourbon and a psychic with silver lipstick?" I raise an eyebrow.

"Spoken like your father. God, I miss him."

"I do too." I gnaw on my lip, a cocktail of emotions swirling in my chest. "You can't ask me to never go back to Wildwood."

"I mean what I said." Mom's expression hardens.

"So do I." Heat touches my cheeks. "Wildwood is all I have left of Dad. Harbor is there, too. It's not like she can live in our back yard."

"No, you are not to go back there."

"I'm eighteen. I graduate in two months. I don't mean any disrespect, but I'm pretty sure it's up to me after that."

Mom lifts her chin. "Be very careful here, Tanzy. You've never been one to sass me and I don't recommend starting now."

Something inside of me, taut and fraying from holding up the weight of both of us for too long, finally snaps. "Well then don't get advice from a psychic," I mutter.

"Tanzy Hightower, you get to your room right now."

"Or what? You won't cook dinner?"

"I am doing the best I can!"

"You're not doing anything at all!"

The kitchen falls to silence, and even though everything in the room is exactly the same as it was before, it feels blown to pieces.

Mom reaches past me and grabs the bottle of bourbon. "Today was going to be my first good day," she says through her teeth.

"I'm sorry I ruined it for you," I retort.

"You did." She walks out of the kitchen and down the hall. I race upstairs to my room and shut the door before sliding down against it. How have we come to this? How do we fix this? I can't leave but I can't stay. I press the heels of my hands into my eyes. Outside, thunder rumbles. I drop my hands and blink, recalling my mother's prediction. The light in my room falls to shadows, and the sky begins to pour.

GRADUATION

"Tanzy Leigh Hightower," the principal says, announcing my name. I keep my eyes on him and walk straight ahead, refusing to look out at the crowd. There's no one here to wave to or take my picture. I only came because the silence in my house was too loud.

I take my diploma and shake his hand.

"Congratulations," he says.

My lips form a tight smile, and I stride toward the off side. With only two steps to go, I can't stop myself from stealing a glimpse of the courtyard. The two seats assigned to my family are empty. I squeeze my eyes shut briefly, and then force my legs to finish walking off the stage.

After the ceremony, I stand under the limb of one of the cherry blossom trees lining the courtyard, and stare out at the people milling around. Families gather together and take pictures. They hug, they smile. They play with the graduation tassels. I take off my cap and rotate it by its corners, and then peer down at the toes of my paddock boots, which are peeking out from under my itchy gown.

I'm not sure why I'm still here. There's no one waiting on me, no pictures to take. I step out from under the tree.

"So, Tanzy, what are you going to do now? Go to Disney World?" Dana's voice calls from the left.

"Where did you come from?" I ask, breaking into a grin as I catch sight of her.

"The back. I don't do the whole assigned seating thing. Sorry I don't do dress up, either."

"I wouldn't have recognized you if you did. You didn't have to come."

"Yes, I did. I'm taking you out for lunch, too. Just me and you. I just need to drop by Wildwood first." She heads in the direction of the parking lot.

"I, I'm sorry. I can't go to Wildwood."

"You don't even have to get out of the truck. It'll just be a second."

I shake my head. "It wouldn't feel right."

"Tanzy, you can't avoid Wildwood forever. We need you. Your horse needs you. You need Wildwood! What are you going to do now, seriously? Are you and your mom just going to sit in the house and stare at each other or avoid each other until the end of time?"

"I'm going to wait tables at Smokey's. I start next week."

"You're going to wait tables?" she practically shrieks. "Your father would have my head if he knew I let you and your talent waste away at Smokey's Barbeque." Her face is the picture of disgust.

"Just for now." I hold up my hands. "Just until I can afford a place of my own. Then we'll see."

"Did you not get into any colleges?" she asks, leaning in.

"I don't know. I haven't opened any of the letters."

Dana reaches up to her sunglasses and pulls them down. Her blue eyes bore into mine. "Are you kidding me right now?"

"I need to be here. Smokey's is fifteen minutes from my house. Mom does best during the day, and I'm going to try to only work lunch shifts."

"This is . . ." she trails off and plants her hands on her hips. "What did the therapist say?"

"Mom fired her."

"Of course she did." Dana rubs her brow. "And there's nothing you can do to force her to get help?"

"She hasn't tried to hurt anyone or herself. She has days where she's better. She's grieving, Dana. I don't think there's one set way to do that. Even the therapist said so."

"This is really what you want to do?"

"Yes."

"Well please, for the love of God, change your mind. And when you do, you will have a job at Wildwood waiting for you."

"Thanks." I squirm under my gown. Between the conversation, and the polyester's exceptional ability to absorb heat, I feel like I'm being cooked. "I think I'm going to pass on lunch. Thanks for the invite though. I just feel like I need to go check on Mom."

"Sure, go." Dana waves at me. "But you better call me soon."

"I will." I make a beeline for the truck, keeping my gaze trained low. In my haste, I fumble with the handle and drop the keys.

"Are you okay?" a man's voice says from behind me.

"Yes, just in a hurry," I say, stealing a glimpse over my shoulder. There's a guy standing at the car two empty spots away from mine. He's nearly a foot taller than me. His hair is dark and messy. His face has a long scar across one cheek, and his hands look like he tried to grab a catfish by the whiskers. I know I've never met him before. He'd be hard to forget.

"Thanks, though." I climb in and slam the door shut, nervousness scampering from the nape of my neck down my spine.

I give him a customary wave through my window, and punch the gas.

The sensation of being followed trails me all the way home. I check my mirrors every few seconds. No one is behind me. So why does it feel like it? My stare moves from the road to the shadows of the trees. Who was that guy? A student I've never met? Someone's relative in town for graduation?

"You need to get a grip. It was just someone trying to be nice. People with massive scars can be nice," I whisper. I look at my own hands, which are crisscrossed with dozens of little scars from farm life nicks and scratches. I sigh. I don't allow my eyes to wander from the road for the rest of the drive.

"I'm home," I call as I walk in the door, and then I head upstairs to my room without waiting for a response. I sit down at my desk and pull open a bottom drawer, where unopened letters from six different colleges are tucked under a scrapbook. I spread them out on my desk. What if I got into one of these schools? Would they still take me, or is it too late? And if I did get in, would I go? Could I leave?

I open the first envelope.

Dear Miss Tanzy Hightower,
  Congratulations! We'd like to welcome you to . . .

My eyes blur with tears. I open the next letter, and the next, until all six are open on my desk. Six invitations to start over. Six places that think I belong with them. I gather up the letters and run down stairs. Mom's door is open.

"Mom!" I burst into her room. It's empty. I approach the windows, a seed of dread taking root inside. Mom is outside, lying flat on her back on what looks to be a patchwork quilt. I lean forward, recognizing some of the patterns. She's made a blanket out of Dad's shirts. His pictures are scattered around her. The tulip has been dug up and cast aside, and she's clutching his dog tags to her chest.

I look from her to the letters and back again. She would be so happy to hear about me moving away. She's about as thrilled with the Smokey's idea as Dana was. But how could I move away with the knowledge she has just as many days like this as she does days where she comes and watches the sunrise through the kitchen window?

I fold the letters, and drop them into the trash can on my way outside, where I lower myself to the blanket of Dad's shirts, and stare up at the sky.

PART II

NINETEEN

I stand in the express checkout aisle at the grocery store, wondering if the cashier can smell the sickeningly sweet scent of barbeque sauce clinging to my clothes and my hair.

"Coconut pancakes, I'm guessing?" she asks, scanning the shredded coconut, the box of instant pancake mix, and a bottle of whipped cream. "I've never thought to make them with coconut."

"Family tradition."

"I'll have to try that some time," she says, and I manage a tight smile as I hand her the cash. I'm pretty sure it smells like Smokey's, too.

I bag my groceries and head home. The sun has already sunk behind the trees. I'd hoped to be with mom before dark, but Smokey's had been busy today, and another server had called in sick.

The house is dark as night. I tiptoe into the kitchen and set out the ingredients and the griddle. Then I climb on a chair and take the smoke detector off the ceiling. For added measure, I remove all the smoke detectors on the first floor. Tomorrow, my mom will cook coconut pancakes, and nothing will go wrong.

I crack my Mom's door open, making sure she's home. She's fast asleep. Lately, her days seem to be divided into fourths. She sleeps part of the night and part of the day. She spends most morning in the backyard, regardless of the weather. She spends the middle of the night roaming the house, tracing a clockwise pattern around the first floor. Sometimes I lie awake at night and try to track her feather-light footsteps as she moves from room to room, wondering what she's looking for.

I find myself tiptoeing to the living room, sitting in his favorite chair, wrapped in his tattered gray quilt, staring at the last picture ever taken of my father. It sits on the mantle in a plain silver frame that I've never liked. I take down the frame and pull off the back, removing the picture. Then I take it to my room and curl up with his blue plaid shirt I stole the day Mom made a blanket out of them.

His picture shakes so hard in my hand I'm afraid I'll tear it. I put it down on the bedside table, but it feels too far away, so I pick it up again. I don't tremble as hard if I don't look at it. Tonight, for the first time in almost a year, the ghost of him feels like it's everywhere. I saw him all day at the restaurant, and again at a stoplight on the way to the store. I ball his shirt in my fist and press it against my mouth to keep from crying. Mom will be up soon, and I don't want to her to hear me.

The moon passes across the width of my window. Mom hasn't started walking. Something's wrong. I creep to the top of the stairs. The bottom floor is dark. The steps creak under my weight. I expect her to come around a corner at any moment, and I wonder if she'll even notice I'm here.

I peek down her hall. Her door is closed. I open it. Her bed is empty, and the window is open. She's in the yard in a nightgown, her whole being turned silver by the moon. She's holding a shovel, digging a huge hole where the tulip once grew. There's a mound of dirt behind it. She steps into the hole, and disappears up to her thighs. She climbs back out, walks the perimeter, and continues to shovel.

Despair seeps through me. Mom's had a run of bad days lately, but this is the strangest thing she's done in a long time. I wonder if she's been seeing the psychic again. I've started scanning the phone bill each month for commercial phone numbers, but haven't seen any. I expected the spectrum of her moods to consolidate, when really, it's only widened. A few of her good days have nearly bordered who she was before Dad vanished. But her bad days have only intensified with time.

I start to call out to her through the window, when clouds pass over the moon, snuffing out the faint light. The darkness around her begins to thicken and crackle. She doesn't look up, doesn't notice the static glow or the fizzing sound.

I hold my breath. Silver fissures spider-web across the black. Still, she doesn't acknowledge them. Are they real? Is any of it? Is my mother really standing outside in a slip of a gown during the first frost of fall, digging a hole big enough to fit a body? Or am I imagining all of it? Is she sound asleep in her bed or pacing the house, and I can't see her? What if . . . what if I'm not watching her lose her mind? What if it's me?

I reach for her bed and run my hand over the comforter. It's flat and cool. I turn back to the window. The cyclone of shadows has vanished, the dark blanket of night returned. Mom goes still. Her head swivels in my direction, and I duck out of sight.

I hurry from her room, easing her door shut behind me, and then continue down the hall, and into the kitchen. The clock on the stove reads three in the morning. I lean on the counter, gripping the edge to keep my hands from trembling. Nausea churns so hard in my stomach I can barely breathe or swallow. What is happening to me? I can barely remember who I was on this day last year. She's a stranger now. What had I wanted back then? Where did I think I would be today? All I can remember is promising Mom I'd come home.

No matter how hard I try to stop it, my mind replays the ride to the ridge, shows me the iridescent rainbow shimmering across the valley, and the flash of blue. Even now, my voice trumpets in my ears. A wave of guilt strikes me center, and I nearly gag. I need proof. I need to know if she sees the shadows, if she reads them the way she reads the sunrise.

I slip through the back door and step out onto the lawn, which is icy and brittle under my bare feet. The mound of dirt she'd made is gone. She must've refilled the hole. I walk to the side, waiting to feel the soft, loose place of freshly turned earth, but I can't find it. I crisscross the yard until I'm dizzy. There's no break in the terrain.

"I swear," I murmur, turning in a circle. I clamp my hands on both sides of my head as a buzz grows in my ears. "This doesn't make any sense." Had I imagined it? Has a year of nearly sleepless nights caught up with me?

Confusion swirls inside my skull. I hurry into the house and traipse down the hall, leaving a trail of dirty footprints. I reach up to knock on her door, when the sound of her sobbing comes through the wood. All thoughts of what I saw outside vanish. This conversation *will* happen—it must—but it can wait one more day.

"Momma? Are you okay?"

"Just leave me be, Tanzy." Her voice is thick and blubbery.

"I brought stuff for coconut pancakes," I say. "We can make them together."

"Not today."

Grief pricks my heart. "But, it's tradition."

"To hell with tradition. It couldn't keep any of you safe." She lets out a jagged sob.

"Safe from what?" I press my ear against the door.

"From . . . from . . . from the darkness in the world, Tanzy. From all of it."

"Please, Mom. Let's make the pancakes. And we can go to Wildwood, just like me and Dad did every year. I can take you to the ridge. We can just walk, we won't ride. He was so happy up there, Mom. Maybe, maybe you'll feel it. Maybe you'll feel him." I rest my forehead on her door. My fingers wrap around the handle, testing it. She didn't lock it. I slowly turn it, easing the door open. Mom is sitting on her bed, a bottle of bourbon in her hand.

"Where did you get that?" I ask, alarmed. I'd poured out all the bottles I could find after the psychic's first and only visit.

"That's not your business." She stands up, and sways to the side.

"This is my business! I help pay bills! I put food in the kitchen. I have given up everything for you! College, riding, Wildwood. Everything! I am trying to help you but I can't do that if you won't help yourself!"

"Help me? It should have been you that day! Don't you get that? It should have been you in that river!"

I stumble away from her, my ears ringing, my heart shuddering in my chest.

"How could you . . . how could you say that?" I whisper. "How could you say that to me?"

"Tanzy, no." Her face sags and her mouth hangs open. "I didn't mean it like that."

"Then how else did you mean it?" I ask, gasping.

"I meant . . . I meant . . ."

My heart quakes in my chest. I spin on my heels and run for the door, grabbing the keys on my way out. She's still shouting my name when I fling open the front door. I jump in Dad's truck. I can't drive away fast enough.

Sheets of rain collide with the windshield. Between the rain, the dark, the pops of lightning, and the halo from the headlights, I can barely see the front of the truck. I don't even know where I'm going, just somewhere that isn't home. I grip the steering wheel. My mind spins. My breathing sounds far away.

Memories from the last year fill the narrow cab—Mom ranting, pacing, blind to my presence; the first time I noticed the bills were past due; and the electricity was two days away from being turned off; Mom staring out the window, her silence louder than her screams; watching the tulip's roots shrivel and the slender stem wither; the time I found Mom's wedding dress, still stained with dirt, stuffed in the fireplace; the hundreds of dinners I've eaten alone; the fifteen seconds of dread I feel between exiting my truck and reaching the front door of the house every time I come home.

"I can't do it anymore!" Tears streak down my face. The turn for Wildwood appears. I wait for the customary nudge of guilt, which has stalled my truck twenty feet from here more times than I can count, but it doesn't come. I steer down Wildwood's driveway, my mind becoming quieter the closer I am to the parking lot. With a start, I realize I've pulled into Dad's old parking spot. I lean against the chair and inhale. I feel his presence more here already than I have anywhere else in the past year.

I hop out of the truck and jog to the doorway, only now realizing I'm still in my pajamas. I pluck the spare key from the garage door track, and unlock Dana's office, where her farm jacket will be waiting on the back of her desk chair, the way Dad's used to. It's a tradition I'm glad she kept, especially tonight.

I shrug on her jacket, pull on a spare ball cap hanging off her bulletin board, grab a couple brushes out of the basket for lesson supplies, and head to Harbor's stall. Her head is sticking over the Dutch door, as if she knows I'm here. She whinnies when she sees me.

"Hey girl." Emotion squeezes my throat. I've only seen her twice in a year and she's not holding it against me. "I'm sorry. I'm so sorry." New tears come, flooding my eyes. I drop the brushes in the barn aisle, let myself into her stall, and sob into her neck. She nuzzles my hair and my sides. Her warm breath works to thaw my heart, still frozen by my mother's words. I have given up so much to be by her side, including Harbor, but it wasn't enough. She wishes the river had taken me instead of Dad.

It should've been you.

I sob, sinking to my knees. Maybe I should've left for college. Maybe without me around she would've found more peace. I have never considered she saw Dad's accident as some kind of choice, an either/or. Teague spooked. Dad could've jumped off. He didn't.

"Why didn't you just jump off?" I whisper.

Harbor drops her head to sniff my cheek. I touch her face, and she noses at my fingers. When's the last time Mom reached out for me? When's the last time she asked me if I'm okay? I'm not okay.

A clap of close thunder startles Harbor, and she moves into me.

"It's okay, girl. It's just a storm," I murmur. Her nostrils flare. She steps to her stall door and peers out. Footsteps echo down the hall. They're too slow to be Dana. I glance down where my watch should be, but I'd taken it off before bed. Is it already time to feed? I back against the front wall, and sink down between Harbor's two hanging water buckets.

A man's silhouette appears in the opening, backlit by the hall light.

"Is someone in here?" he asks. He bends down. When he straightens up, I see he's holding the two brushes I dropped in the aisle. "Hey, girl," he says. I hold my breath, wondering if I've been spotted. Instead he reaches in and scratches Harbor behind her ear. She shoves her nose into his chest. I lean forward, disbelieving. Harbor bites everyone but me.

The man's face shifts, looking into the stall, and we lock eyes.

"What are you doing in here?" he asks, sliding the bolt on the door. Light spills onto his face, revealing two scars that run from his jaw to where his ear connects to the side of his face. Familiarity nips at the base of my neck. Where have I seen this guy before?

"This is my horse." I jump to my feet.

"I know." He smiles.

"You know?"

"Everyone knows who you are. And from what I've heard, the only people Harbor will let hang out in her stall without trying to kick their teeth in are me and you. I've been watching out for her since you've been gone. I hope that's okay."

"What are you doing here? It's really late." I press myself against Harbor's shoulder.

"The storm is about to get really bad." He glances down the aisle. "The radar is lit up like the Fourth of July. I couldn't sleep. I figured I'd rather be here than stare at my ceiling."

"So, you work here?" My shoulders relax.

"I'm Lucas." He sticks his hand over the barn door. I keep mine where they are. "That's fair," he responds, and withdraws his hand.

64

"Dana lets you come to the barn whenever you feel like it?"

"You're here, too." He raises his brow.

"Yeah, but my dad . . ." I trail off, suddenly overcome. "My dad used to run this place."

"From what I understand, it's more like your dad was this place. All I hear is how Wildwood isn't the same without him."

"How could it be?" A gust of wind rips through the barn, and blows rain harder against the metal roof. My mind drifts to the river, and I imagine how fast it's rising.

"Were you planning on grooming her?" he asks, holding out the brushes.

"My tack locker is down the hall. I'll go get my own stuff in a bit," I lie. I stay behind the security of the door, wishing Harbor hadn't taken a liking to this guy. He has to duck to fit inside the door. His eyes are wide-set and almost completely black. His gray shirt is tucked into a pair of jeans and his boots are caked with mud. My gaze travels back to the scars on his face. For some reason, I know if I check his hands I'll find more. I know I've seen him before. But it's a small town, and Smokey's is a local favorite. He's probably been in the diner at least once in the past five months. Maybe he even sat in my section.

"Didn't you want to get your brushes?" He gestures down the hall toward the line of tack lockers, and then slowly looks back at me. "I'm freaking you out, aren't I?" he asks. He steps back and lifts his hands. "Say no more. I want to check the radar again, anyway. I'll sack out in Dana's office. It won't be the first night I've spent on that crappy futon. You won't even know I'm here."

"Thanks."

"Be seeing you," he says, and retracts his looming body from the doorway. I replay his words in my head, and recognition jolts through me. Not what he said, but his voice. *Are you okay, miss?* He was at my graduation.

"Hey, wait!" I blurt. He doesn't answer. I don't know why I need to know why he was at graduation. Maybe he was there for a relative, or maybe he's why Dana needed to drop by Wildwood before lunch. Maybe because it was the first time someone had asked me if I was okay in months. But something inside of me needs to know. "Lucas!" I peer around the door frame and into the barn aisle. He's gone.

I walk out of Harbor's stall. Dana's office door is open. I jog down the hall. He's not there. I head to the parking lot, Except for my truck, the lot is empty. I stop in my tracks. Lucas's boots had been caked in mud, as if he'd walked straight out of the pasture.

Purple lightning forks across the sky, followed immediately by a crack of thunder. Two more bolts split the dark in rapid succession. A fourth hits so close, the air crackles in the aftermath. Each time the lightning flashes, the woods light up in silvers and blues, and the shadows dance and leap.

A sharp creak is followed by the bang of wood on wood: someone's stall has just opened hard and fast. I lean forward in time to see Harbor emerge from her open stall. She holds her silver head high, stepping with caution, and then takes off down the aisle at a trot. I must have left her stall door open.

"Harbor," I hiss at her. "Whoa, girl." One ear swivels in my direction, and her body curls in consideration. Then her back hoof knocks an over-turned bucket, sending it clattering to the side, and she bolts out of the barn.

"Lucas! Harbor's loose!" I shout over my shoulder and then follow her into the storm.

Sometimes The End Comes First

I run through the open gate and down the hill, doing my best to ignore the way the swaying trees and the bursts of lightning cast moving shadows across the wet grass. This part of the pasture is nearly fifty acres across. Any sign of Harbor has been swallowed up by the dark and the rain.

A twig snaps nearby. I whirl around. My gray horse is standing by a tree, regarding me with wide eyes. She paws at the earth, and then crab-steps, craning her neck.

"Hey, girl," I murmur, doing my best to not scare her off. She snorts, and steps in my direction. Finding her was the easy part. Now I have to figure out how to catch her and bring her back into her stall with no halter or lead rope.

I peer back at the barn. Lucas is standing in the mouth of the main door. He brings his hands to his mouth. A roll of thunder drowns out whatever he's yelling.

Without warning, Harbor rocks back onto her back legs, and rears.

"Easy!" I step closer to her, keeping myself at her side so she won't land on top of me. She touches the ground for a split second before going up again. She strikes out this time. Her ears lay back and she bears her teeth. I chance a glimpse behind me. Horror charges through my body as I lock eyes with a massive, black cat solidifying from the shadowy dark. It slinks toward us, belly low, tail long and twitching, shoulders and hips sunk and ready for release.

I smother a gasp and clinch tight to Harbor. She hops sideways, wanting to take off. The air around us builds. A strange, heavy vibration saturates the air, and a buzzing sound builds from the ground. The moment before the pitch reaches an impossible frequency, a thick blade of lightning slices through the sky and strikes the top of the barn. Sparks spray in every direction.

"Tanzy! Run!" Lucas's voice bellows over the pasture.

Panic floods me, making my body feel springy and buoyant. In a single motion, I propel myself onto Harbor's back and swing my leg over her side. Harbor scrambles forward as I struggle to find my balance. It's been a year since I've ridden, and her back is awkward and foreign under me. There's no time to acclimate. The creature opens its jaws, and lunges for Harbor's back leg. A scream catches in my throat. Harbor spins and bucks, kicking the beast square in the chest. I cling to her mane as I right myself as best I can.

I dig my heels into Harbor's side and let out a shout. Instead of moving forward, Harbor leaps sideways and twists in the air, nearly slinging me off her back. I clamp my knee onto her withers and pull myself back to center. Harbor spins again. Why won't she run? She rears nearly vertical. I throw my arms around her neck and stare down at the ground. Another creature is pressing us from the side. The first creature is closing in from the front.

"Go, go!" I yell, blindly urging Harbor into motion. She whirls away from the direction of home and gallops deeper into the woods. The two creatures cackle at each other as they fall in line behind us. I want to look back at the barn, desperate to check how the barn came through the strike, but I can't risk a fall. We rip through the trees. The pasture fencing is somewhere up ahead, reinforced with steel mesh and over five feet high. With no clear place to take off or land, jumping may be more dangerous than whatever is chasing us through these woods.

I fight to ignore the feeling of being trapped, clinging to Harbor's back and neck as she pushes herself faster. Harbor sees the fence in time to make a hard turn to avoid crashing into it, and then gallops flat out alongside it, finally able to stretch out on the clear path. A dark streak gives chase, staying cloaked in the shadows of the trees to our right. Harbor's ears swivel back and forth, listening to it close in. I concentrate on the steady rhythm of air blowing out of her nose like a freight train. Her head flings back, nearly cracking me in the face. I cry out as another black creature leaps at us head on, claws outstretched and huge jaws open. Harbor stumbles and then gathers.

"No!" I scream as Harbor launches herself sideways over the fence. I wrap my arms around her neck and squeeze my eyes shut as my left leg crushes between her sliding body and the fence rail. Sounds of splintering wood fill my ears.

Her legs buckle on the other side and her body flips above me as we roll across the hard earth. Blood and sweat are hot and salty in my mouth. I feel no pain, and though I'm sure I'm screaming I don't hear it.

Harbor's labored breathing sounds somewhere ahead of me. I try to call out to her but no sound comes. *Have to get up. Have to keep moving.* My body writhes in agony as the air slowly returns to my lungs. My eyes train on the gaping hole in the mangled fence. The lion approaches, mouth open, red tongue flicking over its teeth. My brain commands my body to move, but my right leg won't answer. One of my hands is trapped under my body, and is covered in something warm and wet. A low hum builds in my ears. The ground trembles. I lift my head. The rain begins to turn silver. The darkness is lit with platinum, and a bolt of lightning crashes down.

LUCKY

The light is crushing. I can't breathe, can't move. The direction of the pressure changes instantaneously, and the ground beneath me shoves me airborne. The blanket of white fades to gray and then to black, and I am weightless. I inhale a deep breath. The ringing in my ears dissipates, and is replaced with complete and utter silence. The moment I realize I'm floating, I begin to plummet. The darkness whizzes by. I gasp, and fling my arms out to my side, trying to slow my fall. Red earth appears, racing toward me. I'm going to hit it. I'm going to die.

Contact jolts through me, but I feel no pain. I don't feel anything at all. I climb to my feet, which are bare, and shield my eyes with my hands so I can see into the distance. The rust-colored desert touches every inch of the horizon, met by a sapphire-blue sky. The world around me is as quiet as an empty sanctuary. I've never been here. I know I haven't. But I have been here. I have . . .

Gray washes over my vision, and a cacophony of voices floods my brain, shattering the peace. I clench my teeth against the noise and clamp my hands over my ears.

"No," I whisper. "Go away."

Several faces whirl in the sky above me. Shadows lurk behind them. Fear explodes inside of me. I burst into a sprint. The faces loom closer, and the shadows grow. I change direction, but the shadows are faster. They flood the sky, eclipsing the faces that spin faster by the second. There's nowhere to go.

Movement in the distance catches my attention. It's dark and shimmering, distorted by the heat. They're coming for me. I spin and run. A white light appears on the horizon ahead, as if a colorless sun is rising. There. I need to go *there*. My arms and legs pump as fast as I can make them, but everything feels slow and heavy. The ground has become soft, nearly too soft to run across.

"Wait," a voice says, clear and close. I turn, panting. Lucas stands behind me, his image blurring as if he's a heat-induced mirage.

"Where am I? Why are you here?" I ask. My voice echoes between us. Lucas studies me.

"Do you know who you are?" he asks. Before I can answer, the roar of voices overhead intensifies, and words emerge from the noise.

"We're losing her again." I hear. My stare snaps toward the sky.

"Get the crash cart," a male voice calls from farther away. A searing white circle of light appears inches from my face. I shut my eyes, exhausted and overwhelmed. Searing heat begins in my heart and spreads outward. The sensation surges through my limbs. *What's happening to me?*

"Make it stop!" I scream. Lucas takes my hand in his. I nearly yank it away, but the pain vanishes everywhere his skin touches mine. My palm is the only piece of me that doesn't feel like it's on fire.

"Charge to two hundred," another voice batters against my brain.

"Leave me alone!" I hear myself scream again.

"It's okay, Tanzy. It's time for Spera to return," Lucas reassures me, his mouth so close to my ear that his lips brush my skin. Spera. The name whispers through me, and a face blooms clear and vivid in my mind's eye: brown skin, a tangle of black hair, bright, gold, angry eyes. Her lips pull back in a smile. Then she bares her teeth, her face elongates, her ears sharper, and shiny black hair begins to cover her skin. My heart races. I've seen this before.

"Clear!" a voice booms. A bolt of lightning screams down from the blue sky and strikes the ground inches from my feet. Lucas turns his dark eyes to mine and squeezes my fingers in his big hand.

"Be seeing you," he whispers.

Instantly I am flying, falling upwards into a sinking black. The total void liquefies, pressing on my skin, filling my mouth. I can't spit it out. It swells in my throat, choking me. I try to reach inside my mouth but my hand won't budge. The sound of gagging reaches my ears, and the sensation of floating begins to subside.

You're dreaming. Open your eyes. They won't open, glued together by whatever sticky substance I'm covered in. Behind my eyelids, my eyes begin to burn as desperate tears pool across their surfaces.

Wake up!

The weight dissipates along with the darkness. Sensations come back one by one. All of them hurt.

Someone is touching my hand. I curl and flex my fingers, uncertainty passing through me. Where am I? Dana's sing-song voice floats into my ears. Please be real. I latch onto it, and use it to swim all the way into consciousness.

My eyelids flutter as I work to make them stay open. Dana's face, drawn and pensive, comes briefly into focus. I draw in a breath. The air moving down my throat and into my lungs feels like it's splintering my ribcage.

"Dana?" I rasp curiously. My entire body throbs with pain and pressure. Tears threaten to spill from eyes.

"You're awake!" she says.

Awake . . . I was dreaming. Just dreaming . . . Then why do I hurt so much? Why does Dana sound like she's talking to me from the other end of a long tunnel? I try to sit up, but my body doesn't respond. Images of a storm bend and blur in my mind, receding each time I try to focus. The sounds of a galloping horse and rumbles of thunder echo in my skull. Nausea churns in my stomach.

"I don't feel so good," I mutter. "Something . . . I think something's wrong."

"Shh," Dana says. "Just breathe."

I inhale a long, slow breath through my nose. The grayish room comes into focus behind her. Florescent lighting paints my surroundings sickly yellow. There's a rectangular pattern of natural light beaming across the end of my bed, indicating a window behind me. Dana's sitting in a worn blue chair. There's a clock on the wall behind her. The second hand makes a ticking sound with every second, which reverberates in my skull, making my teeth ache.

"Where are we?" My mind spins with confusion.

"We're in the hospital."

My eyes move from Dana to my body. My left leg is in a cast. I raise a hand to my throbbing head. Gauze covers most of my scalp. Pain shoots up my left side every time I move. I wince, curling away from the pressure.

Dana leans in. She reaches across my face and tucks a wayward lock of my hair behind my ears. A green semicircle, the size of a marble, glows in the palm of her hand. The color looks alive, like she's caught a lightning bug. I press myself away from her hand as it passes within inches of my face. Up close I can see the glow resembles the shape of a horseshoe.

"There's something on your hand," I say. My tongue is dry and sticky, and my voice sounds garbled in my ears. She frowns, turning both hands palm-side up, and stares down at them.

"I don't see anything," she says, and then faces them to me.

"It's right there . . ." I trail off as I nod my chin towards her hands.

"There's nothing there, Tanzy." She rests her hands palm-down on her knees. I stare at them, waiting for the glow to peek out from under her hands, but nothing happens.

"It's gone now," I lie.

"I wouldn't worry about it too much." She tries to smile. Her face is heavy. There are purple half-moons under her eyes. I've never seen her look so tired.

"What happened to me?" I try to think back to the moments immediately prior to hearing Dana's voice. I'd dreamed something so vivid. All I can recall is a blue sky. And before the dream . . . my mind is dark and vacuous.

You . . . you were either struck by lightning or it struck near enough to a strike that you that you were electrocuted."

I suck in a breath, reliving the moment the night sky turned white. A shiver takes root deep within me, the chill spreading outward, and even though I'm covered with two blankets, I'm suddenly freezing.

"I'm not your mom, but riding at night in the woods in the storm of the century with no helmet on a horse with no tack? Have you lost your mind? I know you just woke up but it's all I've been thinking for days. You could be dead, Tanzy." She squeezes my arm.

"Harbor got loose. I chased her into the pasture." I struggle to remember more.

"Why did you get on her?" Dana presses.

"There was something in the woods," I whisper, staring into space as the cat's face comes into razor sharp focus. "Two of them. They looked like mountain lions, but were probably double the size and black. It was like a nightmare."

"We haven't seen many cougars in the valley this fall yet, but it doesn't mean they're not out there. It's weird they would be out in a storm though. It's weird that you were out at all. You picked a hell of a moment to make a comeback."

"Mom and I fought. I just needed some space. I drove to Wildwood. I didn't have anywhere else to go. I wasn't thinking."

"Lucas said you seemed upset."

"Lucas . . ." The name rings familiar in my mind, but I can't remember why.

"He started working for me at the beginning of the year. He saw the storm on the radar and went to check the horses. He's a good hire. Your dad would've liked him." Dana's voice sounds far away.

"He was there. Harbor liked him," I murmur. The exchange comes back in bits and pieces, ending with the moment I saw him standing in front of the barn. "Lightning was striking all around. I saw it hit the barn . . ." I lock eyes with Dana, and my heart begins to race. "Lightning struck the barn." Dana's chin trembles, and her eyes brim with tears.

"Wildwood is gone," she whispers.

"The horses?" I can barely get out the words.

"They're all gone, Tanzy," she begins to quietly sob.

"No." I shake my head and my insides quake. "No." Wildwood is all that's left of my father. It's a living memorial, a testament to what he achieved with own hands, what he stood for. He'd touched every wall, walked every inch. Every horse knew him on sight. How could it all be gone?

"I didn't want to tell you so soon," Dana looks away from me to wipe her face. "The barn went up so fast. They haven't even found any remains."

"What about Harbor?" My voice shakes. So do my hands.

"We've searched everywhere, but we haven't found a trace of her. There's a possibility she's so scared that she won't come near the smell of the fire. I'm leaving out feed and hay in the pasture every day just in case. The cats you saw may have chased her across the river, and now she won't come back across."

"Mom said it should've been me in the river," I sputter. "That's why I came to Wildwood. That's why this happened. That's why all of this happened."

"Tanzy, lightning would've struck the barn whether you'd come or not. If Harbor is still alive, it's because you came. Lucas, too. If he hadn't gone after you, he might've been in the barn asleep in my office." Dana shudders.

"That storm was different, Dana. It was . . . angry."

"Have you ever seen a storm that wasn't?" She gives me a teary smile.

"How's Mom?" I ask, and guilt washes over me. She warned me to never go to Wildwood, to not ride. Could the psychic have seen this coming? I shove the thoughts aside. The only thing that psychic saw was an easy target.

"We haven't been able to reach her yet," she answers quietly. "We've tried, Tanzy. I called about a hundred times in the first twenty-four hours after the fire. I've been by your house every day. I've dropped off dinner on your front porch every night, I swear. I even asked your neighbors, but they haven't seen her."

"She probably just isn't answering the door or the phone." I sink into the flimsy mattress, worried. Has she been eating?

"I'll go tonight on my way home. Lucas has tried to check on her, too. I think he feels responsible for what happened," Dana adds.

"It wasn't his fault. I left Harbor's door open. I chased her into the pasture."

"He thinks he upset you by being there, and it's why Harbor got out in the first place."

"But if she hadn't . . ." I murmur.

"If she hadn't," Dana echoes.

"How did he get those scars? I didn't want to ask."

"What scars?" Dana knits her brow.

"The big ones on his face, and there are a bunch all over his hands. They're pretty hard to miss."

"Lucas doesn't have any scars that I've seen."

"I swear . . ." I trail off, questioning my memory of both times I've seen him.

"I'm sure he'll be by soon to visit. He's been in once a day since the fire." She points across the room to a little sink area, which is lined with vases of wild flowers.

"Those are from him?"

"Like I said, he blames himself."

"He shouldn't." I close my eyes and lean back. I want to look at the flowers, to breathe them in, but they remind me of Dad, which reminds me of Mom, the river, the storm, the fire, the fact that I see things no one else does. It all comes circling back to that moment on the ridge, where I looked out at the big, clear valley and wanted to see something in it.

"Don't go to sleep yet. I need to tell the doctor you're awake, and he won't believe me if you're out again when he comes in. I'll be right back," Dana whispers.

I open my eyes in time to see her almost collide with Lucas, who's standing in the doorway with a jar of flowers in his hands.

"She's awake," Dana says, and glances at me over her shoulder on her way out the door. Color touches Lucas's face, and he stares down at the flowers.

My gaze lifts to his cheek. It's marble smooth. There aren't any scars on his hands, either. I blink, confused. I know I saw scars the night of the fire, and in the parking lot at graduation. Didn't I? I catch myself frowning as I stare at him.

"This felt way less awkward when you didn't see me bring them," Lucas says.

"What?"

"The flowers."

"They're beautiful," I reply, catching on. "Thank you, for all of them."

"I can throw them out. The others, too. I just, I want you to be okay. So I keep bringing you things." His jaw shifts beneath his cheek.

"No, leave them. It's nice to have something fresh in here."

Lucas smiles and moves into the room. He sets the jar down on the sink. I spy a flash of sapphire blue on his right palm. The hair on the back of my neck stands up. Why am I seeing these colors and what do they mean?

"Are you okay?" he asks.

"Honestly, I don't know. I'm awake. I know who I am. I can talk. I can remember a lot of what happened . . . but there are pieces of what I think I remember that don't make any sense." I study his face.

"Like what?"

"You had scars on your cheek and on your hands."

"I don't know what to tell you." He turns his hands over. The blue mark in his palm flashes each time he moves. "Sorry to disappoint. Do you have a thing for scars?"

I let out a nervous laugh. "That's . . . uh . . . that's not why I noticed them."

"I'm just kidding. It's nice to hear you laugh, though." He shoves his hands in his pockets. "Sorry, that was lame. I forget that you don't know me and I feel like I already know you."

"How's that?" I raise an eyebrow.

"Since I started working at Wildwood, I've heard more stories than I can count about Travis and Tanzy Hightower. I know all about your show record, and the time your dad taught you how to drive the tractor—"

"And I ran it through the fence?" I finish for him.

"Yep. I think it's cool they painted that section of fence a different color to commemorate the moment," he adds. I shield my face, feeling it flush. "But no, no scars. I thought you were talking about whatever the hell those things were in the woods that chased Harbor."

"You saw them?" I drop my hands and sit up, ignoring a burst of pain in my abdomen.

"Only when the lightning flashed. They looked huge. I wasn't even sure they were real, and then you and Harbor took off. I didn't mention them to Dana. I thought she'd think I'm crazy. They weren't like anything I've ever seen before."

"Way too big to be cougars," I say, nodding.

"I thought so too. I tried to follow you, but I lost your trail. By the time I found you, they were long gone."

"They were there when I fell." I shudder. "The only reason I can think of that they didn't kill me is because lightning struck so close. Did you see any sign of Harbor?"

"No. I searched every inch of that pasture. There's a place on the west border where the fence was down in about a four-foot section where a tree limb fell. The chance she found it is one in a million, but there's still a chance."

"Why did you come after me instead of letting the horses out?" I ask, instantly torn. What would I have done in his place? Chase a stranger into the dark or try to get out as many horses as I could?

"I saw Harbor take off and I just ran after you. I didn't realize the barn was on fire until I reached the trees. It went up so fast, Tanzy. It's like a bomb went off. I knew I wouldn't have been able to get many out, if any. They weren't even . . . they weren't even screaming or kicking the walls. Aside from the pops of the flames, it was snow quiet. It's like they were already gone."

My mind conjures the flames and the silence, and I close my eyes against a new wave of nausea.

"I'm sorry," Lucas whispers.

"Tanzy, my name is Dr. Andrews. I'm the chief of surgery here," an unfamiliar voice calls from the head of the room. I open my eyes and blink away the threat of tears. The name sends off a flare in my memory, but I can't remember why. A tall, lean man walks toward my bed, followed by Dana. He has close-cut pepper-colored hair and wire-rimmed glasses. "Welcome back. How are you feeling?"

I glance at his hands, but, save what's probably my chart, they're empty. I check Lucas and Dana's hands. Their colors are still present.

"I'm seeing things." Above the pain and the blank places in my memory, this is my foremost concern. Something inside of me is convinced if I can understand what these colors are and why I'm seeing them, so much more about the last year will make sense.

"What kinds of things?" He retrieves a tiny flashlight from his lab coat pocket, clicks it on, and shines the light near my chin. "I'm going to check your pupils, okay? You keep talking."

"I see little glowing spots on people's hands." I force my eyelids to stay open as he shines the light directly into my eyes.

"I'll make a note of that. You were struck by lightning, and you had a severe concussion." He stares over the top of the flashlight and into my eyes. "Halos, double vision, abnormalities, strange colors, those are all to be expected. What I need to know from here forward is if anything changes significantly or gets worse. All things considered, you're incredibly lucky. You're awake, you're talking, and you know who you are and who your friends are. This is an amazing start—way more than I hoped for this early in the game."

"When can I go home?" I ask. Dana peers at me from behind Dr. Anderson, and her face clouds over, filling me with trepidation.

"Well, your body has been through a lot. You lost a lot of blood from a significant puncture wound." He points to my left side. "Luckily, whatever you fell on missed every major organ. You did require a considerable blood transfusion. We need to monitor your vitals over the next two or three days. We also need to put a hard cast on your leg, and make sure your burn is healing."

"My burn?"

"As with most lightning strike patients, you have a burn pattern from the contact and conduction. Yours is the most unique I've ever seen. Generally, the burns look like trees or spider webs, and in some cases I have seen fairly straight lines. I can say with certainty this is the first time I've ever seen a lightning strike create a circular pattern. Here, I'll show you." He reaches for the front of my hospital gown. My chest is wrapped in gauze, and I wonder if it's responsible for the pressure I've been experiencing. He loosens the gauze enough to pull down the front of the bandage, but the pressure remains. Three interlocking circles are branded across my sternum. They're fiery red, with spindly red wisps feathering off of them like trails of smoke.

"Lightning did that?" I stare at the burn, mesmerized. Dr. Andrews nods.

"The only explanation I can think of is that the lightning passed directly through you on its route from ground to atmosphere, and didn't travel elsewhere in your body. But it's impossible to know. We haven't seen any indication of an internal char pattern, which makes you incredibly lucky, especially with the proximity of the strike mark to your lungs and heart. My wife actually has a program for lightning strike and electrocution survivors, if you're interested. She's a psychiatrist. She was struck by lightning once, too. She has some unorthodox beliefs about the weather, but I'm a results man, and she's had some remarkable outcomes with former patients. They've often gone on to pursue goals and dreams they never thought tangible before their injuries. I'll have her come and talk to you."

"Okay." I squirm at the thought of discussing goals and dreams with anyone, much less a perfect stranger. I also can't help wondering if she's anything like Mom.

Dr. Andrews secures the bandage, and then turns his attention to the computer attached to the opposite wall.

"We're going to be drawing blood quite a bit over the next forty-eight hours. You'll also be given medication to help with the pain, and to help with any possible infections and adverse reactions to the blood transfusion. I want you to rest as much as you can, but as often as we'll be in here, we probably won't make it very easy." He chuckles, and I manage a weak smile in return. Dr. Andrews stares at the screen and types for several seconds. "I will be back to check on you this evening. If anything changes, anything, call the nurse's station and have me paged immediately. Any changes," he reiterates, and then strolls from the room.

Lucas leans back against the counter, folding his arms against his chest. Dana slides into the chair next to my bed and wipes her hands on her jeans before propping up her chin on her fingers.

"You might look worse than I do," I say.

"You haven't seen a mirror, yet." There's lightness in her voice, but her expression is serious. I glance around the room. There aren't any mirrors. I wonder if it's intentional.

"Go home, Dana."

"I can't leave you."

"Yes, you can. I need you to check on Mom. And to bring me real food," I say, even though my stomach churns, and I can't imagine eating. Dana won't leave if I don't give her a way to feel helpful.

"You're hungry? That's great," Dana says, standing.

"I think it's a good sign. It always is for horses."

"You shouldn't be alone, though," she adds.

"You heard Dr. Andrews. They're going to be in here a lot. And Lucas is here." I glance at Lucas. He raises his brow, surprise lifting his expression. Dana gives me a curious look.

"Okay. Well, I'll make sure you're allowed to eat whatever you want, and I'll bring you dinner."

"What time is it?" I twist to see the window behind me, but a stabbing pain in my side stops me. Dana glances at her watch.

"Just after noon," she says. "I'll run by your mom's, check in at Wildwood, stop by my house, pick up food, and come back."

"Don't rush. I'm not going anywhere. Take a nap or a shower or both."

"Tanzy, you've taken care of yourself and your mom for so long you don't even see when you're the one who needs help," Dana says quietly.

"This is how you help me."

"Okay." Dana points at Lucas. "If she starts acting weird at all, get a doctor."

"I'm on it." He salutes, and Dana walks out, casting one last glance into the room before disappearing down the hall.

Two Of A Kind

Now that Dana has left, the room feels smaller with just Lucas and me in it. There's nowhere to look that isn't in his direction, or purposefully away from him. Still, I need this time alone. I need to learn more about what happened, and he was noticeably quiet in Dana's presence.

"So I look bad?" I ask, in an attempt to lighten the mood.

"I mean, you look like you fell off a galloping horse and were then struck by lightning."

"Right."

"Actually, all things considered, it's not as bad as it could've been. You have two black eyes. The left side of your face is about twice as big as the right, and you have some scratches, but it'll all heal in no time. Trust me, I know a thing or two about . . ."

"About what?" I prompt.

"About bouncing back. I did some dumb things in younger days, had some epic face-plants of my own."

"Ever been struck by lightning?" I ask, only half kidding.

"No." His face falls. "Tanzy . . . I'm sorry. If I hadn't been there, this wouldn't have happened to you. I know I freaked you out. As soon as I saw you, I could tell you wanted to be alone."

"If you hadn't been there, I might be fine, or I might be dead," I say.

"Maybe."

"Things happen. Life goes sideways. Trust *me*, I know. And I know what it's like when you feel responsible for something that's not really in your control." Flashbacks of Teague bolting surface in my mind. "You're right. I wasn't happy to have company at the time. But I'm lucky as hell you were there." My memory drifts to the last moments I remember before the flash. "Tell me everything you can about what you saw when you found me."

Lucas swallows and moves closer. He slides his hands in his pockets, and his eyes find the floor.

"You were flat on your back. Your arms were stretched out. I remember thinking it was weird that your palms were faceup, your fingers were loose. You looked so relaxed. Even . . . even peaceful." He stops to clear his throat. "Then I saw that there was blood everywhere. I knew I shouldn't move you, but I wanted to see where it was coming from. I rolled you over, and there was a piece of the fence sticking out of your back. That's when I realized it went all the way through. Everything slowed down and sped up at the same time. I picked you up. You were so light. And I carried you back to the barn. When we got close, I saw the glow from the fire, heard people shouting. I'd forgotten about the fire. I wish I could tell you I hadn't. But . . . I forgot." His gaze is focused on something far off.

"It's okay," I whisper.

Someone knocks on the open door. I look up. A woman flashes me a smile before stepping into the room. She looks like she belongs in a "Cover Girl" ad. She's wearing a tailored skirt suit and black stilettos. She's not wearing a lab coat, a badge, or a stethoscope. Her blonde hair spills over her shoulders, and her green eyes leap out from under a hood of copper eyeshadow. Who is this woman? Curious, I peek at her hand. A reddish-gold hoofprint shimmers in her left palm, and on her ring finger is the biggest emerald I've ever seen.

"Hi Tanzy. I'm Vanessa," she says, stopping when she reaches the foot of my bed.

"Hi." I cover my abdomen with my arms. Lucas takes a sideways step closer to me.

"Sorry, I thought my husband told you I was coming." Confusion flashes across Vanessa's face. "Dr. David Andrews? I'm his wife. Vanessa Andrews. Dr. Vanessa Andrews." Her voice is lyrical and soft, with a hint of a deep-south accent that elongates a syllable in every word

"You're Dr. Andrews," I say on an exhale. "You believe in a world in the clear," I continue before I can stop myself. "I . . . I heard you on the radio." I flush, glancing briefly at Lucas. He's not watching me, though. His gaze is fixed on Dr. Andrews.

"Oh." She clasps her hands at her front. "It was an early segment on a little radio show. I'm surprised anyone was listening."

"I was." The room falls to silence.

"Well, call me Vanessa. I'm here because my husband said you were struck by lightning." I struggle upright. I don't want to talk about lightning. I want to hear about the world in the clear. I want to know if anything I've seen in the last year is something she can explain, something she has also seen. If the shadows on the ridge were real, then Teague spooked at them, not at my voice. "Can I examine the burn pattern? David said it was quite unique."

"Sure."

Vanessa twists her hair on top of her head and secures it with a pen, which exposes the ivory slope of her neck. Huge purple bruises checker her throat and collar. Her skin is broken open in one place.

"You're bleeding," I say, pointing. "You're really banged up . . . what happened to you?" I ask as I scan the rest of her. She sits back and wipes her neck with her fingers, and then holds up her hand, which is covered in dark blood.

"I don't see anything," she says. I squeeze my eyes shut and then open them again. The bruises are no longer there, and her fingers are clean.

"I'm so sorry. I've been seeing some pretty weird things lately. Your husband said it's to be expected with everything I went through," I explain. Her brow creases, and I sink back against the pillow. She may see a world in the clear, but she doesn't see what I do. Vanessa eyes Lucas.

"Will you excuse us for a moment, please?" she asks.

"I promised I'd stay with her," Lucas counters.

"You can stay close." She levels her gaze at him. Even though she's half his size, he seems to shrink.

"It's okay," I say. Lucas presses his mouth into a line, and then strides from the room.

"Close the door, please," Vanessa calls. Lucas pulls the door, but it doesn't click shut. "That'll have to do." She purses her lips. "Describe to me what you saw on my neck a moment ago."

"Bruises along here." I trace the pattern on my own throat. "Here, too." I draw a wide "U" shape from collar bone to collar bone.

"That's very interesting." She pulls the pen from her hair and taps the eraser on her cheek. "Those bruises aren't there now, but they've been there before. They happened the day I was struck by lightning."

"Why did I see them just now?" My heart races. I feel as if I'm on the edge of a mile-high cliff, looking straight down, my toes hanging over the side, my weight on the balls of my feet, my heels lifting from the ground.

"All of life is a conduit of electricity. I believe that lightning can throw off the linear barriers our senses apply to the world around us. After I was struck, I saw some unexplainable phenomena in the days afterward as well."

"What happened to you?"

"A tornado hit our town, and we weren't ready. It tore through our house like a bowling ball through a china cabinet. I was found a quarter of a mile from home, barely alive, clinging to my sister. We both had lightning burns on our backs. We were the lucky ones. My parents didn't survive." Her bright eyes darken, and she looks away.

"I'm so sorry." Even though I lost my father, I have no idea what to say to her.

"It was a long time ago," she says softly. "But it drives me even now. I have dedicated my life to helping others who are struck by lightning recover and find their own sense of purpose."

"I lost my dad. It was actually the day I heard you on the radio. There was a storm. I saw something." I pause, shaking my head. "For the past year, I have seen things no one else does," I whisper. "I have tried to forget about you and the world you said is in the clear every day for a year. Every day."

"I can tell you it doesn't exist, if you want." She touches her finger tips together. "I can tell you I was wrong, or seeking attention. I can tell you I made it all up. Would that help you?"

"That depends on whether or not it's true," I say.

"Truth is grayer than anyone wants to admit." She tilts her head, studying me. "But I'm not here to discuss my theory about a world in the clear. I'm here because you were struck by lightning."

"I don't want to talk about lightning. I want to know exactly what you see in the clear. I saw unexplainable things before I was struck. Lightning might be part of it, but it's not all of it."

"I never should have gone public with that theory, Tanzy. Going on the radio show was irresponsible. It caused more harm than good for me, and for people who believed me. My reputation took a hit. The world in the clear may exist, but I've let that go, and so should you. You need to focus on healing," she insists.

"That storm wasn't random. That lightning wasn't random. It has to be related to the things I see that no one else does." My voice rises with the escalation of my pulse.

"I agree with you there. I have researched thousands of lightning strikes, and I can say with certainty that lightning strikes aren't random. Points of contact are chosen, premeditated. I know you're searching for meaning in all this. I did, too. And it is there to be found, Tanzy. But it's not the world in the clear you need to focus on. You need to confront why the electric web that holds our world together chose you, and, most importantly, why it spared you. In my experience, those of us who are struck and survive have set a course for ourselves that is less than what we're capable of, what we're meant to accomplish in our lifetime. Every patient who I have worked with has gone on to set and achieve goals they'd long forgotten they had. Does this ring any kind of bell for you?"

In my mind's eye, I relive the moment I threw the college acceptance letters in the trash. I see myself fill drinks, take orders, run food, bus tables. I watch my skin, tan from years in the sun, turn sallow, and shiny with grease. I feel the squeeze at the base of my throat any time another horse person walks in the door at Smokey's and catches sight of me. They always left me bigger tips than they should have.

"I'm on the wrong path," I murmur.

"This is your moment. Your new life can start right now, if you let it. I can help you."

"I . . . I take care of my mom."

"I promise you that when you feel fulfilled, you will be able to take even better care of yourself and your mom."

"I would really like that," I rasp. My thoughts turn to my mother, and I wait to feel the stab of guilt over envisioning a different life. For the first time in a year, it doesn't come.

"It's an intense program," she cautions. "And it will involve continuing work together and on your own after you're discharged. I'll bring literature and paperwork for you tomorrow."

"I'll have to go back to work as soon as I'm able." Reluctance trickles through me, although I'm not sure it's because of the idea of returning to work at Smokey's, or the notion that with just my signature, my life could turn on its head.

"This is a privately funded research program, and I allocate stipends for all participants. I feel certain it will cover your regular expenses. It's all in the paperwork."

"Okay." Questions swirl in my head: Do I want my life to unequivocally change? I know I'm on the wrong path, but I have no idea what the right one looks like. How will she know? Will I know it when I see it?

"I'll see you tomorrow." She stands. Her gaze falls to her hand, and she rubs a thumb across her mark. For a split second, I'm sure she sees it, too. Then she shakes out her wrist, as if alleviating stiffness, and walks out.

Lucas peeks his head in.

"Coast is clear," I say, attempting a smile. Vanessa may have left, but her voice lingers in my head. Why wouldn't she discuss the world in the clear? Could she be right about the weather? I can't help imagining a conversation between Vanessa and my mother. What does Mom think about lightning strikes? I make a mental note to ask her. I wonder when we'll speak again, and what she'll say. This is the longest we've been apart in over a year. I don't want her to see me like this, but I wish she was here. Would she want to be?

"Hospitals make me nervous," Lucas announces. He claims the blue chair, but he's so tall he has to sit sideways to fit.

"Why's that?"

"We're surrounded by people who like to cut on other people, and have a lot of practice doing it." He makes a face, and I burst out laughing.

"They like to fix people," I counter.

"Whatever helps you sleep at night." He grins. I manage a smile, but inside, the brief lightness has left, and I feel simultaneously hollow and yet filled with lead. I find myself wishing I could see out the window. I hope it's a natural thing to want, and not a by-product of the buzzing sensation growing under my ribs each time my thoughts slide to the utter upheaval my life is facing. If I'm being honest with myself, I know the upheaval has already begun; I recognize its inevitability to continue. But in this room, within these walls, I don't have to face it yet. And just like that, all I can think about is Mom.

"I know Dana told you to stay, but I could use some time by myself," I say.

"Yeah, sure. I get that." He rises. "I mean you just met me. I'm probably not the guy you want hanging out in your room."

"I just met you, but you saved my life." I look him square in the eyes. "So go, but come back. I mean I want you to come back. If you want to." My cheeks begin to burn, and I am tempted to pull the worn hospital blanket over my face.

"You do?"

"Well, you know a lot about me. I'd like to hear more about you. Fair's fair. I won't lie. I'm hoping you wrecked something at some point in your life."

"I did. And you got it." He runs his hand through his hair, an open-mouth smile on his face. "Do you need anything before I go?" The word "no" is on my lips when I spy the rectangle of light burning a slow path down the opposite wall from where it shines through the window behind me.

"Can you . . . can you turn me around?"

"I don't think the bed moves." Lucas looks under the mattress. "This one isn't on wheels."

"No, I mean turn me around."

"Are you sure? I don't think you're supposed to move a whole lot yet."

"You carried me half a mile through the woods in the dark. I think it'll be okay."

"Okay." He assesses the IV stand and my leg. "What if I hurt you?"

"You won't."

"Are you sure?"

"Yes. I'm sure the nurses won't do it, and Dana is strong but she's tiny. You're all I've got. I just want to be able to see outside."

"I get that. Go ahead and lower the head of your bed," he says. I push the button until the bed levels completely, feeling entirely more exposed when I'm lying flat. Lucas wheels the IV stand to the opposite side, guiding the tubing over the bed slowly so he doesn't put pressure on where the needle is inserted into the top of my wrist. "Okay, here we go." He bends down and slides one arm under my knees, and the other behind my shoulders, and carefully lifts me from the mattress. Pain rockets down my leg, and I clench my teeth together to keep from crying out. He slowly moves around the bed, his focus ping-ponging from me to the tubing and back again. "Almost there," he says as he begins to lower me back to the mattress. I exhale the second my back touches the bed. I hadn't realized I've been holding my breath. The hole in my side throbs. I check my gown to make sure I'm not bleeding.

"Thank you," I say, suddenly chilled. He rolls the cart to the new head of my bed so I can reach the phone and a thermos of water. "Can you push the green button to raise the foot of the bed?" I shiver, and my teeth clatter together. I place my palms flat on my stomach to try to trap any heat.

"Sure." He pushes the button, watching for me to nod when it's high enough for me to see out. "I hope it was worth it. It's not a great view." He stares through the glass. All I can see are the tops of distant pines and a cloudy sky. Still, peace settles through me.

"It's worth it."

"Good." He peers down at me. "Be seeing you, Tanzy," he says softly, and then backs out of view.

"Be seeing you." I watch the clouds roll by, thinking back to the bruises I saw on Vanessa, and the correlation between what I saw and her old injuries. Could the scars I saw before on Lucas indicate something he'd been through years ago?

I pick up the phone. I want to tell my mother everything. I'm desperate to ask her one more time about her past, and about what she sees in the sky—how she knows the weather like a mother knows a child. I dial our number, my heart fluttering. The phone rings, and rings, and rings.

I can't sleep.

The dinner Dana brought me is still sitting on my cart. My stomach twists with emptiness, but I can't bring myself to eat when I'm not sure where my mother is or if she's had dinner. Dana left a sack of fruit on the porch. There's still been no sign of her.

The waning moon stares back at me through the window. On its face, I relive the chase on Harbor—the whistle of the frigid air stinging my ears, the rhythm of her stride and breathing. I can feel the heat of fear pulsing through me. I close my eyes and start to count in an attempt to stop the thoughts from consuming me.

Outside my room, the hospital grinds on with carts and stretchers rolling past my door. Nurses' shoes squeak on the polished floor. Even though I should be sleeping, they still tap before they enter. My vitals are to be checked every four hours for the next thirty-six. Each nurse also brings a little plastic ramekin with a rainbow of medicine—muscle relaxers, anti-inflammatories, and a sleep aid. They dull the pain, but they also make me feel loopy.

The skin between my shoulder blades tingles with the warning of someone watching, but I haven't heard the routine taps. I roll over. A man in scrubs stands beside my bed, a bottle in his hands. He's wearing thick-rimmed glasses, which cut a dark line across his angular face. His stature is similar to Lucas's, but his skin is paler than the walls, and his hair is long and raven black. His resemblance to my mother startles me. They could be siblings.

"Sorry to wake you, Tanzy" he says. "My name is Asher. I'm the head nurse for the night shift in the ICU," he introduces himself. "Your last complete blood panel showed that your red blood cells are producing a little slower than we'd like to see. This is a normal side effect considering the large blood transfusion you received. We caught it early, so it shouldn't become an issue. We just need to give your body a little encouragement to produce new red blood cells at a better rate. They're very important for healing." He pulls the safety seal off a bottle, hands it to me, and makes a note in my chart. The bottle is warm, the liquid deep red. I smell it, and my stomach turns.

"It smells bad," I remark.

"I'd hold my nose if I were you," he replies. I pinch my nose closed with one hand, and chug the bottle as fast as I can. It's thick and sticky and I gag more than once.

"That was awful." I hand him the empty bottle.

"Some patients actually learn to like it," he teases as he sticks his tongue out. "Someone will be by in an hour to draw blood from your catheter line. If you're asleep you probably won't even know it's happening."

"I doubt I'll be asleep," I reply, but then I yawn for the first time all night. "Does this stuff ever make people tired?" I ask, everything feeling a little heavier.

"It affects everyone differently," he says. He stares at the computer screen, marking a couple boxes. "Don't be surprised if we repeat the dose tomorrow night. Staying ahead of this is important."

"Does that stuff come in different flavors?" I ask, making a face.

"I'll see what I can do," he says. "Get some rest."

"That's what they all say," I reply. As I begin to settle, a thought strikes my brain: I didn't notice a mark on Asher's hand. I open my eyes to check for confirmation. He's already gone. Thoughts about the symbols try to rouse my curiosity, but my mind would rather sink into sleep. I roll onto my side, welcoming the slow, spinning feeling of approaching slumber.

FLIGHT OR FIGHT

Sunlight warms my face, drawing me to consciousness, and for a moment, I forget where I am. My entire body aches with stiffness. I push myself up on my elbows, longing to stand and stretch.

"I see they didn't turn you back around," Lucas's voice whispers from behind me.

"What are you doing here?" I twist to see him.

"You said to come back."

"Isn't it early?" I glance out the window. The sun is halfway to its peak. I'm not sure I've ever slept this late in my life.

"Not that early. I brought you breakfast but it's probably cold. I brought you a couple extra blankets and another pillow too." He spreads the blankets across my bed.

"No, thank you. It's really chilly in here. How did you get them?" I ask.

"I asked for them. No, that's a lie. I like to wander. I found the supply closet. I noticed you shivering yesterday. Is that weird?"

"I'm not sure," I say, giving him a sideways look. He hands me the pillow and slides the chair around so we're facing each other. "Dana wanted me to come first thing. She won't be by until later because she had an appointment."

"I'm sure there's a lot to do at the farm." I flinch at the thought, and my mood plummets.

"Well, yes and no. I've actually heard talk of the owner not wanting to rebuild. Apparently, he thinks the property is cursed."

"That's ridiculous." I scoff.

"I think so too. Dana's pretty upset about it." He scoots the chair closer to the window. I chew on the inside of my cheek, a storm of emotions rolling inside me. I never considered that Wildwood would never be rebuilt, that I wouldn't one day be able to return. My gaze lifts to Lucas. His focus shifts from me to the view outside. He moves his hands from the armrests to his knees and then back to the armrests. His mark casts a sapphire glow on the threadbare upholstery. Could these marks I see hold a real meaning, like the bruises I saw on Vanessa? Something as simple as a favorite color, or maybe some deeper meaning, like an aura? I can't stop myself from rolling my eyes at the thought.

"Do you want to tell me what you're thinking about, or do you want me to start rattling off fun facts about myself to change the subject?" he asks.

"Tell me about you," I say, relieved to not be the one answering questions.

"What do you want to know?"

"Well . . . what's your favorite color?" I ask. "Actually, can I guess? I'm testing a theory." I steal a glimpse of the crevice between his pointer finger and his thumb.

"Sure," he says with a smirk.

"Turn your hands palm side up," I say, demonstrating. Lucas stiffens in the chair, drawing his back robotically straight. He puts his hands out and slowly turns them over.

"You seem nervous," I say. "Is your favorite color pink and you don't want me to know?"

Lucas busts out laughing. "No, my favorite color is not pink," he says. I stare at his sapphire-blue horseshoe. I'm tempted to touch it.

"Is it blue?" I ask, and glance at his face. His expression clouds over as he closes his hands.

"No," he replies. I sink back, more disappointed than I thought I'd be.

"Okay, I give up. Tell me." I press my thumb into my palm, wondering what color I would hope to have if one ever shows up.

"I don't think I should say."

"Why's that?"

"It has to do with storms."

"Tell me anyway," I whisper.

"You know the silvery purple that forked lightning leaves behind in the sky for just a second after it's struck? That's my favorite color." He turns back to me, and I realize I've been holding my breath. He clears his throat. "So, what's your favorite color?" he asks.

"Charcoal gray," I answer, forcing a smile. "Not nearly as cool as yours."

"Mine is pretty cool," he says, and laughs. "So, horses and gray, huh? That's your story?"

"That's it. That's all there is to know about me," I say.

"Why charcoal gray?"

Because there's a charcoal gray quilt Dad had as a kid that still hangs over the back of his favorite chair, and neither Mom nor I have dared to move it since the day he disappeared, but I've spent more nights than I can count tucked under that quilt, breathing in the last scents of him, pressing down the random short auburn hair I find stuck to it so it won't fall off, because mom sleeps better in that chair under that quilt than she does in her own bed without him, remembering how he would use his "special blanket" to tuck me in at night when I was a kid and had awoken from a bad dream, or the time he used it for an impromptu picnic dinner on my twelfth birthday when work ran late, or how it was the first thing I slept on when we moved here and the rest of our furniture hadn't arrived yet.

I blink away the thoughts and the burn in my eyes they evoke. I have to find a different way to describe my father.

"You know how when a storm comes in, a real storm, one where the temperature drops, and the wind picks up, and the clouds are that deep, heavy gray? I love how that color changes everything. It's like those clouds bring a box of highlighters and color everything. The grass glows, and flowers look so vivid. Even the old, peeling paint on the barn walls looks fresh when it's against that deep-gray backdrop. It's what that color does to everything else around it that makes me love it so much."

"Nope, you win," he murmurs. "That was way more interesting than mine."

"Alright, Tanzy. Time to check your dressing," a nurse says as she steps into the room, breaking the spell.

"Right," I say, and shake off the warm buzz of connection. Lucas glances at the clock.

"I have to get to Wildwood anyway," he says.

"What are y'all doing there today?" I ask, hope flickering inside. If they're still working there, maybe there's a chance the owner will decide to rebuild.

"I'm going to look for Harbor." He stands. I stare at him, open mouthed.

"Thank you," I whisper.

"Of course." He stands, and brushes his knuckles along the back of my hand, as if he's done it a hundred times before, and then leaves me with a two-inch streak of goose bumps and a hundred new questions—none of which have anything to do with colors.

"He seems really sweet on you," my newest nurse replies.

"He's nice," I respond, my mind replaying our conversation, my hand still tingling. I'm no stranger to a boy's touch, but something about Lucas's touch was definitely a first.

My nurse begins to gingerly unwind the bandage from my leg. The skin on her arms is loose and wrinkly, and her wedding band slides on her finger. I wonder how long she's worn it, what it's seen and been through. I wonder if my mom will wear hers, a simple braid of copper, forever. I can't imagine her ever looking at another man the same way she looked at Dad.

The nurse tsks under her breath.

"This isn't good, sweetie," she says. I look at my leg. The surgical incision is flame red and oozing. Red lines extend from the site and up my leg. "Stay as still as a statue, and I'll be back with the doctor."

"Okay." My pulse accelerates and my hands become clammy. I stare out the window, wishing Lucas hadn't left. If he's still in the parking lot, I wonder if there's any way I could get his attention.

"Tanzy?" Vanessa's smooth voice calls from the head of the room. "Are you in here?" I want to turn and look at her so she'll know I'm here, but the nurse told me not to move.

"Still here," I say.

"What did you do to the bed?" she asks, coming around the side. She's wearing leggings and an oversized green tunic. Her hair is pulled into a top knot, and a plain leather satchel is slung over her shoulder. Aside from her face, she looks like a completely different person.

"I wanted to see out the window."

"You could've just asked to change rooms." She smiles down at me, then her eyes shift to my leg. "That looks infected." Worry creases her brow.

"The nurse just went to get a doctor."

Vanessa works the corner of her painted mouth through her teeth. She fiddles with her necklace, which has a little, cylindrical charm on the end.

"Do you want me to fix it?" she asks.

"Excuse me?" My brow knits together. "Aren't you just a psychiatrist? I mean, no offense."

"I can fix your leg right here, right now. No waiting. No recovery. No rehab," she says quietly.

"How is that possible?" I shake my head, wondering if I've misheard her. Vanessa glances at the door. She moves quickly across the room to close it, and returns to my bedside.

"I wasn't completely honest with you before. I still believe in the world in the clear, something I've begun to call the Unseen world. I haven't stopped researching it. I'm close to proving its existence. I think you can help me do it."

"Why are you telling me this now? What does it have to do with my leg?" I hiss. Alarm scurries across my skin.

"I have long suspected that lightning is a tool the Unseen world uses—weather, specifically lightning, to catalyze change and send messages on our side. But I've never had concrete proof until you."

"What kinds of changes and messages?" The hair on the back of my neck stands on end. Nothing she's saying makes sense, and yet, her words pull at something inside of me like a magnet to metal.

"I . . . I'm not entirely sure yet. But they wrote one on you." She opens my chart and turns it so I can see the note where her husband sketched the burn mark the lightning made on my sternum. "This mark is one of the most important symbols in the Unseen world. It can't be a coincidence that it's on you. Lightning doesn't travel this way naturally. This was on purpose."

"What? Why? What the hell are you talking about?" I ask her through my teeth, my mind spinning.

"I'm sorry, Tanzy. I will explain as much as I can to you later, but if you want me to try to heal your leg, I need to do it now, or they're probably going to keep you in the hospital longer and delay your start in my program until this clears up. Right now, I need you to trust me. I met someone who claims to have come from the Unseen world. She gave me something they use to heal the injured, and I can use it on you. With your help, I can learn so much more about the Unseen world."

"No way." I cross my arms.

"If I can prove to you that I know what you see, will you let me try?" she asks. Possibility stirs inside me. Proof of anything would be a relief.

"Maybe," I say. Vanessa holds up her right hand with her palm open. Her fingers spread apart as her golden horseshoe leaps from her skin like a candle flame.

"What color do you see?" A knowing grin grows on her lips.

"What?" I ask, startled by her question. Did she really just ask me that?

"What color do you see?" she asks again slowly. She wriggles her fingers. Her eyes dart from her hand and then back to me, unfazed by my shock. "I see a color too. I want to know if we see the same thing."

"I . . ." I hesitate. Is she for real? In all this time, I've just wanted someone to believe me. Now that someone claims to see it too, it doesn't feel real.

"Tell you what," she starts, dropping her hand. "I had a feeling this was going to take some convincing. I mean, why wouldn't it? I've already picked the crayon that best matches the color I see in my hand, and I've colored a notecard with it." I watch as Vanessa pulls a big box of crayons out of her bag and carefully plucks a folded notecard from the front pocket.

"Now it's your turn. Pick which color you see," she says with a warm smile. She flips the top off the box. "It's a brand-new box, so don't try looking for the worn tip. There's no right or wrong answer, but I know you see something." My gaze leaps from her mark to the burnished-gold color smack in the middle of the reds and oranges. It's not a perfect match, but it's really close.

"Do you want me to close my eyes?" Vanessa asks.

"No, it's okay," I say, and slip the crayon from the box. I wrap my fingers around it. Vanessa opens her notecard and faces it so I can see the color. I open my hand. The color is the same.

"It's not an exact match to my hand," she says, showing me her right palm. "But it's as close as we can get, right?"

"What . . . how . . . ?" I stammer. "Your husband said everything I was seeing was temporary. A crossed wire . . ."

"A by-product of a brain injury?" she says, rolling her eyes. "Science explains what we already accept as truth. There's so much more to our world than what we've been told. All science has done is limit our understanding, not expand it. We've been looking for extraterrestrial life billions of miles away, when there's a whole second world coexisting with ours, completely unseen, divided by some kind of impenetrable plasma veil."

"How do you know?" I ask in a whisper.

"The moment I was struck by lightning, I was teleported somewhere completely different, somewhere I knew I'd never been before. Yet I had this sensation of remembering. Then the clouds cleared and sunlight shone through, and the picture faded into the light. But for a few seconds, I could see both worlds, and the glittery barrier that separates us."

In my mind, I see the rainbow that painted the valley the day Dad disappeared. I watch the dark thing swoop through it and soar up, disappearing as it came close to the surface, and my heart begins to race.

"I know how easy it would be to say it was because I'd hit my head, or it was the electrocution, or any number of excuses," Vanessa continues. "I wish I could say any of those felt like my truth. But in my heart, in my soul, I understood what I was seeing."

"A world in the clear," I murmur, my mind jumping forward to the place I saw after I was struck. "So what do the colors mean? And why do only some people have them? I don't have one."

"I believe the colors are indicators of the path we're supposed to be on, kind of like bus lines. When you intersect with someone who has your color, you're supposed to walk at least a piece of your paths together. Just like us."

Vanessa shows me her mark. I stare at my empty palm, for the first time wishing I saw something there.

"Our colors are the same?" I ask, imagining the same golden glow.

"That shouldn't come as a surprise," she says softly. "I have a feeling we are going to discover a great deal working together." She steals a glimpse of the door, and worry flashes across her face. "As much as I'd like to spend all day discussing the Unseen world with someone who might actually believe me, I need to redirect us here. If you want me to try to heal your leg, I need to do it right now, and I will tell you everything I know later. Otherwise, you could be looking at months of physical therapy and possible complications from this infection. Will you let me try?"

"Yes."

"Good." She pulls a small bottle from her satchel.

"What is that?" I ask as I look at her concerned.

"It's called Tenix," she begins. "Everything in our world is made up of a combination of four elements: earth, air, water, and fire. Tenix is like the glue. It makes them stick together. Creatures in the Unseen world use Tenix to change the way elements bind together to repair something broken, or make something new. I can use it now to heal your body."

"How?"

"By realigning your elements." Vanessa tips the bottle, spilling a small amount of Tenix into her palm. It looks like liquid sand, and has the same baking scent of summer sunlight. Even though she's still a few feet away from me, I can feel the heat it generates. She rubs her hands together, and the substance bursts into a glowing, pale-gold orb. It's the same color as our marks. My breath stills in my chest. Vanessa looks to me, as if she's seeking my approval. I nod in response. She settles beside me and closes her eyes, pressing her hands into a prayer position. Then she places both hands on my leg. The substance is warm, tingling where it touches my skin.

"Sana," she whispers.

"What does that mean?" I ask quietly.

"It's Latin for 'heal.'" She opens one eye and peeks at me. "I prefer the formality of Latin." She refocuses on my leg. A dull ache spreads through it, followed by a growing sting, as if circulation is returning. Within seconds, my leg begins to burn.

"This really hurts," I hiss as my muscles lock in a cramp.

"It's going to," she answers. "I'm accelerating a month's worth of healing into about a minute. It works better if you don't talk yourself out of the pain's existence," she says softly. "Accept it for what it is. Allow it to do its job. Visualize it. It helps me when I give it a color."

I draw in a long breath through my nose and let it out through my mouth. Dana taught me to use visualization to focus my mind at horse shows, and it improved my performance every time. I close my eyes, imagining the Tenix going under my skin, finding the bone. The Tenix turns deep silver, the color of the screws and plates holding my legs together. In my mind, my bones turn the same color. The screws back out and dissolve to tiny fragments about the size of sand grains, and then disappear altogether. Slowly, the vice-like grip relaxes. The ache is there, but the intensity lessons.

"Well done," Vanessa says calmly.

I open my eyes. What Tenix remains on my legs is the color of steel. She wipes down the front of my thigh and the Tenix disappears, replaced by a subtle shimmer. I draw both knees up to my chest, staring at my feet as I wiggle my toes.

"Any pain now?" Vanessa asks.

"No," I whisper. The scar is still there, acting as proof that the accident happened, but the swelling and drainage are gone. How is this even real? And if it is, if my leg is healed, cured by Tenix, what else can Vanessa do? What else does she know? I can't wait to find out. For the last year, all I've had are questions. Vanessa's research could be a treasure trove of possible answers. Does she see the shadows, too? Are they part of the Unseen world? Vanessa is right, if I can help myself, I can help Mom. We can be whole again.

I swing my legs over the side of the bed, preparing to stand, ready for movement, for progress.

"Whoa, no way," Vanessa says, stopping me with a hand.

"But you said . . ." I deflate.

"You're healed, trust me. But if the doctors walk in and see that you're standing up . . .? And you're just a few days out from being impaled. The Tenix I used will likely circulate through your body and heal any places where your elements have been divided, but I can't be sure how fast the puncture will granulate."

"Oh, right," I say, realization dawning on me. "So, what do we do now? Can I get out of here today? I have so many questions. I want to know everything."

"I'm going to work on getting you discharged soon. For now, go back to looking broken. The doctor should be here any minute. Play dumb, okay?" She gently tosses my legs back onto the bed. I try to settle back into my previous position, but new energy hums through me. Everything is about to change. I can feel it. And for the first time in a year, I can't wait to see what happens next.

ENEMIES CLOSER

Dana sits across from me, her left leg propped on her right knee. Her foot is twitching twice as fast as the ticktock from the second hand on a clock. Her eyes roam the room. I can tell her mind is a million miles away. I can't imagine what all she's seen back at Wildwood. I'm grateful I don't have a memory of it burning down, nor a picture of what it looks like now.

"So they're keeping you in a soft cast for a while longer?" she asks after a long pause.

"They just want to keep an eye on the incision overnight and make sure it's not looking infected," I say, keeping both legs straight and still. "They'll put on a hard cast in the morning."

"Okay. That's good."

Silence swallows up the room again.

"Dana... what's wrong?" I finally ask. Dana looks at me. Her fingers drum a rhythm on the arm rest.

"I . . . I went for a job interview today. Just in case. Wildwood probably isn't going to reopen for at least a year, if ever. I have to find work. I have bills.

I have—"

"Dana," I cut her off. "You don't need to justify anything to me. I couldn't make myself go back to Wildwood after Dad's accident, even when all I wanted to do was walk those aisles and be with my horse. I can't imagine being back there with no barn and no horses. I'm honestly not sure I will go back," I whisper, suddenly overwhelmed with emotion.

"I'm not sure I can go back again. The smell, Tanzy. It's . . . They still haven't found any remains, but I swear it smells like death."

"It's time for us to move forward," I say softly. "All of us. We can't keep treading water. We can't let our lives stall on the tracks. We both still have so much more to do, don't we? Wildwood was my father's dream, and I will keep his memories close to my heart. But he isn't there anymore. Even . . . even if he is physically. He isn't there." These thoughts that have plagued my brain for the last few months at last become sound—they become the truth. It is a boulder lifted from my shoulders, and placed briefly upon my chest, yet somehow the pressure is easier to carry this way.

"I know." Dana's eyes brim with tears.

I look at her, and I repeat the words my father told me the day he died:

"Whatever it is that makes you happy to get out of bed in the morning, you go after it, and don't you let anyone or anything stop you. Distance, time, stepping-stones, setbacks—they're all a part of it. You can make mistakes. You can take wrong turns and the long way. But if you get your sights set on something, something that really, truly moves you, don't you dare quit. You promise me?"

"I promise," she answers, smiling. "It's still not a done deal, but it felt like a good interview, and it's a great opportunity."

"Tell me about it," I say, and rest against my pillows as she begins to talk.

Once Dana leaves, I dial the number for my house again—just like I do every time I'm alone for long enough—and then let the phone ring for two solid minutes before hanging up. I check the clock, noting the time, and plan to call again in an hour.

"I found a new flavor for you," Asher says, appearing in my room.

"I didn't hear you come in." The similarity to my mother is bittersweet. He breaks the seal on the bottle before handing it to me. "Thanks," I say. He turns his back to me, scrolling through a series of notes on the computer while I swallow down the medicine, which isn't as bad as last night.

"Your red-blood-cell count is up. That's good," he says. "Shouldn't be long, now."

"I'm hoping to be out of here soon." It takes all of my self-control to keep my legs still under my sheet. I watch him, expecting him to leave, but he paces around my room like a ghost, silent and fluid. His face is angled slightly to the ground, as if he's studying the floor immediately in front of his feet. "Is . . . everything okay?"

"I'm tired of waiting." He pulls off his glasses and stares straight at me. His eyes are colorless, white marbles dropped into his sockets. It's impossible to tell what he's looking at. My heart pounds, and I suck in a breath. "Is anything coming back to you yet, *Spera*?" he asks in a growl. His body blurs at its edges, and in the center of his chest, inky black bleeds outward.

"This isn't real. This isn't real." I whisper, gasping, pinning myself to the back of my bed.

"You in this mortal body. That's what isn't real. It's time for you to come home," he growls, his voice echoing as his form fades into a shadow, and dissolves into the darkness of my room. I swing my legs over the side of the bed. My heartbeat pounds in my ears. *Run. Run. Get out of here now.* The thoughts flood my nervous system. Adrenaline pours into my bloodstream. My body hums. I touch my toes to the ground. My calves tremble. To get to the door, I'm going to have to run straight through the shadows. Will I even be able to walk without falling? The wrap on my leg is flexible and light. It shouldn't stop me. I push off the bed, and stand up. My leg threatens to buckle, but it holds, me up. I steady just as two more shadows solidify on either side of the door. Instinct bursts inside of me, propelling me forward. I punch off the ground and leap through the sliver of a gap between them. Nurses startle as I land in the hallway.

"Tanzy! Stop!" I hear someone shout from behind me. I can't stop. Any of the staff here could be another shadow, hiding behind a human face. Are these the creatures who live in the Unseen world? How can I outrun a shadow? How can I trust anyone I see? I catch sight of an exit sign on the other side of the nurses' station. I take off down the hallway. A nurse steps in front of me, arms spread wide. I dive to the left, and throw myself over the desk, cracking my ribs against the side before landing on my feet. Disoriented and grunting for air, I find the sign again. I sprint through the counters, squeezing between the last desk and the wall, and then stumble through the door and into a wide corridor.

Elevators appear to my right, and a sign for a stairwell is posted on the wall just beyond them. I push the "UP" button for the elevator, and then run past it to the stairwell. I gently push open the door to the stairs and slip through, then ease it shut so it doesn't make a sound. I flatten my back against the wall, and silently tiptoe down the stairs.

On the next floor down, the door slams open and two people in white coats enter the stairwell. I freeze in my tracks and hold my breath. Pain laces up my sides and pulls tight. The doctors start up the stairs. Suddenly their pagers chirp on their hips. They stop talking, glance at their pagers and turn around, backtracking the way they came.

Where am I going to go? I start down, when a hand grabs my arm. I whirl around, jerking my arm free. Lucas stands there, his fingers on his lips.

"Not that way," he whispers as he points up. He grabs my hand and sprints up the stairs. We exit the stairs on the top floor. The long hallway is dark and empty, and checkered with closed doors. We duck inside a closet. He grabs a blanket, two pairs of scrubs, and a surgical cap.

"What are you doing here?" I ask, gasping for air.

"Helping you."

"I don't even know what I'm doing."

"You look a lot like you're trying to leave. I'm good at leaving. Practically an expert."

"Don't you need to know why?"

"Hospitals are freaky as hell, and you look like you just saw a ghost. Plus, you're up and running around. Looks to me like it's time to go. Now shut up and put these on." He hands me a set of scrubs and a surgical cap. He steps into the hallway, pulling the door semi-closed. I pull off the hospital gown, toss it into the corner, and step into the scrubs. My limbs throb with effort and fatigue.

"How did you know where to find all this?"

"I told you. I wander," he hisses. "I like to know my way around."

I step out. He's changed into scrubs, too. He gives me a once-over.

"You need shoes, or at least to look like you have them on," he says. He grabs a pair of shoe protectors, and kneels down to secure them on my bare feet. "At least now it's less obvious. Come on," he says, and walks down the dark corridor to the opposite side. Windows line the far wall. He stops and peers out, studying the ground. We're directly over the ambulance bay. An ambulance pulls in now, lights flashing. He takes my hand and hurries for another stairwell door.

"I'm going to stay a half-flight ahead of you. I stop, you stop. Got it?" he says, tugging me along.

"Got it," I repeat.

"When we get to the E.R., we'll separate. You walk out of the automatic doors to the far right. That'll put you out at the ambulance bay. Hang right, stay against the wall, and walk straight back. The back parking lots are dead at night. You shouldn't run into anyone back there."

"You aren't coming?" I ask.

"Not yet. I'm going to see what I can find out about how hard they're going to look for you," he says. He puts his hand in his pocket and pulls out his cell phone. "Keep this. I will call you if I find out anything."

"Where should I go?" I ask.

"There's a little garden behind the hospital. It's not well kept, but there are bushes and ivy, and a little gazebo. You should have plenty of places to hide."

"And then what?" I ask, desperation clawing up my throat.

"And then . . . then you come home with me. Just for tonight," he says. I pull back and stare at his face, heart thudding in my chest.

"I can't do that," I say. "I barely know you." Still, the want to tell him everything throbs in my mind. He saw those creatures at Wildwood—he saved my life. Will he believe everything else?

"But you do know me. You know exactly who I am."

"I've known you for less than a week," I sputter. "I never should've run out of that hospital room. There was a nurse who turned into . . . into pure darkness, Lucas. I swear it's true. I'm not going crazy. I'm not. It was real. He gave me something. Last night, too. There was this surge inside of me, and I just had to run. It wasn't even a choice. I just took off. I don't know how to fix this. I've screwed up everything." The expression on Lucas's face shifts to something dark, and I can't tell if it's the flicker of the red lights from outside, or his mood.

"Everything was screwed up long before you came around. And for the record, you're not crazy," he says, and strokes the side of my face with his thumb. I stare at him, marveling at the novelty and familiarity his touch evokes from me. He drops his hand and steps back. "If you want to stay, then we can just walk back to your room. I'm sure people have freak-outs all the time in here."

"I want to talk to Vanessa," I say before I can stop myself. She's the only person I am absolutely certain will believe me. She'll know what to do.

"I can take you to her. I saw her downstairs."

"What is she doing here in the middle of the night?" I wonder aloud, simultaneously grateful and suspicious. "What are you doing here in the middle of the night?"

"I . . . I can't leave you here alone." He shoves his hands in his back pockets. "You died in my arms, Tanzy. I didn't tell you that before. I watched the paramedics bring you back. Then you died again when you first got here. I just feel like if I leave for too long, you're going to die and not come back. I know you don't remember any of that, and probably not much from the accident, but I remember it. And this is not going to end with you not coming back." His eyes shine. "Not this time." He lets out a hard exhale and drops his gaze, working his jaw side to side as if he's trying not to cry.

"What happened to you, Lucas?" I ask, seeing the pain on his face, and wondering what memories must haunt him. Those same memories must be why he feels a responsibility for what happened to me. He and I might just be two of a kind in that regard. "You might not have scars now, but I think you used to. How did you get them?"

"I . . . You . . ."

"Tanzy!" Vanessa voice fills the room. "I heard you ran out of your room. What happened? Are you okay? What are you doing up here?" I whirl around, fresh adrenaline sprouting needles on my skin.

"I have to get out of here, Vanessa. Something is here. Something—" I pause, glancing at Lucas. "Something from the other side."

"Come on, let's go," she says, and pushes the door behind her open.

"I don't want to go back to the room."

"Where do you want to go?" she asks gently.

"Home. Take me home."

"Okay. I just need to sign a couple forms and you can walk out of here." She steps back into the door, opening it wider. "Well, roll. You're going to have to be in a wheelchair until we get to the car. It's standard hospital procedure, and it'll help reduce the number of questions we're about to face." She winks. I stare at her, unblinking, wondering how she can be calm enough to joke.

"And I can just go?"

"My husband isn't going to be happy about it, but you're an adult. You can refuse or stop treatment at any point. Come on, let's go talk to him. He just had a big surgery go quite well, so he's in a pretty good mood tonight. I'm going to have you go ahead and sit in a wheelchair though, just so we don't have to try to explain why you're standing."

I look at Lucas. I have a startling urge to reach out for him, to touch his skin. Our eyes meet, and his expression turns solemn and resolved. He takes a small step backward.

"Be seeing you, Tanzy," he says, and I follow Vanessa down the stairs.

HOME

I wait in the stairwell while Vanessa retrieves a wheelchair from the nurse's station. Each time I hear footsteps, I crane my neck to look up at the floors above, wondering if Lucas is coming down, and wondering why he didn't just follow right behind us.

The door opens, and Vanessa appears with the chair and a rumpled blanket.

"I grabbed this from your room. We'll spread it over your legs," she says. I sit in the chair, confronted with a wave of exhaustion the second I relax. "Do not, under any circumstances, speak of what happened in your room until we are out of this hospital and alone," she orders softly. "Let me do the talking. If my husband asks you a question, then answer, but keep it short, and keep smiling. He's a sucker for pretty girls who smile," she says, rolling her eyes. I nod and scrunch deeper in the chair, wishing I had a hat to pull down over my face.

Vanessa pushes me down the hall. My pulse accelerates the closer we get to my room.

"I can't go back in there," I whisper.

"We won't. I paged my husband. He's going to meet us in the sitting area on your floor."

"Okay." Still, I grip the arms of my chair so hard my knuckles turn white as we pass by my open door. My eyes slide unbidden to their corners. The room is dark and still.

Dr. Andrews is waiting for us in the sitting area. He stands when he sees us, and his brow knits across his forehead.

"Is everything okay?" he asks.

"Tanzy is ready to leave," Vanessa announces.

"It's the middle of the night."

"I checked her records. Her vitals have been perfect for twenty-four hours. She's ready to move forward with my program."

"I'm not sure she's there yet. And even if she is, this could've waited until the morning." He narrows his eyes.

"I don't like hospitals," I blurt. "They're . . . freaky." I can't help but think of Lucas and how funny his face looked when he'd said the same thing. The idea of such a big guy being afraid of a hospital almost makes me smile. Remembering Vanessa's advice, I force my mouth into an apologetic grin. Dr. Andrews's face softens the moment he sees it.

"There aren't many patients that do like hospitals," he says. Behind me, Vanessa clears her throat, as if warning me to stick with the plan. I press my lips together. "That's not a reason to leave before you're ready," he adds. Vanessa huffs.

"She's ready, David. She's remembering moments immediately prior to and after the lightning strike. I don't want her to lose the purity of those memories before I have a chance to work through them with her."

"Vanessa," Dr. Andrews says, a note of warning in his voice. "I know your research is important to you, but need I remind you that Tanzy's health comes first."

"Mental health is every bit as critical as physical health. If these memories are mismanaged, she could suffer from anxiety, agoraphobia, depression . . ."

"That's a big leap." Dr. Andrews frowns, rubbing his eyes.

"There's a family history," I whisper, wondering if there's any truth in Vanessa's claims. Betrayal slices through me as I envision my mother staring out of the kitchen window, roaming from room to room, stopping just shy of the front door.

"David, I have seen it happen. You know I have. I wouldn't take her out of here if I thought for one second leaving would do her more harm than staying. She . . . she can stay at our house, if it makes you feel more comfortable. Maybe you could even come by to check on her."

I tense in the chair, my spine becoming rigid. I never agreed to go anywhere but home. And why would David have to come by to check on me at his own house? Doesn't he live there?

"I don't think—" I start, twisting to look at Vanessa. She gently knees the back of my chair.

"No, Vanessa, I'm sorry. My answer is no."

"She's seen things, David," Vanessa pleads. "She's seen . . . it. With her, I finally have proof."

I hold my breath, realizing she's talking about the Unseen world, the very thing she'd told me unequivocally to avoid mentioning. Dr. Andrews folds his arms and a scowl puckers his mouth.

"I hope you're not referring to what I think you're referring to."

"I am. But David, I'm desperate. This is my first break in years. If you would just let me—"

"No." He shakes his head. "I thought you had let this go, Vanessa. We agreed that you would."

"It's real, David."

"This conversation is over. Take Tanzy back to her room." He turns away.

"I saw a ghost," I say, practically shouting. "This place is haunted. It made me drink something. I can't go back in there. If you make me go back . . . I'll . . . I'll sue." Dr. Andrews spins around.

"Those are big words, Tanzy," he says, his voice low, anger flashing in his eyes. The hair on my arms stands on end as a shiver of regret passes through me.

"This is an easy fix," Vanessa soothes, stepping around to the front of me. Her hands are open and slightly raised, as if she's trying to distract a mad bull. "Tanzy will agree to be in the inpatient portion of my program. She will have her vitals monitored, any meds administered, whatever you want. I can even bring in a nurse, if that helps."

I wonder how much of this promise she's going to try to insist we follow, and uncertainty gnaws at me. She puts a hand behind her back and crosses two fingers, as if reading my mind, and I have to stop myself from smiling.

"She could just leave against medical advice," Dr. Andrews says, exhaustion settling on his face.

"She's going to need insurance to cover this," Vanessa answers quietly. "If she leaves AMA . . ."

"Okay." Dr. Andrews puts his hands up. "If this is that important to you, and you really think you can handle this, and Tanzy has made it clear she's leaving either way, then okay. Tanzy, I will have you sign an additional liability waiver addendum before you leave. And she'll need to make an appointment to have a hard cast put on by the end of the week."

"Of course," Vanessa agrees. I'm so thrilled I nearly stand, stopping myself just before my toes touch the ground.

"I'll get the paperwork," Dr. Andrews says, walking forward. Then he stops. "Did I hear that you ran through the lobby?" he asks.

"I . . . I hopped. I held onto things," I answer. He gives me a wary look.

"Any pain, anything at all," he says, directing his gaze to Vanessa while he points at me.

"I will bring her back right away if there's any concern. And Tanzy won't protest." She glances at me. I nod, too afraid to speak for fear I'll say the wrong thing. Dr. Andrews lets out a sigh, and we follow him down the hall.

VANESSA WHEELS ME ACROSS THE LOBBY. I'm not sure if she's pushing me twice as fast as she did before or if it's just my imagination and my want to be out of here making everything feel rushed. The main doors are twenty feet away. Ten. Then they open in front of me. Winter air rushes in, eliciting goosebumps from the skin my forearms as we burst through the sliding doors.

The moonless sky is plum purple, and scattered with stars. I sink against the back of the wheelchair, keeping my face turned down. I press the extra blanket Lucas gave me against my chest. I can't imagine Asher or another shadow would reemerge in the crowded hospital lobby, but I can't shake the feeling of being watched.

Vanessa grabs her keys out of the front pocket on her satchel, and pushes a button. The lights flash on a black Maserati. She pulls open her door and slides inside. I duck into the passenger side and pull the door shut, finally feeling a little less vulnerable now that I'm inside something that can move quickly, and the hospital will soon be miles behind me.

She collapses the wheelchair and stows it in the trunk, then turns on the engine. The tires squeal as she makes a hard turn, gunning the gas the second the car returns to nearly straight. I grab the door handle and the console, anchoring myself to the seat. Had we been in a truck, we would've rolled over. Where is my truck? Realization sinks heavily onto my chest: I'd parked right next to the barn. There's no way it survived the fire. Wildwood has claimed my father, Teague, probably Harbor, the barn, all of the other horses . . . maybe the owner is right. Maybe that land is cursed. I stifle a sob, acknowledging that Harbor is probably dead, making me feel like a traitor. *There's no proof, no body* . . . Suddenly, I understand my mother on every level, and I burst into tears.

"Are you okay?" Vanessa asks. She begins to reach for me across the console, and then retracts her hand.

"I don't know," I whisper.

"Do we need to turn around?"

"No," I answer sharply, and then exhale hard in an attempt to settle my breathing. "Thank you for getting me out of there."

"I really think you need to come home with me. I said what I said to my husband to help you get out, but there's truth in all of it, even in what David said."

"I need to go home. I need to check on my mom. I'll do everything you ask me to do, but from my own house."

"Okay," she says softly. "Tell me how to get there."

I don't say much on the drive to my house, other than the usual directions on where to turn and which roads to take. The quiet is nice. So is the movement—the world whizzing by my window. Everything is dark, and most of the trees are winter bare. I want to be able to crawl into my bed and listen to her shuffle from her room to the kitchen or press my ear against her door just to make sure she's in her room and breathing, just so we can go back to the way we were before. I used to wish that life away. I would give anything to have it back now. The Unseen world seems like it's been destined to come for me. My old reality has been on borrowed time for a year.

We turn onto my street. My heart begins to pound the moment my house comes into view.

"I just realized I don't have a key," I mumble. "My keys were in my truck. I parked it directly in front of the barn. I don't think there's any way it came through the fire." I scan the front of the house for it, but there's no sign of it on the street or in the driveway.

"Do you have a hidden key outside somewhere?" Vanessa asks.

"We do," I say, brightening. "It's under a rock on the side of the house."

"Let's go check," Vanessa says and puts the car in park. We climb out, leaving the engine running.

I head for the side of the house. The medium-sized gray rock sits by itself in a patch of dirt. I roll it over. The key box is lodged in the ground underneath. I slide it open. It's empty. I drop the box and jog to the front door to test the handle. As I climb the steps, the memory of running down them and into the night pulses in my head. *It should have been you . . .*

But I hadn't locked the door.

I twist the handle. It doesn't budge.

"Is there a back door? Maybe she left it open," Vanessa offers from behind me.

"Maybe." I'm unwilling to register the note of hope in her voice. We traipse around to the back of the house and up the porch stairs. I feel foolish standing in the shadow of my own home without a way in. I pull the screen door, but the latch on the inside has been closed. I pry at a loose place in the screen with my finger until it gives, and then reach in and pop the latch. I stride across the porch floor, urgency breathing down the back of my neck. I grip the handle and try to turn it. The back door is locked.

I spin on my heels and fly down the steps.

"Something's wrong," I mumble.

"Tanzy, it's the middle of the night. She didn't know we were coming. It's completely reasonable for someone to lock their house."

I circle back to the front of the house. The lights are all off. A glow from the opposite side of the house paints a faint yellow circle on the lawn. I run in its direction, gazing up. The light in my room is on. I beeline for Mom's bedroom window, press my fingertips under the lip, and lift. The pane slides up. I shove it open enough to slide through, and then hoist myself over the sill.

"Do you want me to come in with you?" Vanessa asks. I peer back, having momentarily forgotten her presence.

"No. Stay here."

"What if—"

"I'll be okay," I say, cutting her off, and then drop into Mom's room.

Her bed is made. I stand stone still, unable to look away. Mom hasn't made her bed since Dad's accident. I touch it, just to make sure it's real. The comforter gives under my hand, leaving an indention when I pull back. I smooth it out, and then step into the hallway on trembling legs.

"Mom?"

She doesn't answer.

I check the kitchen first, flipping on the light switch. The light doesn't come on. I open the fridge. It's empty and silent. I travel room to room, but none of the switches work. I wrap my arms around myself and my teeth chatter. I can see my breath. I haven't been gone but a week. Even if the electricity bill was past due, they wouldn't have turned it off that fast.

I pass by the stairwell and freeze: *there was a light on in my room.*

I take the stairs two at a time, keeping my eyes fixated on my door as it comes into view. The yellow glow is visible under the door. I reach for the door, suddenly terrified it'll be locked, too. *What if she's in there … what if …?*

I twist the handle and throw my shoulder into the door. The handle turns, and my momentum sends me sprawling through the opening door and into my floor. I land on my side, wincing, and then look up. My room is completely empty, save a single lantern and piece of paper sitting under the window.

I sit up, blinking. I rub my eyes. My room doesn't change. I slowly stand and turn in a circle, digging my nails so hard into the skin on my arm I draw blood.

"This isn't happening," I mutter. I walk to where my bed should be, certain I'll crack my shins on the wood frame. I only stop when I reach the corner and can go no further. I turn around, expecting something, anything to be different, or for my mother to be standing there in the open door. I'd give anything for her to scream at me, say whatever she needs to say, if it meant that she was here.

I'm alone.

The lantern light flickers, making shadows dance on the wall. I step forward, eyeing the piece of paper. Seeing her handwriting makes my heart begin to hammer even harder. I bend down to pick it up.

Tanzy,

This house is no longer your home. I am no longer your responsibility, and you are no longer mine. Don't look for me. You won't find me. Our paths will not continue unless we walk them alone. Leave, Tanzy, and don't come back.

Hope

She signed the letter with her name. Her words knife through my heart and begin to twist. My heart shudders in my chest, and I gasp with pain. I drop to my knees, catching my face on the heels of my hands, and choke on a deep sob.

"How could you?" I cry out. "How could you!?" Where am I supposed to go? What am I supposed to do? I grab the paper from where it fell to the floor and tear it down the middle, letting out a scream. My eyelids crush shut, sending down two rivers of tears. "How could you?" I whimper. Could this just be another bad day? Will she snap out of it and come home? Where is she? What if she's truly lost her mind? Do I need to call the police and report her missing? *What's the point?* I press my knuckles to my chest, wondering if my heart could still be beating with such a cold thought taking root in my brain.

A gust of air whips through the room. My eyes fly open as the lantern flame roars, and then snuffs out, plunging the room into darkness. I scan my room, the raspy sound of my breathing echoing in the empty house. A prick of fear sends a shiver down my spine.

"Tanzy?" Vanessa's voice calls from far off, stirring me to motion. "Is everything okay?"

I push up to my feet, staring down at the torn paper and the dark lantern. I back out of my room. The wood floor creaks under my steps.

"Tanzy?" Her voice is louder now.

I pass through my doorway and turn before I collide with the banister. Vanessa is standing in the foyer, peering up.

"I thought you'd fallen asleep," she says.

"No." I blink away the image of my empty room. Should I stay here anyway? Sleep in her bed or in Dad's favorite chair? How long would I have to wait to have the electricity turned back on? It's bitter cold, and from the looks of my room, Mom didn't leave me any clothes. This wasn't a whim. This took planning, conviction, follow-through.

If she left the house, why couldn't she come see me? If she's this angry, why couldn't she have the courage to tell me in person? She left a note in the empty floor of my room like a coward. The heat of anger laces through me, and I clench my teeth to keep from screaming.

"It's cold in here." Vanessa shivers where she stands. "Why is it so cold?"

"I can't stay here," I say.

"What's going on?" Vanessa asks slowly.

"I'm not welcome here anymore," I say, squeezing my hands into fists.

"Is your mom here?" Vanessa looks up the stairs. "I can talk to her."

"No."

"No, she's not here, or no you don't want me to talk to her?"

"Can we just go, please?" I say, my voice breaking.

"Of course. We can call someone . . .? Friends? Family?"

118

"Vanessa, no," I manage to say, my insides quaking. My mind is a storm, my body a ship. I stumble to the front door.

"It's the middle of the night. The only place I can think to go is my house. Is that okay?" Vanessa asks hopeful.

"Anywhere but here," I whisper. I pull the door open and walk into the night.

THE WITCH AND
THE DEVIL

We wind our way back to the main road. Vanessa glances at me every minute or so. She doesn't say anything. She's probably waiting for me to be the one to break the silence. I have no idea what to say or where to start. My mother's note swells in my mind, taking up all the space, but I can't bring myself to recite it. What does it say about her, about me, about us? Even after she said it should've been me instead of Dad, I held tight to a tiny piece of hope that there was a way back to who we used to be. But those words on that paper, her decision to rid the house of any trace of me . . . they can never be undone.

"Do you want to tell me what happened back there?" Vanessa finally asks after we pull onto the highway.

"No."

"Okay. What about in your hospital room?" She changes lanes without signaling—my father's pet peeve. I have to look away to keep from commenting. I let out a hard breath, staring through my window, and refocus on the man who turned into a shadow. My mind paints his picture in the dark of night.

"A nurse came in both nights," I start. "Last night seemed completely normal. He gave me some medicine, he checked my chart on the computer, and he left. But tonight, he seemed agitated. After I took the medicine, he asked if I remembered anything. He called me a name . . . Spera, I think." Beside me, Vanessa stiffens, and inhales sharply through her nose.

"That's a very unusual name. Are you sure that's what he said?"

"Positive. He said he was tired of waiting, and something about how I don't belong in a mortal body." I wrinkle my nose, recognizing how funny this must all sound. But when I glance at Vanessa, her face is stone still, her eyes wide.

"You said he gave you medicine?" she asks in a rush.

"Yes."

"How did he give it to you? What did it look like?"

"It was red. I had to drink it. It tasted awful last night, but he said he found a new flavor tonight, and it wasn't as bad."

"Why did you think he was from the other side?" she presses.

"He . . . dissolved," I say, blinking in disbelief at the memory. "His edges looked like they were smoking. He turned completely black, like a living shadow, and then he disappeared. That's when I ran."

"Did he tell you his name?" Vanessa's voice is strangled.

"Asher. His name was Asher."

"This is much, much worse than I thought," Vanessa mutters, and floors the gas. The car leaps forward, pinning me to the back of my seat.

"Vanessa, you're scaring me," I say.

"You should be scared. I'm terrified." She points the car at the exit ramp, taking the curve without slowing down, and then re-enters the highway going the opposite direction. "The one Unseen creature I know can work magic. She can create something out of nothing using Tenix. She can use blood to see the future. She can see the past. She can dissolve into pure water. She's as old as time itself. And she's afraid of one thing. One." She steals a glimpse of me. "She's scared to death of someone named Asher."

"Where are we going?" I ask, bracing myself on the door, my mind racing as fast as the car. I glance at the speedometer. We're traveling a hundred miles per hour.

"We're going to see her."

"It's four in the morning," I say, checking the clock on the dashboard.

"I'm sure she knows we're on our way," Vanessa mutters.

"If she knew this was coming, why didn't she stop it? Or warn you?"

"You should ask her when we get there," she says with a growl.

We travel south for a solid hour. Questions about Asher, the Unseen we're going to see, and the world they belong to pile up in my head. Vanessa is a statue in her seat. Even though she's silent, her nervousness fills the little car, and I can tell her mind is spinning behind her fixed eyes.

"I have a confession to make," she says without looking at me. "I saw what happened to you the night of your accident."

"You were there?" I ask, swiveling in her direction.

"No. I didn't see it like that." She shakes her head. "I dreamed it. In my dream, you chased a white horse out of the barn. There was lightning all around you. Two monsters followed you. You didn't see them. The horse saw them first. You jumped on and the horse took off through the woods. Then everything got really fast and choppy."

"Did you see what happened to my horse?" I ask, emotion swelling at the base of my throat.

"No." Vanessa blinks away the shine in her eyes. "I saw you flip over the fence. She was trying to stand up. Those beasts were coming toward you. And then there was a bright purple flash and a deafening boom, and I woke up."

"Her name is Harbor," I whisper, reliving the sounds of her struggling to her feet. "Why didn't you tell me before now?"

"I wasn't prepared. I didn't think we'd meet so soon. My husband said he had a patient who matched my research qualifications. I walked into your hospital room and there you were. I didn't think you were ready, and I didn't think you'd believe me," she says quietly. "I didn't want to lose you at the very start."

I shake off the nudge of resentment. I know how she must have felt.

"When did you dream about me?" I ask.

"A couple weeks ago. It's how I find people I'm supposed to work with. I don't treat every person struck by lightning or electrocuted. It happens more often than you'd think," she says, managing a wry smile. "I didn't know your name or where you were, but I knew, I *knew* we would cross paths. I knew we would find each other somehow."

"How is this even possible?" I murmur.

"I believe, when you are targeted by the Unseen side, as we have been, it's either because of a gift we've always possessed, or a gift they intend to bestow. My prophetic dreams began shortly after I was struck. Everyone I have encountered who can see these marks," she pauses, flashing her palm at me, "also develops an extraordinary gift or talent. Maris, the Unseen I'm taking you to see, has, in her own way, confirmed this."

"In her own way?" I ask quietly.

"Maris speaks mostly in riddles. It's not always obvious what she's telling you, but usually, if I stop trying to overthink what she's telling me and just listen, the message is loud and clear."

"What is she like?"

"She's a voodoo priestess, like a marsh or swamp witch. At least that's what other people call her. Sometimes people will ask her to read their palms or tarot cards, but she just messes with them, and then charges two hundred dollars a pop to do it," she says with a laugh. I think back to the day I found the two glasses in the kitchen, the half-empty bottle of bourbon. Could Maris help my mother? I have a feeling she'd be more receptive to voodoo than a shrink.

"So, she doesn't see the future?" I ask.

"No, not like that. But she . . . she reads people. She knows how to set things in motion. She understands how to predict what someone will do. It's hard to explain. She . . . she isn't an oracle of the future, she's an oracle of the past."

"How does that work?"

"Maris believes in reincarnation, especially for humans connected to the Unseen side. The Unseen world is eternal, unchanging. She calls it the land of sea and stone, and says that change of any kind is nearly impossible there. So when a human is marked by the Unseen side, it's thought that there's something in their soul that will offer change to their world," she explains. "Sometimes, Maris can literally help a person see their past lives. She wasn't able to do that for me." Her shoulders droop.

"How did you find her?" I ask curiously.

"Let's just say I'm two hundred dollars poorer because of Maris," she says, smiling ruefully. "I had just begun work with the second girl I ever had in my program. I had a dream that she was being chased by something very similar to what chased you and your horse. In my dream, a woman rose out of a pond and drowned the beast, saving the girl. The next day I was in an art gallery in town. I saw a painting of her, exactly how I'd seen her and I contacted the artist. He told me she was a fortune-teller and how to find her. She's taught me everything I know, and she sells me Tenix. She's the one who taught me how to use Tenix to heal injuries. How's your leg, by the way?"

"A little stiff," I say, stretching. "But great, otherwise. So, did you save her?" I ask, rubbing the scar through the scrubs.

"Who?"

"The girl."

"No. I didn't. She disappeared." She glares at the windshield. "That's when I learned of Asher."

"What do you know about him? Why is Maris afraid?"

"Do you know how I said change is nearly impossible in the Unseen world?" she asks. I nod. "It's not just new life that is impossible. Death is also nearly impossible. There are only two ways an Unseen creature can die. First, they can die here on our side of the veil, so a stronger Unseen can force a weaker Unseen through the veil and kill them here. Second, Asher can end an Unseen's life on either side of the veil. He doesn't have to force them here first."

"Why?" I ask, smothering a gasp.

"Because over there, he's king."

"The man in my hospital room, the living shadow . . . that's a king?" I ask, disbelieving.

"Unseen creatures don't look like me and you—not in their true forms. When they cross through the veil, they have to take shapes humans recognize, and with it, all the mortal risks that come with a mortal body. A human stands a chance of killing an Unseen when they take a mortal form. Although Maris swears Asher would never cross the veil. Our world is the only place where he's vulnerable. So he usually sends his guards to do his dirty work."

"What does he want over here?"

"Two things. Tenix, which is only available in its raw form here, and . . ." she pauses, "if Maris is right, he's searching for Spera."

"But he called me Spera." My head swims with confusion. "I'm not Spera. Asher's wrong. Can't we just prove I'm not who he's looking for?"

Vanessa presses her lips together and stares straight ahead. "What if he's not wrong?"

"Vanessa, I'm not Spera," I say, nearly laughing. "What am I missing, here?"

"You're not Spera now." She steals a glimpse of me. "But what if you used to be?"

"What the hell are you talking about?"

"Maris once talked about Spera. She's a legend in the Unseen world. I don't know much about her, only that she was a human who had captured Asher's heart hundreds of years ago. She became royalty. But she betrayed Asher. There were rumors she was in love with someone else. Whatever it was, she disappeared soon after. If Asher thinks you're Spera, he's not going to stop. This is way beyond proving an Unseen world exists and my stupid research program. This is the king of the Unseen world standing on your front door step with a torch in his hands. I am scared to death."

"If he fell in love with Spera, why is he a danger to me?" I ask

"Maris is convinced he killed Spera for loving another," Vanessa whispers.

"What would he do to me now?" I ask, every inch of me on edge.

"I don't know!" She slams the steering wheel. "But Maris will."

"Are you sure Maris doesn't work for Asher?"

"She hates Asher," Vanessa replies. "She even tried to arrange his death here once, but he didn't fall for it."

I hug my knees to my chest, the fear in Vanessa's voice trying to burrow its way inside of me.

"It's a harsh world on the other side of the veil. Lawless, ruthless. From what Maris has told me, the Unseen way of life is to take what you want, by any means necessary."

"And Asher thinks he wants me. But why?" I murmur. I can't see the world beyond the clear, but I'm beginning to feel it, ice cold and razor sharp.

We exit the highway halfway between Richmond and Charlottesville onto a dilapidated two-lane road, which quickly changes from cracked asphalt to gravel. Vanessa points to a dirt road with no street sign. She slows down and then makes the turn. The road carves a path through an overgrown field, and then down a long, slow hill. The ground levels out as the fields end and a dense line of trees begins.

Vanessa pulls a U-turn, and then backs the little car into a gap between trees. She kills the engine and we are plunged into utter darkness. Then she digs a flashlight out of her glove box and hands it to me.

"Shouldn't you hold it? I don't know where we're going," I say.

"I see pretty well in the dark. I'm more worried about you than me," she says. I take the flashlight and we climb out of the car. Even though my heart is pounding in my chest, I can't help but notice how the stars shine brilliantly overhead with no light pollution to dim their visibility.

"So, where are we exactly?" I ask.

"It's an unincorporated bank-owned piece of property and has been pretty much since the Declaration of Independence," she says with a snort. "Maris comes to this place when she wants to be alone."

"How do you know about it?" I ask, searching for Unseen shadows. There's no point. The forest is uniformly black. How does Vanessa see out here?

"Once I decided I wanted her help, I followed her everywhere. I learned about all of her hiding places. It might seem rude in our world, but I've learned it's the way Unseens operate," she explains. "The last time I saw her, she told me she'd be here the next time I needed her. Like I said, she knows we're coming."

I follow her in, and even though I can barely see my hand in front of my face without my flashlight, I somehow feel entirely exposed. The trees thin, and the ground turns soft under my feet. We step through a tangle of shrubbery, and then onto a sandy bank. Ahead of us runs a wide, slow river, turned dark silver by reflecting the light from the moon. The opposite bank is nearly vertical.

"There's a river on my property that eventually connects with this one," Vanessa says, nodding at the water. "I've actually seen Maris in my yard before."

"Does she kayak or something?" I ask.

"No." Vanessa laughs. "I forget how much you still have to learn. Maris is an elemental Unseen, which means her elemental makeup is almost pure water. She can take a human form to speak to people, but she spends most of her time on this side of the veil as water. If she goes too long on this side of the veil without contacting water, she could die."

"Who do we have here?" A woman's voice rasps from close by. I spin around. A short woman stands ankle deep in the river, a silver hooded cape draped over her shoulders and trailing in the water. Her pale blue eyes glow in the dark, narrowing to slits as she stares at me. I startle at how similar her eyes look to my mother's. Their similarities begin and end there. Her skin is coal black and deeply wrinkled, reminding me of hardened lava, and flecked with tiny white dots like freckles. Her hair, by contrast, is white as snow. It hangs to her waist in waterfall curls, and is streaked with shades of silver and blue. A thin silver strip of metal coils around her throat. She brings her finger within a hair's width of my coat, then snatches her hand away.

"You are something special, aren't you?" she says. I hold my breath. I want to step back and bolt, but my feet remain frozen.

"That's why we came," Vanessa says, breaking the intense spell that had settled in the sliver of air between us. "But then you know that already, don't you, Maris?"

"Let me take a look inside." Maris stares straight through my eyes. Her pupils dilate so far that they blot out her pale irises. I can see myself on their surfaces. I look openly at myself for the first time in years—the sadness, the exhaustion, how young I appear . . . how old.

In her eyes, my reflection sharpens. My cheek bones become severe, my eyes shift into a wider set and double the size, my hair thick and black. It dances around my face, then swirls away as if driven by wind and the rest of me turns black. My face stretches long and morphs into a horse's head. The horse throws its nose in the air and screams. I smother a gasp and shut my eyes, shaking and overwhelmed. Where have I seen that horse before? Why am I seeing it now?

"It's you . . ." Maris murmurs, and her pupils recede.

"Me?" I ask, shrinking back.

"The girl chosen by the black horse, the soul Asher can't break. The heart he can't fool. It's you." A brisk wind kicks off the river face, sending my hair flying and a chill through my body. "Come, now. Let's get you inside and I'll tell you all that you need to know." She leads me toward a little tent tucked between the limbs of a fallen tree at the water's edge. Vanessa follows close behind us.

"Ah-ah, *Bella*. This one is not for you," Maris scolds Vanessa. I expect Vanessa to argue. Instead, she steps back. I've never seen her concede to anyone. I cast her one last glance over my shoulder as Maris takes my hand and pulls me forward.

We step inside the little tent. Half the floor is submerged in shallow water, and the other half is dry sand. There's a thick blue blanket folded into a rectangle at the water's edge. A weathered wooden chest is nestled in the corner. Crystal prisms dangle from the low ceiling. They catch light from somewhere, and paint dark rainbows all over the canvas walls. Maris strikes a match and brings it to the wick of an antique lantern. The rainbows fade a bit in the new light. With a start I realize that the prisms had been reflecting Maris. She takes a seat in the water. She motions for me to take a seat in front of her on the blanket.

What are you, exactly? I wonder as I lower myself to the ground.

"I am the hand in the undertow. I am the rainbow in the mist," she responds.

"You can read my mind?" I ask, leaning away.

"I can read a lot of things," she says. "You, though, reading what is right in front of you isn't your gift." She tilts her face, studying me. "You are standing on a chess board, dear girl, and the game is happening all around you."

"What piece am I?" I ask, remembering what Vanessa said about Maris and preferring to speak in riddles.

"A pawn doesn't worry about being a pawn, it worries about the pieces within striking distance. Any piece can be taken off the board by any other piece. There's beauty in it, don't you think?"

"I guess so," I offer.

"There's a reason the king can only move one space at a time, but it is important to remember he can move in any direction. He's perhaps most deadly when he's ahead of you. The queen however, the queen is the piece that is used best when she's quiet and hides behind others. Her reach is so great, she can cross the board in a single turn if the way is clear."

"Am I a queen or a pawn?" I press, doing my best to keep up with her.

"Which piece you are isn't nearly as important as making sure you're choosing allies whose colors match yours."

"I don't know who to trust," I admit aloud, grateful Vanessa isn't in the tent to hear me say that. I didn't even realize it was true until right now.

"Trust no one," she says, leaning forward. "Only yourself and perhaps your mother," she responds, sincerity touching her voice for the first time.

I tense. "My mother?"

"Yes, your mother," she says with a knowing smile.

"Do you *know* my mother?" I ask sarcastically.

"We go way back," she replies, a wistful smile drawing up her cheeks. I'm startled by her answer. She brings her thumb to her lips. When she drops her hand, she's left a silver streak on her mouth. Immediately, I see the glass on the kitchen table, the streak of silver that I thought was lipstick.

"You were at my house. She called you a psychic."

"She knows better than that," she answers.

"How could she know what you are? She doesn't believe in a world in the clear."

"She didn't come to me about a world in the clear. She came to me about you. I haven't seen her in years, until very recently."

"You saw her? Is she okay? Where did she go? Why did she leave?" I end in a whisper, seeing her letter in my mind.

"When Asher closes in, the fewer things you stand to lose, the safer you are. Your mother was a piece of wind and sky, and to the sky she returned in order to help you."

"Are you . . . are you trying to tell me that my mom died?" I stammer, my throat squeezing with the threat of grief. Maris shakes her head.

"She is more alive now than she has been in years. I could not help her the way she needed, but she found someone who can. I do know she is safe. But this is not about your mother. This is about you and Spera."

"Asher thinks I'm Spera," I say quietly, relieved to hear news of my mother, and equally relieved to move away from the subject of her. I'm not sure how much longer I can hold myself together when she's in my mind's spotlight.

"I thought he might," Maris says, raising an eyebrow. "What do *you* know of Spera?"

"Vanessa told me she was royalty in the Unseen world, and a legend ever since. That's all I know," I say.

"Spera was a girl, just like you, a thousand years ago. Through Asher's influence, she became royalty, but she never became Unseen or crossed to the Unseen world in her lifetime," Maris says. "Asher must believe Spera has been reborn in you. He will come for you over and over, because there's something on this side of the veil he wants. Something he can only have if the veil dissolves, and he believes Spera is the only one who can open the veil for him."

"Why does he need the veil to dissolve? He can come through it just fine now," I say.

"The veil keeps Unseen creatures from destroying your world. In order to pass through the veil separating the Unseen side from your side, all Unseen creatures must take a form humans will recognize, and with it, that form's weaknesses and mortality."

"Vanessa told me about that."

"If an Unseen can cross in its true form into your world, its immortality will follow, as will its strength and size. The beasts you conjure in your worst nightmares are no comparison to what will appear in your world should the veil collapse. Your world would never survive."

"Why?" I ask, trepidation climbing my spine like a ladder.

"Tenix." Maris reaches behind her and searches her box with her fingers. She picks up a silver tube. "Do you know what Tenix is?"

"Sort of. Vanessa used it to heal my leg," I say, eyeing the bottle. "She said it's like the glue that bonds elements together, but I don't really understand how it works."

"She is right. All mortal life is comprised of percentages of the four major elements: earth, air, water, and fire. When a person dies, what does its body become?"

"Earth?" I guess, shifting where I sit.

"Yes. When a person dies, the elements that make your body break down. It's mostly earth and water, and a fraction of air and fire, depending on the personality," she says, winking. "Tenix is left behind in its raw form, visible only to Unseen eyes. But finding it is the easy part. Asher and his guards are the only creatures with the correct elemental breakdown to be able to absorb Tenix in its raw form, and carry it through the veil into the Unseen world for purification and processing. The mortal forms they must take when on your side limits how much Tenix they can absorb and transport. It also slows down how fast they can kill things. If they are allowed to cross into your world in their true forms, they would dismantle all mortal life in your world within a matter of days."

"So Tenix is . . . Tenix is life itself?"

"In a way, yes. It's what makes life possible."

"Does Vanessa know that?" I ask, stricken. I wonder what had died to give me the ability to walk again.

"Of course she does," Maris says, shrugging.

"And you sell it. So do you . . . do you harvest it?" I ask, guarding my front with my arms. "Do you kill things?"

"I'm more of an opportunist," she answers. "Remember, only Asher and his guards can harvest Tenix from a living creature here. But every Unseen creature values Tenix, and will do whatever they can to possess it."

"So how do you get it?" I ask, staring at her box.

"I am a trader. Tenix is a popular currency, but it is not the only one. Although it's certainly Asher's favorite."

"What does Spera have to do with this?" I narrow my eyes, inwardly searching for a link, but these puzzle pieces of information could fit a thousand different ways, or not at all.

"Words carved into diamond," she says. She splashes handfuls of water on her thighs, and then trails her fingers along the surface of the puddle. The water glows in response to her touch, and she paints a wavy line.

"What words?" I ask, mesmerized.

"A prophecy of a mortal who can open the veil. In my world, they call this mortal the Vessel." She draws a spiral in the water. It begins to throb the second she lifts her hand.

"And Asher thinks this mortal is Spera?" I ask, trying to solidify one fact at a time.

"Yes."

"Why?"

"The veil itself is a living thing. It would not allow for a way to be destroyed for the simple act of harvesting Tenix. That throws off the law of balance. The price your world would pay would be too great, what Unseens would gain would be too great. There's no way to rebalance the scales. It would need something truly spectacular, something ... once in an immortal lifetime."

"And what would that be?" I ask slowly.

"An immortal birth. There are only two laws in the Unseen world that not even Asher can break. The law of balance, and the law of permanency. Unseens cannot die naturally, except at Asher's hand. Likewise, no Unseen can give birth to real, new life. We can only temporarily mimic it with creations made from Tenix." She reaches into a bottle. When she withdraws her hand, her fingertips glow gold with Tenix. She pinches the water and draws it upright, and then makes a bulb shape with her hand. When she opens her fingers, two roses appear, one white, and one black.

"Why would Asher care about ..." my voice fades away, and the flowers blur in my vision. Asher fell in love with a mortal woman. And whether it's out of that love, or out of desire to be above an unbreakable law, Asher wants a child.

"Yes," she confirms, reading my mind. "Asher has declared that he alone will sire the one immortal birth in all of history."

"And he thinks Spera has to be the mother," I murmur, recalling how agitated he became, the words he used: *do you remember anything yet?* "Vanessa says you think Asher killed Spera, though."

"I said Asher loved Spera. I never said Spera loved him in return."

"So he killed her?" I ask, my eyes opening wide.

"You can't force a prophecy into being just as you can't force love. Spera would have to want to open the veil and deliver his child. If she didn't want it, he couldn't have it. But, because of the law of balance, one person can't hold all the cards. Asher has found a way around Spera's reluctance. Long before her time, he learned how to mark and reincarnate mortal souls. I believe when Spera refused him, he ended her life in hopes that she would return in the future in a more agreeable form."

"Me." The pieces fall into place all at once, and I can hardly breathe. "You."

"There has to be another way," I whisper in a rush. "If there really is a law of balance, my option can't be to either open the veil or die and come back until I am willing to open the veil."

"Very good." She raises an eyebrow. "The veil can also be sealed, the door never to open."

"What would happen then?" I ask.

"Unseen creatures will never be able to cross into your world ever again. All the Unseens living in your world will be pulled through the veil and trapped on the Unseen side, permanently."

"That doesn't sound so bad," I say.

"There is no change in the Unseen World—no birth, no death, no seasons. It is the land of sea and stone. Can you fathom what it would be like to live for eternity and wake to the same day, the same room, over and over, with no chance for change in sight? Can you imagine how much power Asher wields, as the only creature who can end the life of another Unseen in our world?"

"That's not really our problem, is it?" I ask tentatively. "This is our world. You have yours. Isn't that the way it should be?"

"Each mortal life is a blink of an eye in comparison to an eternity. Most Unseens don't believe Seen creatures deserve the access to what you have. They believe that you squander what we could use to create so much more."

"Whose side are *you* on?" I ask, suddenly wary.

"Neither. Both," she answers. "I want the veil to remain in place. I want to keep Unseens in check, yet the Seen world available."

"What did Spera want? Why didn't she seal the veil?" I wonder aloud.

"Regardless of what she wanted to do, she first had to find the door in the veil. There's only one small place in this entire world where a mortal can pass through with a choice in her heart. No one yet knows where that door is. And if they were to find it, the price of closing the door is the permanent death of the Vessel. Sealing the veil will cost your eternal life. If you choose to open the veil, you will become as immortal as Asher, untouchable, for all of time. This choice is not simple."

"How could Asher kill Spera if he truly loved her? How could he put her in that position at all? If he loved her, wouldn't she be enough?" I ask softly. I think of how my father loved my mother, wholly and unquestioning. He let her keep her secrets. He let her have her window. She shone even brighter when in his presence. He was the charcoal storm, and with him behind her, she was the brilliant garden.

"No one knows for sure what happened. But there might be a way *you* can see it, Tanzy. You might be able to find answers for us all," she says, leaning toward me.

"How?"

"I can send you back," she whispers. "If Spera's soul truly looks through your eyes and Spera's blood runs through your veins, you can witness her life. You can find the answers that evade the rest of us. You can help us stop Asher from changing the veil, maybe even destroy him all together."

"How can I go back?" I ask, wonder filling me.

"I know a way to use your blood and Tenix to create a key to send you back to your first life. You will be met by a guide, who will show you the most important decisions Spera made during her short life. Surely you will gain knowledge of how she died, and what her plans were for the veil."

"How can we be sure I'm Spera?" I ask, my skin tingling with warning.

"The door will only work if you and Spera are one and the same. If you need some reassurance, I can check your elemental color. Hold out your hand," she instructs, and places a small cauldron between us before lighting the contents on fire. I reach out over it, watching the trails of smoke curl around my fingers. She gathers a pinch of Tenix, and then sprinkles it over my hand. It falls through my fingers and into the little fire. The flames spit and spark, and the orange glow deepens into reddish purple, and then lavender, and the smoke turns silver. With a start, I remember it's Lucas's favorite color. I am the color of lightning.

"What's an elemental color?" I ask.

"Every mortal creature has a unique blend of elements. Your color depicts this blend, and how much Tenix you require to maintain form. You have a high ratio of water to earth, and quite a bit of fire. It seems you take very little Tenix to maintain your form. Almost none. In fact, you wouldn't be a target for your Tenix, because there would be very little to harvest if you died."

"This is Spera's color?"

"It's an exact match."

"How can you be sure?"

"I would never forget anything about Spera. The Unseen world has awaited and dreaded her return since the day she vanished. Most of us are satisfied with the worlds existing the way they do now, and we don't want anything to change. With your return, that threat returns. You are Spera reborn. The fates of two worlds rest in your hands."

"I want a key. I want to see her life," I say, my heart drumming with new purpose.

"I will need a few drops of blood for the key, and then we will need to find the door to your past. That shouldn't be too hard though. I have an idea of where to start."

She presses the fleshy part of my palm with her thumb, and pricks it with the tip of a short dagger. It doesn't even hurt. She turns my hand over into the cauldron and squeezes out a few drops. Then she wipes the tiny wound with the Tenix on her thumb. It glows for a full second before vanishing. My palm is smooth, as if she'd never stuck me.

I watch on in silence as she adds a few more ingredients, and then pours the smoking concoction into a little stone vial.

"Now for the door," she says. "Hold your hands out and make a bowl." I do as I'm told. She scoops water from her sides into my hands, and stirs it with her fingers. The water glows. Before my eyes, it turns murky brown and begins to churn, splashing over the sides of my thumbs. In the distance, I swear I hear someone scream. I jerk toward the tent door, and my hands fall.

"Did you hear that?" I say.

"It was you," Maris answer softly. "I was there that day in the river."

My entire being trembles, and I am transported to the river at Wildwood. I hear my own screams in my ear. I feel the hands lifting under my arms.

"You saved me," I whisper. "You're who Mom called. You searched the river."

"Like I said, she knows I'm more than a psychic."

"Where is my father?" I ask, my voice breaking.

"I don't know. I swear on my life, I don't know," she says gently. My chin falls to my chest, and my eyes burn with the threat of tears.

"Mom said you said he was somewhere beautiful."

"I tried to channel his soul for her. I saw an incredible menagerie of colors and crystals, somewhere I've never been before. I can only imagine it's a place where souls go when they're finished. It was peaceful there, I can tell you that much. I hope it brings you comfort. It seemed to help your mother."

"Thank you," I whisper.

"Your door is in the river at Wildwood. Can you return?"

"I have to, don't I?" I say, lifting my gaze to hers.

"If it's knowledge you seek, then yes." She nods, a sad smile softening the lines of her face.

Another scream echoes in the night. I sit up, alarm coursing hot through my veins.

"That wasn't from my memory of the river," I say.

"No, it wasn't. Take this." She shoves the key into my hand. "Wait for the black moon. Go to the river. Drop in the key. Jump through the door." She rises, and hurries through the door, when Vanessa screams again.

ALL IN

Vanessa lies on the river bank, my flashlight in her hand, which illuminates her golden hair spilling across the sand.

"Vanessa!" I run to her. Her eyes are open and fixed, and her breaths come in little gasps. "Can you hear me? What happened?"

"It's okay. It's a vision," Maris says, taking a hold of my arm.

Vanessa blinks, then licks her lips, coming to.

"You scared me, Vanessa," I say, sinking down beside her. "What did you see?"

"We have to run," she rasps. She looks up at Maris, her green eyes wide and wild. "She really is Spera, isn't she?"

"Yes," Maris hisses.

"Something's coming for her," Vanessa gasps. With a start, I realize I don't hear the river. Adrenaline shoots through me. The water is still as glass. On the other side, a crackling shadow distorts the dark. Maris shoves something in Vanessa's bag, before grabbing me by the arm, and hauling us both to our feet.

"Go. You have to go now. Your Tenix is in the bag. Run!" Maris orders.

Vanessa shoves me ahead of her, and we take off up the hill. The sound of footsteps and snapping twigs echo all around me. I don't know if I'm hearing us or someone else. Even though I'm running, I swear I hear Harbor's breathing roaring in my ears—her pulse pounding in the night, driving me faster. I could surge past Vanessa if I want to, but I don't know my way back to her car.

A flash of light catches my eye in the trees ahead.

"There's something there!" I shout up to Vanessa, but I'm too late. A solid form takes shape in the dark. Vanessa crashes into it. Huge, gray hands grip her by the shoulders and sling her to the ground. She yelps and rolls over, grunting as air leaves her lungs. She crawls forward on her elbows and covers her satchel with her body. The burly form steps over her. A staff with a bladed end is slung across its back. The creature reaches for it, keeping its gaze trained on Vanessa.

"I'm what you're after!" I scream. The thing turns. It has a man's face, although it's charcoal gray in color. His frame is similar to Lucas and Asher. I shift my weight to the balls of my feet, preparing to run. I'm smaller, but I know without a doubt I'm faster. Size isn't an advantage when maneuvering through close trees. The Unseen narrows his eyes, assessing me. Vanessa shifts. The bottle of Tenix rolls out of her satchel. The Unseen samples the air, and his attention returns to Vanessa. His fingers grip the middle of the staff, sliding it out of position.

"I'm Tanzy! I'm what Asher wants!" I scream but he doesn't respond. He raises his staff. He's going to kill Vanessa. Terror races through me, igniting every nerve ending.

"Stop!" I shout. "Help! Maris!" My screams echo through the trees. The Unseen doesn't turn, and Maris doesn't appear. I charge forward, and throw myself between the Unseen and Vanessa.

He stares down at me. The flicker of surprise on his face turns to a crush of anger. He snatches the front of my coat and lifts me off the ground. I slap and claw at his hands, kicking uselessly at his body. He clasps my throat with his other hand and begins to squeeze, staring me straight in the face as he tightens his grip. He's just watching, waiting for me to die.

I wheeze, gasping in a breath. My brain quiets. The world around me slows down. Something clicks inside my head, blocking out hesitation. I let go of his arms, gather my knees to my chest and then push off his torso with my toes. He leans forward, caught off guard just as I crank one arm back and send a fist through his teeth. His head snaps back. A second swell of strength drives my left hand through his jaw. He releases me, grabbing his face in pain. I sink my weight back of one foot and send a kick on a diagonal through his diaphragm. The force of the blow sends him reeling backward. He crashes against the thick trunk of a tree and slumps in a heap on the ground. I stand stone still, panting and dizzy.

"Finish him Tanzy," Vanessa moans, clutching her side. "Or if he comes to, we're as good as dead."

"I . . . I can't do that.," I stammer.

"Yes, you can! You have to!" Vanessa pleads, pulling herself up to standing. "I can't . . . I don't think I can run yet."

"I can carry you," I say, moving for her. A rustle sound draws my ear. The Unseen rises to his feet. He flexes his hands and shakes his head, and then he trains his sight on me. I freeze for half a second.

"Run, Tanzy!" Vanessa shouts. I pedal backward. My heel catches a root, and I fall flat on my back. My head strikes a rock, sending a white starburst across my vision. My eyes squeeze shut, and then fly open as I suck in a hard breath. The Unseen steps over me. I push off with my hands, trying to propel myself away, but I back into a tree.

"Tanzy!" Vanessa shouts. She holds up the staff. She throws it to me. I catch it with trembling hands, and as the Unseen reaches for my throat, I shove the bladed end into his chest. He staggers back, shock on his features.

"Finish him, Tanzy!" Vanessa screams. I pull myself up and run after him. Grabbing the end of the staff, I push as hard as I can. He wraps his fingers around the staff, still fighting to reach me, when the light leaves his eyes and he sinks to the earth. I catch myself reaching down for him, wondering if he's in pain.

"Is he dead?" Vanessa asks, hobbling closer.

"I . . . I think so," I whisper, shaking with exhaustion and fear. "How did I do that?" I whisper.

"I don't know," Vanessa answers. "But whatever it is . . . you saved my life." She stops in her tracks. "Tanzy, Unseens are incredibly strong. There's no way you should've been able to fight him off. I think we have found your gift."

"Fighting?" I ask, my hands shaking.

"Strength," Vanessa says, leveling her stare at me. A noise comes from the Unseen, making us jump. His lines blur and then his form becomes grainy, as if turning to sand.

"Let's get out of here," Vanessa says in a hushed voice. I can't take my eyes off the disintegrating Unseen. Could I do that again? What if it was Asher? Would I if I were given the opportunity? They're monsters, aren't they? Even if they're wearing human faces? Uncertainty wriggles inside me.

"Tanzy . . ." Vanessa's voice reaches me. She's staring at my chest, motionless. "Look," she says. My coat has pulled open and my sweater torn, revealing the skin below my collar bone and the three circles burned into my chest by the lightning. At the top of the first circle, a bright black spot appears, and traces the ring, leaving a shimmering black trail. Once it returns to the top the ring begins to throb, glowing in time with my pulse. I stagger backward, covering my chest with my hand.

"What's happening to me?" I gasp. "It really burns," I press my palm against it.

"Let me help," Vanessa says as she grabs her bottle of Tenix.

"No," I wave her off. "Something died for that Tenix. Save it for when we really need it." I push harder against my skin. The pain lessens and then all but vanishes, leaving behind the sensation of a sunburn. The mark fades back to red, the first circle only a touch brighter than the other two.

"This has to mean something." I say, staring down at the burn.

"I'll ask Maris first thing tomorrow. I just don't think it's a good idea to go back down there," she says, staring down the hill.

"No. I don't think I have another fight in me," I say.

"So Maris told you how Tenix is collected then?" she says, her shoulders slumping.

"Yes," I say with a firm nod.

"I only buy it from Maris, and she's very selective about sources," Vanessa explains. "I only use it for good, Tanzy. I swear I'm not careless with it. I respect where it comes from."

"You don't have to justify anything to me," I reply. "Just don't use it on me unless it's a matter of life and death, okay?"

"Okay," she says and stows the bottle in her bag before we turn up the hill.

"What was that thing?" I croak. My feet ache beneath me, and only now do I remember I've been effectively barefoot since leaving the hospital, the flimsy shoe protectors hanging in tatters on my feet. I reach down to gingerly peel them off my raw, sore soles. How had I just fought off someone nearly twice my size when I can barely take a step now?

"I don't know. I've seen Unseens before, but never that color, or that . . .

feral. Usually when they come across, they enjoy pretending to be a person, the manipulation aspect," she explains.

"Maris is right. I have to see if I can go back as soon as possible. Asher and the Unseen world are coming after me full force. I can't sit around and wait. We need answers now. She said I needed to wait for the black moon."

"She probably means a night with no moon." She checks the warming sky, where the sliver of crescent moon is still visible in the coming dawn. "That's probably tomorrow night. If you want to go back this soon, we have a lot to do. Well, I have a lot to do. I'm going to take you to my house so you can rest. I told my husband I'd take care of you. If we were to take your vitals now they'd probably be off the charts. I haven't even fed you since we left."

"I'm okay. I can do this."

"I don't think it's a good idea. Not with what just happened." Vanessa limps ahead. "There's nothing wrong with waiting until next month. Or even a couple extra days. I think there are two or three dark nights in a row."

"What happened to you wanting me to do this? Are you trying to talk me out of it?" I ask.

"It's not that. You know how bad I want these answers and to find a way to get ahead of Asher. But this kind of magic isn't always foolproof and it isn't always rooted in good. Maris . . . Maris is operating from her own playbook. Sometimes it works in my favor. Sometimes . . ." But her voice drifts for a moment. She tucks a strand of her hair behind her ear. "An Unseen is an Unseen, end of story. No matter how human they try to be, or how long they live on this side, they will always put themselves first. She may be encouraging you to do this time travel thing knowing full well you might not come back. And then what?"

"She said she knew my mom," I whisper. "It sounded personal. I don't think she'd risk my safety. Honestly, I'm not safe anywhere. Tonight just proves it."

"Good point," she says with a sigh. She settles against the back of her seat and stares at the place where the road meets the horizon. I follow her gaze, watching the sun rise, wondering if my mom is somewhere doing the same. I don't know what's coming, but I have a feeling it's going to take everything I've got.

A CASTLE FOR
A QUEEN

"**A**re you coming?" Lucas asks. "There's something you need to see."

I turn toward the sound of his voice. He's standing on a rock beach, bathed in silvery white light. He guides me to a large, black rock. It's layered with sand. I try to wipe it away. Six stick figures ringed in red spirals appear. Even though they are identical, I focus on the last one. I trace it with my finger. Heat sizzles through my hand and I instinctively draw it away. Blood seeps from my skin. A drop of it falls to the beach. The ground beneath me trembles. The sea churns as the ocean floor quakes, and the waves that crash ashore grow increasingly powerful.

A towering wall of water charges for the shore and as it breaks upon the sand, thousands of white horses emerge from the surf and cover the beach like the spill from a wave. They gallop in tight formation and then circle around Lucas and me. I hold my breath as the horses halt in perfect synchronization and turn to face us.

"They've been waiting for you. We all have," Lucas says. "I wasn't sure it was really you. Never believed Asher could do it. But he has. You're here now. And he's coming for you."

The moment the words leave his lips, the horses dissolve into a wave.

"Be seeing you," Lucas whispers and disappears as the foaming water flows back to the sea. The water rises, climbing my legs, reaching my thighs. I stand, rooted to the spot. I should move. But there's nowhere to go. There's nothing but water as far as I can see. I look down, wanting to see if the black rock is still underneath my feet, but it's not. I plunge downward, and the ocean swallows me.

I jerk awake, gasping for air.

"Are you okay?" Vanessa asks from beside me. My surroundings come into focus, and pain spreads across my back and my neck. I'm scrunched against the car door. My arm has gone numb from being used as a pillow.

"Just a bad dream," I mutter, trying to mentally grab the bits and pieces as it scatters.

"I'm glad you slept a little, but that doesn't count. You're going to bed as soon as we get to my house. We're right up here," Vanessa says, and points at the only green lawn I've seen on the whole drive. The unblemished land is neatly dotted with hardwoods and rolls on as far as I can see. No house is visible from the road. She slows the car down and whips expertly onto a cobblestone driveway, which is guarded by an iron gate hung between two stone pillars. She presses a button on her visor and the gate swings open. We pass through the gate, and it closes behind us. Mature trees line the drive in checkered rows. We curve to the right and then back to the left, cutting a gentle switchback climb across the steep terrain.

A stone mansion sits atop the hillcrest. In front of it, a diagonal divide slices through the driveway as the cobblestone changes to a fiery-colored marble. The driveway loops in front of the spectacular stone house and doubles back on itself, leading back to the tree-lined entrance. An ornate fountain made of the same rust-colored stone stands in the center of the circle drive. In its center slowly spins a metallic statue of a woman. Water flows from one hand, and some kind of liquid flame drips from the other. Steam rises from the pool beneath her as the drops of fire are extinguished at her submerged feet.

I open my door as Vanessa pulls the key out of the ignition. Land rises and falls around us. Wind whips across the tall grass. The morning glow stripes the gray sky with gold.

"You have a lot of property," I say, a whisper of freedom lifting my spirits.

"Almost a thousand acres. It's been in my family for a very long time."

"Do you use it for any kind of farming?" I ask, and immediately know the answer. Vanessa purses her lips, suppressing a laugh.

"Do I look like I farm?" Her brow lifts.

"You'd be surprised," I say, tilting my head. "The only part of you that's a dead giveaway are your hands. Your nails are long and manicured, and they're smooth as a baby's butt," I say with a snort. "Farm girls can clean up with the best of them, but it's hard to hide the toll farm life takes on a person's hands." I inspect my hands. Even though it's been a year since I last worked on a farm, I have the hands of someone three times my age, my joints more pronounced than Vanessa's, the skin loose and textured.

"Actually, I've wanted to own a horse for as long as I can remember," she says, and then looks at me. "I had a barn built behind the house a few years ago, but I know I'm not ready to have a horse yet. One day, though. I've always loved them. Our guest room is a loft apartment above the barn. I hope you'll like it. I'll take you on a quick tour of the house so you know your way around, and then we'll get you settled."

I walk forward, drawn to the mention of a barn despite the winter wind slicing through my thin clothes, and peer behind her house. The corner of a stone barn peeks out from behind a cluster of willow trees.

"You must be hungry. I'm starved." Vanessa moves toward the front entrance.

"Not really," I reply. Between the events of the last twenty-four hours, the pressure of what lies ahead, and sheer exhaustion, I can't imagine eating.

"Maybe some tea, then? You need something in your stomach."

"Tea sounds good." I follow her inside. She closes the doors behind us, and a wisp of fear passes through me. The interior is dark, the tall windows shielded with thick velvet curtains. There are shadows everywhere. I back up until my heels touch the wall, and nearly jump at the chilly contact.

"Tanzy, you're safe here," Vanessa says softly.

"It's just . . . it's so dark," I say.

"My husband prefers to keep the curtains drawn. He says sunlight fades the floor and the furniture." She rolls her eyes. Vanessa moves to the closest window and throws the curtains open. Light floods the foyer. The pale-green marble stair case that curls along the curved wall glitters in the dawn. The stone railing is engraved with roses and thorny vines. I reach out and touch it, finding it cold.

"It's jade," Vanessa explains as she slips her shoes off and uses her foot to arrange them by the door. "Let's throw those away," she continues, eyeing the muddy bottoms of my scrubs. I look behind me. A few crumbles of dirt litter the entryway. I bend down to pick them up, but the motion shakes more dirt and debris loose from my pants.

"Tanzy, no. Don't worry about that," Vanessa says, and pulls me up by my elbow. "Just roll them up for now. I'll get you a change of clothes."

We cut through a spacious oval-shaped room. The curve of the wall is made out of glass. An oriental rug takes up most of the floor space. I stop and stare upward. The ceiling is glass, too. The glow from the rising sun tints the glass with gold. I feel ridiculous standing in its center, which reminds me of heaven itself, in stolen scrubs and bare feet.

"This is my favorite room," Vanessa says. "I refused to put drapes up in here. It nearly became a war."

I follow her out of the atrium and into the kitchen. She moves around the room, opening every curtain. Dawn filters through the windows and casts streaks of light across a huge marble island. She fills a teapot with water and sets it on a burner.

"I'll give you a quick tour of this floor while the water heats up," she says. "There's one room in particular I think you're going to like."

Vanessa leads me into a great study. Books line the built-in shelves climbing the treacherous height of the room.

"See, kindred spirits," she says, and shows me a life-sized black marble statue of a horse. His head is raised, his eyes defiant. The stone radiates warmth and life. I almost expect him to snort in annoyance. I move toward him and reach out to see if he feels as real as he looks. Why does this statue look so familiar? I know I've never seen anything like it before.

"Don't touch him!" Her words come out in a rush, and I jerk my hand away. "Sorry. He's very valuable. The stone he's made of is very porous. Any oil from our fingertips would decrease his worth tremendously," she explains.

"Got it," I say, squeezing my right hand with my left, massaging my fingers where my pulse beats against my skin. Vanessa continues down the hall, but I chance a last glimpse of the black horse. His smooth ears seem to be pricked harder than before, more focused. His gleaming eyes are trained on mine. Even after we leave the room and walk down the hall, I can still feel his presence.

"So here's the plan," she says once we return to the kitchen. "You need to rest. I'm going to give you some tea with a little valerian root to help you relax. I know it sounds like something a hippy would suggest, but I swear it works."

"My dad used it all the time to help calm anxious horses," I say, nearly laughing. "Herbs are the kind of medicine I believe in most."

"Good," Vanessa responds as she mixes in a spoonful of powder into my mug, and then hands it to me. "Once we're done, I will show you the barn and the loft. It's already set up as a guest room, so you're good to go. I'll grab some of my clothes for you to borrow, and bring some snacks, too."

I take a sip of the hot drink, enjoying the feel of warmth that fills me.

"I have some errands to run in town," Vanessa continues as she stows a few packs of crackers, cookies, and some fruit in a reusable shopping bag. "When I get back, I'll tell you what I know so far about Asher and the Unseen world. I'll answer every question you have. And if I don't know it, I know someone who does."

"Shouldn't we start now?" I ask, stifling a yawn.

"No, you are going to rest now," she says. "At least try to sleep. As soon as you wake up, we will begin. You have my word."

"Okay." I yawn again.

"I have one favor to ask. My research about the Unseen world didn't just cost me pieces of my professional life, it took a toll on my marriage as well. Honestly, it nearly ended it. My husband is driven by results. It's why he's so good at what he does. However, he also needs to see results to believe in something. When it comes to the Unseen world, that's something I couldn't give him."

"You couldn't just have him stand outside with a lightning rod in a thunderstorm?" I joke, nearly delirious with exhaustion.

"I've been tempted," she says, mustering a smile. "This is serious, though, unfortunately. We cannot discuss Asher, Maris, what happened tonight, the world of the clear, any of it in his presence."

"Ten-four," I say, offering a salute.

"If I didn't know better, I'd say you were tipsy," Vanessa says, giggling. I smile, a warm tingling sensation moving through me.

"This must be why the horses like it," I mumble.

"Come on, let's get you to the loft before you pass out," she says.

She leads me through her house, collects a bagful of clothes from her room, and then heads to the back door.

"You can change clothes in the loft, but I'm sure you'll want these for the walk across the yard." She hands me a pair of paddock boots that don't have a single scuff on the leather or a grain of dirt in the tread. They're a little small and stiff. They'd probably rub a blister if I wear them long, but at least they're warm and dry.

We step outside. A gust of fresh air breathes life and clarity into my cloudy mind. I blink away the mental fog. The barn I'd glimpsed earlier comes into full view. The walls are crafted from polished, black stone, which catches the morning light. The barn doors look to be made of iron, and stand wide open. There's an empty iron plate over the archway, and a small metal balcony above that. I catch myself looking forward to standing out on that balcony, surveying the pasture, imagining horses running across a thousand acres. I force the thoughts aside, uncomfortable with the sudden rush of longing.

"What are you going to name it?" I ask, pointing at the plate.

"I don't know yet," she says, following my gaze.

"Make sure to name it before you bring a horse home. Dad always said it was bad luck to have a barn with no name."

"Well we can't have that," Vanessa says as she plants her hands on her hips. "Any ideas?"

I stare at the structure, which resembles a fortress more than a barn. Horses would be safe here. I wish Harbor could be in one of the stalls, and I envision her head emerging from a window.

"High Harbor," I whisper my horse's full name.

"What?" Vanessa looks at me.

"Nothing."

"No, you said High Harbor," she responds. "High Harbor Farm . . . I kind of like it. Where did that come from?"

"It's my horse's show name," I say, forcing the words past a pinch in my throat.

"You'll find her," Vanessa says gently. "I have a good feeling about it."

I give her a small smile despite the feeling of defeat settling in my heart every time I think of where Harbor might be. I make a mental note to call Dana as soon as I find a phone.

We walk inside the barn together. I try to ignore the cedar scent, and the row of empty stalls.

"I haven't shown you the best part," Vanessa says. She moves toward a little black box mounted by the staircase. "When I have horses here, I will make sure they are completely secure." She presses a button. Thick metal doors drop over every door and window. Automatic lighting kicks on as the sunlight is completely snuffed out.

"Isn't it great?" she asks, grinning.

"It's definitely effective," I respond, instantly fighting claustrophobia.

"The loft is equipped with the same security set up. You will be completely safe up there. I'm trying to learn how to use Tenix to create a barrier that Unseens can't pass through," she says and presses the button again. Sunlight bleeds back into the barn, and I release a breath.

"That would be great," I confess. Vanessa heads up the stairs. I glance back at the barn aisle. Sunlight cuts across the walkway in laser beams, but something's missing. Dust. There's no dust in the air. Maybe it's because no horses have been here yet, but there's no warmth in this perfect place. The stalls are jail cells, with only the small square windows cut into the back walls, and a similar square opening above the Dutch door. The horses won't be able to smell each other or touch noses. Predators seek caves, but prey animals like horses want wide open space and visibility. They would feel vulnerable in these stone enclaves. If Vanessa is serious about bringing horses here, I wonder if she would consider a few structural adjustments, because as the barn stands now, I can't imagine a horse living here. For now, I keep these thoughts to myself, and follow her to the loft.

The loft has the same dimensions as the barn. A small kitchenette and a bathroom are situated closest to the door. An antique metal frame bed sits along the far wall, along with a weathered chest of drawers, a bedside table with an old-fashioned phone, a stack of books, and a lamp.

"Your snacks are in here in case you get hungry. I also grabbed a bottle of over-the-counter sleeping pills, just in case you have trouble falling asleep." She pats the bag before setting it down on the counter. "The clothes are too. I'm sure you want to change. Just throw those scrubs in the trash." She makes a face.

"I don't know how to thank you," I say softly.

"We don't know each other all that well yet, but you strike me as the person who takes care of the people you love. I have a feeling you'd do the same for someone in need," she answers. "Get settled, get some rest, and I'll see you in a bit." She waves, and disappears down the stairs.

I walk to the narrow pair of glass doors that leads to the balcony, but I don't open them. I'm standing in the middle of a proverbial seesaw, only safe and balanced if I don't move an inch. But I can't stand still. I can't wait for the Unseen world to knock me off my feet again. What was that thing that attacked us in the woods, and why didn't it come for me first? The morbidity of the thought isn't lost on me. I wrap my arms around myself and turn away from the window.

I lock the door, then pull off Vanessa's boots and stow them under the bed. I thumb through the stack of clothes she packed. Fabric so soft it feels like liquid brushes against my fingers. I pull out a white, jersey-knit slip of a night gown. I want to rub my face on it, but I'm filthy. My arms are covered in streaks of dirt and gray grit from that Unseen creature. Suddenly, every inch of me is itchy.

I strip off the scrubs and toss them into the trash can under the kitchen sink, and then crank the hot water in the shower. Steam builds quickly in the little room, blanketing the mirror in a fog. I wipe at it, realizing I haven't seen my reflection since my accident, but beads of water streak the glass, distorting my face. I bring my fingers to my cheeks, checking for swelling. If anything, they feel leaner and sharper than before, but then again, I haven't eaten much in a week.

I step into the shower and under the spray, letting out a sigh as the hot water pelts my back. I prod at the wounds on my side, which I'd all but forgotten are there. Vanessa was right, the Tenix has practically healed them too. The stitches are loose and useless, the skin having already resealed. Still, something died for the Tenix she used on me.

Gray granules swirl in the floor of the shower, and the fight with the Unseen creature bursts to the front of my mind. Terror floods my veins, and suddenly I can't catch my breath, the air too hot. My eyes move to my hands. I killed something tonight. In my heart, I know if I hadn't, Vanessa or I, or even both of us would be dead. But I can't help wondering if there had been any other way to survive.

I turn off the shower and lean against the tiled wall, waiting for the wave of heat to dissipate. *There was no other way to leave those woods alive.* My pulse quiets, and my breathing slows, but I can't stop shaking. I towel off and slip on the night gown. Maybe I just need to eat something. I grab an apple from the bag, and take a bite. My stomach stops churning. I sigh, relieved, and finish the rest.

Even though the high-noon sun is streaming in through the double doors, weariness pulls on every fiber of my being. How long has it been since I really slept? I climb into the bed, which is cloud soft, especially compared to a hospital mattress. I reach for the phone and dial Dana's number. As the phone rings, I try to mentally separate the world I'm building with Vanessa to the world I knew before it. I can't mention any of this to Dana. Maris cautioned that the more people who knew about Asher and the Unseen world, the more leverage Asher would have. Not to mention I would sound completely insane. The phone clicks with connection.

"Hello?" Dana's voice comes through the receiver.

"Hey, it's Tanzy," I say. Even my name sounds strange in my ear.

"Tee! God, I've been worried sick. I called the hospital but they said you'd been discharged, so I went to your house and you weren't there. Where are you? Are you okay?"

"I'm good. Everything is fine." My tongue is dry in my mouth. "Mom . . . Mom is finally getting some help. So I'm resting at a friend's house."

"Who?"

"Just someone from work. You haven't met her." The lie makes my cheeks flush. I press my hand against the side of my face.

"I'm glad for you, and for your mom. This is a big step for both of you."

"You have no idea," I murmur. "Is there any news about Harbor?"

"A guy on the east side of the valley reported seeing a loose white horse grazing along a back road, but the horse wouldn't let him catch it. It sounds promising."

"It really does." I sit up straight.

"I'm going to have Lucas go with me to search the area. Your horse seems to have a thing for him. He kind of seems to have a thing for you," she teases.

"Do you have his number?" I ask.

"And, maybe you have a thing for him?" Her voice lifts.

"Something like that." I smile to myself.

"I'm taking you to lunch soon, and I want all the details."

"There really aren't any."

"Not yet, maybe. Now I'm definitely going to bring him with me. He's easier to pump for information than you are. Do you have something to write with?" she asks. I open the drawer in the bedside table. There's a little spiral bound notebook and a pen.

"I'm ready."

"540-555-0713," she says, and I jot down the number. "Tanzy, there's one more thing I need to tell you. They're closing Wildwood. The property is going up for sale. It's way underpriced. I don't think it'll be long before someone snaps it up. Probably a developer," she adds bitterly. I close my eyes and inhale slowly. I have to stay focused. I can't let the fate of Wildwood distract me from what's coming, even with the idea of the pasture being graded and leveled making me ill. If I go back in time tomorrow night, how much time will pass before I'm home again? Will the farm have already sold? What if they finally find Harbor, and they can't find me?

"Tee, are you there?" Dana asks.

"Yeah, I'm here," I answer quietly. "Listen, if you find Harbor, and you can't get a hold of me, just keep her with you until . . . until you do."

"Why wouldn't I be able to get a hold of you?"

"I'm not sure where I'll be," I answer. "I have some decisions to make."

"I'm sure that's an understatement," Dana offers. "Is this the best number to reach you with for now?"

"Yes." I scan the desk. There's no answering machine. "It's one of those old-timey rotary phones, so there's no way to leave a message. Just call back when you can."

"A rotary phone? Where the hell are you?" Dana asks with a laugh.

High Harbor Farm. The thought stirs in my mind, my heart.

"Just a friend's house. She has . . . eccentric taste."

"Sounds like it. Tanzy, it was good to hear from you. Keep me posted, okay? I'll let you know if we find your horse."

"Thank you," I say, choking up again. I wonder when I'll be able to have a conversation without a sudden wave of emotion catching me off guard.

"And get a cell phone already. Join the twenty-first century," she quips, and I let out a laugh.

"I will as soon as I can. I promise."

"I haven't heard you laugh in a long time," she says quietly. "I hope this is a new beginning for you."

"I hope so, too," I say. "Bye Dana."

"Bye Tee."

The line goes dead. I hang up the phone, doing my best to ignore the thought rising in my mind that I might not talk to Dana again. What if I go back in time and get stuck there? What if another Unseen attacks me and I lose? What if Asher decides to take me by force? Why didn't he before? If Maris is right, the prophecy is true, and I am Spera, my human life is on borrowed time, no matter what happens with the veil.

I lie back against the pillows, suddenly dizzy, and watch the clouds track the width of the glass doors. My mind is a mash-up of pieces of information and adrenaline-laced memories, and even though I don't want to admit it, the idea of closing my eyes for too long scares me.

I pick up the phone again and dial Lucas's number. On the fourth ring, I start to hang up.

"Hello?" his voice comes through the receiver.

"Lucas? This is Tanzy," I say. "I got your number from Dana. I hope that's okay."

"Yeah, of course it's okay."

"Okay." I bite my lip. "She said y'all are going to look for Harbor soon."

"Really? I haven't heard from her today."

"Well, she'll probably call you soon."

"Did she tell you about Wildwood."

"Yes."

"I'm sorry, Tanzy."

"Me too."

Neither of us speaks. I fiddle with the phone cord, struggling to think of how to say what I want to say to him, when I'm not even sure what that is.

"Are you okay?" he asks.

"Yeah. I'm okay."

"What's on your mind?"

"Where do you think we go when we die? Do you think there's some kind of eternal place like a heaven or a hell? Or do you think there are floors in between?"

"You're the one of the two of us who has died. You tell me. Was there a light at the end of the tunnel? What did you see?"

"I saw you," I whisper.

"Where are you right now?" he asks.

"I am going to stay with Vanessa Andrews for a while. My mind came back a little scrambled from the lightning strike."

"I heard some nurses talking about how you said you'd seen a ghost." The note of jesting in his voice brings a smile to my face.

"I lied."

"Good for you."

"Lucas, have you ever had scars on your face before?" I ask. For a few seconds, he doesn't answer, and I wonder if he's decided I'm crazy.

"Yes," he whispers.

"How did you get them?" I ask, bolting upright.

"I have to go now."

"Lucas, wait." I squeeze the phone in my hand, listening. He's on the other end, but he's not saying anything. He's connected to all this somehow. I know he is. Why else would I see traces of his past, the same way I did for Vanessa? But where does he fit in all this?

"I dreamed about you again," I say before I can stop myself.

"Be seeing you," he responds, and the line goes dead.

I stare at the receiver. I'm not sure who I'm more shocked with: Lucas or myself. How else did I think the conversation would go? On the other hand, he didn't bat an eye when I ran out of my hospital room on a leg that should've been broken. I don't know what piece he's playing on this chess board, but he's definitely in on the game.

I have half a mind to call him back, but I doubt he'll answer. More than anything, I need to rest if I'm going to stand a chance of surviving another attack from wherever it may come, and I'm guessing traveling back a thousand years into the past isn't easy-breezy either.

I stand and retrieve the bottle of sleeping pills, and fill a glass of water. Vanessa wouldn't have left me in here if she thought for one second some Unseen would find me. I need to take this opportunity to sleep while I can. I don't know when I'll be this safe again.

HAVE A LITTLE FAITH IN ME

I am surrounded in thin blackness. It begins to push down on me, and then crush in at my sides. The darkness turns brown and frothy, and a rushing sound floods my ears. I'm under water. I'm in the river. I can't breathe. I can't breathe! A twinkle of light appears above me, but the harder I reach for it, the faster I sink.

"Tanzy!" The sound of my name sends a jolt through me. I still can't breathe. Then I realize there's something on my face. My eyes fly open and I jerk upright. Lucas is sitting on my bed, his hand over my mouth.

"Shh." He brings his finger to his lips.

"How did you get here? Why are you here? Did you find Harbor?" I ask. I glance at the main door. It's closed. So are the glass French doors. It's pitch black outside. What time is it? How did he get in here?

"I didn't go with Dana."

"Why not?"

"I need to show you something." He takes my hand in his and presses it against his cheek. His skin feels like it's burning. When he pulls my hand away, the scars from my memory are now etched in his face. My mouth falls open. I reach out for them, and he stays still as I run a finger over the two raised ridges that mar his face from his ear to the corner of his mouth.

"How did you do that?" I whisper. I pull his hands down to stare at them. On his fingertips glitters a trail of Tenix. I gasp. "Did you just create the scars, or have you been hiding them all along?"

"I hid them."

"Why?"

"They make me too easy to identify."

"For who?"

"For . . . anyone."

"You're talking about Asher, aren't you? You know about the Unseen world."

"Yes."

"Are you . . . are you a human, or are you an Unseen?" My whole body tenses. His chin falls to his chest.

"I am an Unseen," he whispers.

"Do you work for Asher?"

"I used to."

I swallow hard, and draw my knees to my chest. If he once worked for Asher, chances are he can harvest and transport Tenix. I find sudden comfort in what Maris told me about my elemental arrangement. Regardless, I know he won't hurt me. He's had too many opportunities before now. He saved my life. He tried to help me escape Asher in the hospital.

"And now?"

"Now, I protect you." His gaze lifts

"Why?" I lock eyes with him, and my pulse accelerates.

"Because you need it."

"I know about Spera."

"Then you know why you need protection."

"Asher could've killed me before. He didn't."

"He won't kill you."

"Then what do I need protection from?"

"What he'll turn you into, the darkness he'll turn loose inside of you. Trust me when I say you need to be shielded from that far more than from Asher himself."

"That doesn't make any sense."

"Good. The less you know, the less he can sway you."

"That's not true. I'm going back," I say quietly. "I met an Unseen named Maris. She gave me a key, and found a door to see Spera's life. I'm going to see what happened."

"You can't go back!"

"I have to."

"Tanzy, no. It's too big a risk. This . . . this is how it happens." He closes his eyes. "You can't go back. Asher will know you if you go back."

"He already does!"

"Please, I am begging you, do not use the key. Do not go through the door."

"I have to. I can't just sit around and wait. Don't you see? This is my only way to figure out what's happening to me."

"It's not."

"I have to see how Spera dies. I have to know how to stop it from happening again."

"I know how she dies. I was there!"

"You were there?" I assess his face, and his gaze falls to his lap. Clips of our interactions pass through my mind like a highlight reel: knowing I was upset at graduation, knowing who I was at Wildwood, his devotion to me at the hospital, telling me I knew him well enough to stay the night with him. He's known me much longer than I've known him. "Spera didn't love Asher, because Spera loved you," I wonder out loud.

"And I loved her." He lifts his eyes. "Please, don't do this." He leans toward me, and cups my face in his hands. His mouth moves to mine. His lips are warm and full. The connection is electric and magnetic. He exhales and I breathe in, my hands exploring his sides. He brushes my cheek with his thumb, and then pulls away, and stares into my eyes. "Please, Spera," he says, and a cool current spreads through me, snapping me from the spell.

"I'm not Spera." I sit back, and withdraw my touch from him. "Not like that."

"Didn't you feel it?" he asks.

"I felt something with you. But you were searching for a ghost. I can't live like that. I have too many ghosts of my own. I need to see Spera's life so I have a chance of saving mine."

He reaches into his pocket, and pulls out a tiny silver chain, with a simple horseshoe charm dangling from it.

"Go, then. But promise me you'll wear this."

"Why?"

"Because if you need me, I'll know, and I'll be able to find you." He presses the necklace into my palm and then stands up. He opens his mouth, and I wonder if he'll say what he always says before parting, I wonder if he'll kiss me again. My lips still tingle with the taste and feel of him. But he presses his lips into a line, turns on his heel, unlocks the door, and leaves.

Maris was right. This is a chess board, and there are far more players than I realized. I stare at the open door, my mouth growing cold, and an emptiness spreading through my chest. I fasten the necklace around my neck. I squeeze the horseshoe charm in my fist, grateful for the prick of metal against my flesh, proof it's real, that I'm real. I wish Lucas had kissed me because he wanted to, instead of hoping to find the girl from a thousand years ago.

I SIT CROSS-LEGGED IN THE MIDDLE OF THE BED, pinching the horseshoe charm between two fingers. Thoughts about Lucas fill my head, and I retrace every interaction we've had, adding back the fact that I now know he's Unseen. I've nearly concluded he's on my side when a train of thought strikes my heart: Lucas was present when Spera died, and Lucas doesn't want me to see it. He claims Asher won't kill me now. Would Asher have been the one to kill Spera, then? And if he wasn't, who did?

I catch myself staring through the glass doors from where I sit. They face west, so I can't see where the sun is on its climb, but the sky is bright, despite a thin layer of clouds. I can hear my mother's prayer in my mind, hoping today's sunrise was clear, and that night ahead will be, too. I'm not sure I can face Wildwood's river with a storm raging above and within at the same time.

"Hey! I thought you'd still be asleep," Vanessa says, peeking through the open door. I hadn't heard her come up the stairs. I never imagined someone would be able to walk as undetectably as my mother. She strides into the room with a tray of food in one hand, a garment bag slung over an arm, and her satchel over her shoulder. "I'm glad I decided to bring coffee."

"I don't need it. I'm wide awake. I had company," I say slowly. Vanessa nearly drops the tray.

"Company? Here?"

"Have you ever heard of an Unseen named Lucas?" A hint of betrayal whispers in my mind, and my lips remember him.

"I remember Maris mentioning someone named Lucas once, but she thought he was long gone. From what she described, he was almost as bad as Asher, and maybe even more ruthless. He was his right hand. Then he just up and vanished."

"Are you sure?" I whisper, dropping my hand from the necklace.

"That's what she said. Oh, my God, Lucas." Vanessa's eyes go wide. "The guy from the hospital, his name was Lucas, wasn't it? He's an Unseen? I didn't see a mark on his hand. He must've disguised it with Tenix."

"I saw one," I whisper.

"What color was it?"

"I don't remember." The lie comes as naturally as breathing, yet I have no idea why I've told it. If they're both here to help me, wouldn't we benefit from all working together? I'm assuming there are only two teams at play here, which is a fool's assumption to make.

"Why did he come here?" Vanessa asks, breaking through my thoughts.

"He says he's protecting me because he loved Spera."

"Honey, everyone loved Spera from what I hear." She purses her lips.

"He saved my life at Wildwood, Vanessa. He's an Unseen, but I don't know if he's who Maris is talking about."

"Maybe you'll see for yourself when you witness Spera's life."

"I hope I do."

"We have some work to do before it's time to leave. Are you up for it?"

"Yes."

"Are you absolutely sure you want to do this tonight?" Vanessa pushes.

"Vanessa, yes. I'm tired of being told secondhand who I was and why I'm important. I need to see it for myself. I need to understand what I'm up against. I need to understand who everyone thinks I used to be." I wonder if witnessing Spera's life will make her feel more a part of me in the here and now, or if we will still feel just as separate.

"Okay. First thing's first. I had a little fun with Tenix this morning. I know what you said, but we need a way to communicate without speaking." Vanessa drapes the garment bag across the kitchen counter, then opens her satchel and pulls out a little velvet pouch. She turns it over, and two rings spill onto the bed. I pick one up. The band is a simple braid of ivy, which twists around an oval gray stone.

"How are we going to use these to communicate?" I ask.

"Whenever two people are wearing these rings, they can communicate telepathically. No one can track us or listen in."

"Are you serious?" I ask, peering at the ring.

"I charged them with Tenix. It works. I've done it before," she says, and slides the other ring on her finger. I put mine on. The surfaces of both rings begin to glow a burnished gold: the color of our marks. A buzz grows inside my ear, and then there's a tiny rush of air.

Tanzy, let me know when you hear me, Vanessa's voice sounds in my brain.

"I . . . I hear you," I whisper, shock blooming in me.

Vanessa laughs. "Don't talk, silly. Think it back."

I hear you, I repeat.

Well done, she sends back, and then smiles. She pulls the ring off.

"Wait, shouldn't we practice?" I ask.

"The Tenix will wear off faster if we keep using it to communicate. I don't want to use them unless we have to. I just wanted to make sure you could do it. Removing the ring will break the connection until one of us calls out for the other again. You should keep yours on. The more you wear it, the more natural the connection becomes when you do use it," she explains.

"I will," I say, twisting it on my finger. The fit is tighter than it was only minutes ago. "Is it making my finger swell?" I ask.

"It can, but it will only be temporary," she answers, and slides her ring back on. "I'm glad they're as pretty as they are useful. Now, let's get you dressed and ready. You always want to show respect when you're using magic. I've never done anything like what you're about to do. I just use Tenix to make pretty things. This is way out of my league."

"You haven't done this before?" I ask.

"No. Maris couldn't be sure who I was in my past. I guess no king from another dimension is looking for me, so my old identity isn't as obvious." She gives me a rueful look.

"Do you know how long I'll be gone?"

"I have no idea. Maris didn't tell you?" She furrows her brow.

"No. She wasn't done explaining everything when we heard you scream."

"I'm sorry I interrupted." Her expression falls.

"I'm glad you did. If you hadn't, you'd be dead on the bank, and we would've been sitting ducks in that tent."

"Well, that's true. Okay, let's go to the main house. I picked out a dress for you."

"A dress? You do remember we have to hike to the river."

"You *do* remember we are messing with powers as old as the universe itself?"

"Okay. A dress it is," I say.

"Don't worry. I think you'll like it. I picked it out with your personality in mind." She retrieves the bag and unzips it, revealing a long, white, lace sundress.

"It's beautiful," I say, touching the fabric. "It's also November."

"So wear a jacket." She makes a face. Her eyes drop to the mark on my chest. "That's pretty. I don't remember you having it before." I press my hand against my sternum, feeling the horseshoe. It's so light I've forgotten it's there.

"Lucas gave it to me," I say softly. "He said if I wore it, he'd be able to find me."

"That's either really sweet or really creepy." She frowns.

"He's good, Vanessa. I don't know who he used to be, but he's good. I can feel it."

"Okay," she replies, nodding. "I trust your judgement. I'm going to fill Maris in though the next time I see her. As soon as I make sure your key works and you get through the door, I'm heading straight back to her."

"She might be at Wildwood," I say, envisioning the river. "She's been there before."

"That'll cut down on my drive time, then. For now, let's get you ready." She pulls out a black leather travel kit and unzips it. She hands me a compact mirror. I flip it open. A stranger's eyes stare back at me. It's larger than mine, and bright amber. My pupil is a pinprick in the vibrant color of my iris. My lashes are thick, and the rims of my eyelids are dark, as if I'm wearing eyeliner. I bring the mirror closer to my face. I blink. So does the eye in the mirror. I press my fingers against my cheeks. Now that the swelling has receded, my cheek bones are sharp and angular.

"What are you doing?" Vanessa asks, looking at me like I have two heads.

"I don't look the same," I whisper.

"How did you used to look? Do you have an ID picture or anything?"

"No. My wallet was in the truck . . ." I study myself. "I looked sort of like this, just, not quite the same." I catch sight of my hair. I pick up the ends in my fingers. "This is a lot longer," I say. "And darker. My hair is usually just plain brown. And it came a little past my shoulders."

"Not anymore," Vanessa says, tugging at the ends, which nearly reach my elbow.

"Is it the light in here, or is my hair black?" I ask.

"Your hair was black when I met you," Vanessa says.

"Are you sure?"

"Positive." Vanessa sits back and drums her fingers on her thighs. "I wonder what Spera looked like."

"You think this is her coming through?" I stare at my hair. It's identical to my Mom's hair. I wish my change had more to do with my mom and less to do with a thousand-year-old soul.

"What else would it be?"

"I guess I'm going to find out soon. How am I going to tell you where I am when I wake up?" I ask. She holds up her hand and points to her ring.

"Use this. Do exactly what you did last time, and mentally call out for me. You may have to do it a few times to establish a connection, but it should work."

"I can't believe this is really happening," I whisper, staring down at myself—my hands, the circles burned into my chest. My hair is black as ink against the white nightgown.

"Let's finish getting you dressed. I have a surprise for you, and I want to get to Wildwood with plenty of daylight to spare."

"Okay," I agree. I slip into the lace dress and simple leather sandals. Vanessa retrieves a long, knit, hooded cardigan for me to wear, and we head down the stairs together. "Remember that these Unseen types are very literal. Be careful what you say and how you interpret what they say. They're different than we are." She casts an apprehensive glance at me over her shoulder.

"Got it."

"Tanzy," Vanessa starts.

"Yes?"

"You look beautiful." She smiles, and then continues down the stairs.

"Thank you," I whisper.

As we walk through the barn aisle, she tosses me a set of keys. "You're driving," she says.

"I can't drive your car. I've only ever driven a truck," I reason.

"That's why you're driving," she says, and leads the way down the stairs. "That's what I was really doing in town yesterday. You need a way off and on this property when I'm not around. I'll need it one day when I have a horse here. But for now, you can use it. I didn't tell you because I knew you'd think it was about you and you'd feel bad or try to talk me out of it," she says in a rush.

"Okay, that's . . . that's all true," I say, staring at the back of her head.

"Good, I'm glad we agree."

Vanessa walks out the back door of the barn. Parked behind the barn is a new model black Ford F150—my father's favorite color, make, and model. Tears spring to my eyes.

"I can't drive this," I say softly, shaking my head.

"No, I can't drive this. I nearly wrecked it twice on the way home. I can barely turn it without running off the road, and I had to do a five point turn just to pull into the drive way without hitting the gate. You can drive it," Vanessa replies. She takes me by the shoulders with a small smile. "This is how you respect the past and those you lost. You take pieces of them with you into your future, and you fight like hell to own your life. Can you do that?"

"I think so," I whisper, staring at the truck behind her. In my mind, I can imagine my dad running his fingers across the shiny, spotless hood—a whistle rounds his lips. He looks up at me and smiles.

"Yes." My voice comes out firmer. I walk to the driver's side door and pull it open as Vanessa climbs in from the other side. The past comes roaring back as memories of my father flood every inch of the truck. I can picture exactly the way he would sit in the driver's seat. I know what radio station he would pick and how he would adjust the mirrors. I know he would use the far cup holder because he would complain about bumping the close one with his knee. I squeeze the steering wheel with both hands and try to steady my breathing so I don't cry.

"Don't force the past out of this truck," Vanessa says softly. "But don't let it keep you from moving forward. Bring it with you everywhere you go instead."

"I can do that," I say, remembering the way Dad's face would light up when we drove somewhere new and beautiful. Mom would shake her head and laugh, calling him the romantic of the two of them. I blink away the tears, and cling to the memory as I force the sting in it to leave me. I inhale through my nose and let the air out slowly through my mouth.

"Are you good?" Vanessa asks with a hopeful smile.

"Better," I say, nodding. I adjust the rearview mirror. On auto-pilot, I move to stow my wallet, which I don't have. "I don't have my license, remember." I offer her the keys.

"So don't get pulled over," she says. She takes the keys from me and leans over to start the ignition. "You drove to Wildwood the night of your accident, right?"

"Yes." My mouth goes dry.

"You need to do this, Tanzy. Not just because I'd probably wreck the truck, but because you need to prove to yourself that you can, and that nothing bad will happen just because you choose to drive to the farm. Okay?"

I close my eyes against a surge of nervousness. I let out a long exhale through my mouth.

"I don't know how to get there from here," I say.

"I do," Vanessa answers.

In my mind, I see the countless times I tried to drive to Wildwood and stopped short. I can do this. I have to do this.

I shift the truck into gear, let off the breaks, and begin the journey back to Wildwood.

LEAP

I stop the truck on the far side of the parking lot. We climb out. When I close the door, the bang echoes. Wildwood is lifeless and silent, the walls that once housed its heartbeat crumbled and blackened. Even the trees stand eerily still. The air smells heavily of stale smoke, and even though it's cold enough to see my breath, I break out in a sweat.

"What do I do?" I ask Vanessa, who's trailing behind me.

"Whatever your soul tells you to do. But I think you need to do this part alone."

I glance over my shoulder. She's stopped in the parking lot, her toes an inch behind the line where the fire scorched the asphalt. I look down at my feet. They're already covered in soot, as is the hem of my dress. I walk forward, picking a path along the outer edge of the rubble. This was where I grew up. This is where I learned who my father really was in his soul, where I learned what made me tick.

I keep walking. Gray dust billows in my wake, leaving smoky trails on the skirt of my dress, but I don't care. If the ancient power that chooses whether or not to allow me through to Spera's life doesn't like it, then they're the ones who need to brush up on their understanding of respect. This place built me, nurtured my soul, Spera's soul. The Unseen world came for me here, and they didn't claim me. Wildwood burned to the ground, yet here I stand. Wildwood is gone, but it's inside of me, a part of me forever. I touch the necklace Lucas gave me. My connection with Spera is much like my connection to Wildwood. If only I knew her as well as I knew Wildwood. Maybe after witnessing her life, I will.

I stop, realizing I'm in the dead center of what was once the indoor arena. I gaze out, retracing the spiraled path I took to get here without even knowing it. Has this journey been the same? Has every move I've made lead me here?

"You look like you're ready," Vanessa calls out, keeping her voice low.

"I think I am."

"Lead the way," Vanessa says.

I turn toward the pasture, my gaze set on the trees beyond the meadow, and the shadows growing beneath them as the sun begins to set. I'm tempted to tell Vanessa she's in for a long walk, but the quiet has a reverent spell, and I won't be the one to break it. I check back on her a couple times as we cross the meadow. Her face is solemn, her eyes looking down at the tall, dead grass.

We step onto the trail that leads to the ridge, and my pulse jumps. The ground beneath my bare feet feels colder here, sending a chill through my body. We round the first bend, and the bank where my mother stood and failed to feel my father comes into view. My heart aches for her.

A gust of wind rustles the trees overhead. The branches crack and scrape as they collide. The river, calm moments before, begins to chop and froth. Another breeze comes straight down the path, as if pushing me back, and blows the loose hair out of my face. Something is out here, something that doesn't want me reaching the river with Maris's key in my hand. I squeeze the bottle in my fist and keep walking.

I hear Vanessa's footsteps stop. I look back at her. Hesitation is plain to be seen in her eyes. She touches her ring with her opposite pointer finger.

This doesn't feel right, her voice calls in my head.

It feels pretty right to me, I call back.

I don't know. I think we should go back.

Go back if you want to. I'll be okay.

No. I'm coming with you.

166

I push forward through the next gale force wind, which kicks up sand from the path. I shield my face with my arm. Every obstacle just proves this is right. This is what I need to do. If something Unseen is trying to stop me, that's a hell of a reason to keep going.

I blot out the world around me, focusing instead on my last ride with my father. In hindsight, I should've known it would be the last of something. He broke tradition, and he gave a big speech. He wasn't one to do either of those things. A sad smile plays on my lips. I hope I'm honoring him with this journey. I won't back down. I won't let anything stop me.

A salty taste floods my mouth, and I realize I'm crying. I grit my teeth together, stifling a sob, and drop my arm. I'm standing exactly where Teague went over. For some reason, I thought I'd be able to still see the indentions in the dirt where he planted his back feet and spun. For the last year, the only sound I can remember is the roar of the river. Now, I hear the shuffle of Teague's feet, the shouts of my father, my own voice screaming in my ear.

"Jump off!" My voice echoes through the trees, and my throat burns.

"Tanzy, who are you talking to?" Vanessa asks. She hurries to me. I stare over the lip of the cliff at the river below. It's twice as far down as I remember. Even from this height, I can feel the frigid air coming off the water. I remember the smothering cold, the way it fought to be inside my nose, my mouth.

"I don't think I can do this," I say, my heart pounding, my mouth dry. I gasp for air, but it still feels like I'm drowning. Vanessa steps to my side. She takes my hand in hers, and we watch the current roll by.

"Yes, you can. You're the strongest person I have ever met."

I pull the cork out of the bottle, and heave it into the river. I strain to hear it hit the water, but there's no sound. For a second, nothing happens, and I don't know whether I'm devastated or relieved. Then, a silvery glow emerges in a single speck, stationary while the water rips and roars around it. It moves upstream, painting a wide arch, and leaving an electrified trail. Once it completes a circle, the water inside turns black as ink.

"It worked. It really worked," Vanessa says on an exhale.

"What do I do now?" I look at her, clenching the cork in my fist.

"Jump."

I shuffle closer to the edge. My toes hang over the side. Chunks of dirt break off under my weight and tumble down the vertical bank. My heart roars in my ears, louder than the river. I lean out further, keeping my weight on the balls of my feet. The black circle below seems to pulse in time to my heart beat. The water inside it swirls in a vortex, and crackles with flashes of silver. Wind shoots up at me straight from the bottom of the river, flinging my hair back behind me, and almost knocking me backward. I pinwheel my arms to regain my balance.

"The hole looks like it's closing," Vanessa says, pointing. Before my eyes, the sides illuminate, and shift inward. "It's now or never." I look at her, wanting to say something, anything, just in case I never come back, but I can't find any words. She nods, green eyes glistening. I turn back to the river, and leap.

PART III

A Path To Where
I First Began

I hold my breath, bracing for the frigid temperature of the river so I don't gasp and inhale water upon impact. I keep my eyes open. The circular door rushes up at me, and the vortex turns faster. I watch in disbelief as I fall past the surface of the river, the water chopping all around me. The door is louder than the river, whirling like a centrifuge, and burning hot. The second I pass all the way through it, my entire being begins to spin. My hair flies above my head, and my arms are drawn skyward, yet my feet are pulled down as if weighted.

The twinkling blackness slows its rotation, and all around me lightens to navy, and then to deep teal. I draw in a breath, spellbound, only now realizing I'm dry. The moment I do, my hands and feet are released. For just a moment, I am suspended in a silent, turquoise vacuum. I exhale. The rush of air echoes in the cylinder, and it collapses. I clamp my eyes shut a fraction of a second before I am pummeled by water on all four sides.

I open my eyes and wait for the blur to clear. Pale gold twinkles above me. I take the chance it's the direction of air, and kick upward. My face breaks through the surface, and I draw a coughing breath. The water is crystal clear and smooth as glass, my movements creating the only disruption.

I turn myself around. A red beach emerges from the ocean fifty yards from where I tread. A woman stands near the water's edge, watching me. She's tall and lean as a willow, with waist-length white hair, and a white robe that pools at her feet. She must be the guide Maris told me would meet me, because she's the only other living thing as far as I can see. Farther inland stands a graveyard of a forest, bare limbs twisted by heat and drought.

I keep my head above water and swim toward her. Without the distraction of something obvious fighting against me, my earlier nervousness rears its head. Vanessa warned me Maris follows her own playbook. This could be a trap just as easily as it could be a lesson. On the other hand, Maris's face conveyed pure sympathy when she spoke of my mother. She wouldn't just be betraying me, she'd betray her, too.

My feet touch the sandy bottom of the ocean. I stand and walk the rest of the way in.

"We've been waiting for you," the woman says. She scans the length of me with eyes the color of water under ice. I examine myself, self-conscious under her stare. My lace dress has transformed into a simple linen slip, and my feet are bare. Unfortunately, so are my hands. No ring. No phone number. I check for the necklace, but it's gone, too.

"Is this the Unseen world?" I ask, remembering how Maris described it as the land of sea and stone.

"No. This place where we stand now is only a bridge between your life and Spera's. Her life began in a little village in Eritrea. Your journey will start there."

"How do we start?" I ask. My guide steps back. Behind her, a narrow, rocky path divides the dying trees like a scar. Without giving me any further instructions, she turns away and starts down the trail. I hurry to catch her.

"You are here to witness decisions Spera made which altered the course of her life. You are purely a spectator. You are not permitted to touch anyone while you are here, with one exception. You must claim ownership of your previous incarnation by touching Spera once, and only once. Otherwise, you will not remember anything you've seen here after you leave. If you touch the wrong incarnation, you will be cast from here immediately, so choose wisely," she says over her shoulder. "You will see thirteen memories from Spera's life. There is a lesson in each memory, which you must decide for yourself. You may ask me questions, but I may or may not provide an answer. When I close my eyes, we will leave one choice, and move on to the next. Do you understand?"

"Yes," I answer automatically, and then list the rules in my mind. Find Spera, touch her. Don't touch anyone else, and don't argue when she says it's time to go. I think I can handle that.

"Good luck, Spera."

I'm not Spera. "Thank you," I say instead.

The trees thin as we reach the edge of a clearing. The rust-colored earth surrounding us is as vast as the sky, and carved with fissures and canyons. My guide pauses and steps aside, allowing me in front of her. I check behind me, the sensation of eyes on my back making my skin crawl. The forest and the path have vanished.

"Your journey begins now," my guide says.

The scuffle of horse hooves on dirt draws my ear. I cover my eyes to block out the glare from the high noon sun. In the distance, shadowy forms move across the sand. They solidify, as if mirages becoming real. I move toward them, and the haze of heat coming off the ground clears, allowing me to focus on them.

A teenage girl stands between an older boy and a small band of nervous, bony horses, which are a few perilous feet from a canyon ledge. She's slight in frame. She's clothed in a tea-colored sleeveless shirt and skirt, and her feet are bare. The joints of her shoulders jut out from her skin, and her lanky arms hang at her sides. Her straight black hair falls to the middle of her back. Her gaunt, brown face is pulled back in a scowl. She bares her teeth at the boy, who's nearly a foot taller than she is, and looks to be several years older. A tattered, open cape is draped over his shoulders. His knees are knobby, and his sandals are too small for his feet. He has a cane in his left hand and a rock in his right.

The girl and the horses are boxed in on both sides by massive rock formations, the only way out blocked off by the boy. He raises his cane out to the side and steps closer to them. The girl screams at him in a language I don't understand, but the want to scream rises in my throat all the same. If these horses are spooked, they could run right off the cliff. The boy chucks the stone in his hand at the closest horse. I realize with horror that it's exactly what he intends to do.

The girl picks up a handful of rocks and throws one back at him. He ducks. She throws again, and it strikes him in the face. He covers his nose with his hand. Blood trickles through his fingers. Rage darkens his eyes. He screams and kicks at the dirt. She yells back. He grabs a handful of rocks and flings it at the horses. They spook and whirl, but don't run away, as if they realize they have a place of safety behind the girl.

"Why does this man want to scare the horses?" I whisper to my guide.

"His father is a farmer. This area is in a horrible drought and many farmers believe these wild horses are competing with their cattle for what little forage remains."

"So he's trying to drive the competition off a cliff?" I ask.

"He is. It would bring him honor."

"Will he hurt the girl?" I ask, worry creeping into my voice. She's younger than me, but not by much. Every part of me wants to plant itself between her and that man. I'm behind him. He'll never see me coming. My guide seems to sense my plan and places an icy hand on my shoulder, rooting me to the spot.

"Keep in mind that this has already happened. They can't see you. You can't affect the outcome. That's not why you're here. You must remember why you are here," she insists.

"Is this Spera?" I ask, confused. I thought I was here to see what happened between Spera and Asher. I'm supposed to find out why he thinks she can open the veil, and how she died. What does this have to do with it?

"You tell me," my guide responds. I watch him move a step closer. The girl backs a step and throws her arms wide. The herd stallion, a black horse, paws at the ground. He's covered in dirt and sweat. Blood drips down one of his back legs, and he won't put the hoof square on the ground. Several of the mares are also wounded. I look back to the boy, who draws a dagger from his belt. My stomach drops. The boy positions the dagger at his front and then sprints at the stallion. The girl rushes sideways and tackles his legs. He falls. The knife skitters across the ground and drops over the cliff. The horses take off at a dead gallop, disappearing seconds later into the brown stretch of nothing.

The girl glances up and watches their trail of dust, a delirious smile on her face. She doesn't see the boy storm towards her with cane pulled back like a bat. He swings at her. She reacts just in time to catch the cane with her hands, but the force takes her to her knees. He shoves her backward. She's a body length from the edge of the cliff. He kicks her in the stomach and she curls into a ball, protecting her head with her hands. He draws his leg back again. Her little hands fly out and wrap around his ankle, and she barrel rolls toward the cliff. He tumbles to the ground. My heart leaps into my throat. They're both too close to the edge. I can't help leaning for them, reaching out.

She pushes up to her hands and knees. He scrambles to his feet, but steps down on the cane. His ankle wrenches, and he falls sideways. The girl lunges forward, grabbing the back of his cape, but his weight takes him over the edge, and drags her forward. She claws at the ground and tries to push her feet into the sand, but before my disbelieving eyes, they both disappear over the ledge.

"No!" I cry out, and sprint toward the edge. A hum builds in my ears, becoming so loud I can't think past it. The sky crackles with energy and a brilliant bolt of lightning spears down from the heavens, striking somewhere on the floor of the canyon. I jump at the crack of thunder, and everything in me wants to run for cover, but I have to find the girl. The mark on my chest begins to burn as the glow straightens between the earth and the sky, widening into a purple column of energy.

I stumble to the edge of the cliff and peer over. The boy is face down on the canyon floor, his limbs splayed out at odd angles. The girl is suspended just a few feet above the him, floating limply in the center of the bolt of lightning. I watch spellbound as a spider web of electricity rolls across her skin, and she begins to drift skyward. She passes the top of the cliff. The column of light bends over the ledge and eases her to the ground inches from my feet. She draws in a jagged breath and tears of relief prick the corners of my eyes.

What have I just witnessed? Did this really happen to someone however many years before? How is it possible? How is any of this possible? Could this be Spera? I bend down, tempted to wipe the sweaty hair from her face. Up close, she looks close to my age, her features made both more childlike yet more weathered by how gaunt she is.

"We are done here." My guide's nimble fingers square my shoulders to hers, turning me away from the girl on the ground. I keep my gaze trained on the girl, but my guide brings my face around with a finger on my chin. The world behind her distorts.

"Look at me," she orders. Her dazzling blue eyes are like a vacuum. Once mine lock onto hers, it is impossible to see anything else. "It is time to move on."

Before I can protest, my ears are filled with a murky quiet. Suddenly, the thick void is ripped apart by angry screams. Although I can't yet focus, the tension in this new place is tangible. In a single breath, the water-color images sharpen, and I let out a gasp. We are standing in the middle of a huge group of people. They are all staring in the same direction; their faces gaunt and hard. I stand on my tiptoes, straining to see what they're glaring at with such fever, but I can't see over the crowd.

Simple stone buildings line the sandy courtyard, leaving a narrow path along the edge of the crowd. I inch along the meager space. On instinct, I try my best not to bump into anyone, even though I know they wouldn't feel it. But I feel them—their want and their needs. I'm treading water in a sea of rage.

I reach the front of the courtyard. Two cloaked figures huddle over something on the ground. A few feet away, a man and a woman throw themselves against the chains keeping them fastened to a wall. It sounds like they're begging. An urge to touch the woman, to wipe the tears from her face, fills me with such longing that it scares me. I lock my hands around my elbows and look away from her. I can't risk making contact with the wrong person.

Up front, the dusty cloaks flutter with motion as two men stand, each with a vice grip around a girl's arm. Dried blood and dirt crust her bare skin. Her knotted hair spills over her slumped shoulders. She won't lift her head. The men bind her hands with a thick rope, and then cover them with a heavy black cloth. They shove her hard from behind and she falls to her knees. I stifle a cry, and force myself to stand still. Everyone in the crowd raises their fists into the air and breaks into a menacing chant. Each person is holding something round and gray stones in their hands.

"They want to stone her to death?" I gasp.

"That is their intention," my guide answers.

My next question stills on my tongue as the man and woman held captive, scream out in pain. No one is physically harming them. In fact, people closest to them are reaching out to them in sympathy. My eyes drift back to the girl. Her chin lifts reflexively toward the sounds coming from the two people crying in the corner. Their connection becomes clear immediately: they're her parents. Grief washes over me—I know what it's like to watch a loved one die.

She lifts her head, and I go stone still. It's the girl from the canyon. The same pull I experienced in her presence during her attack returns. I step toward her. The closer I come, the stronger the need to close the distance.

"Spera," I whisper. Her empty stare falls back to the dirt. Blood might still course through her veins, but her spirit is nearly dead.

"I don't know why you're here. I don't know what to do," I plead with her, automatically reaching my hand for her dirty arm. My guide's instructions from the beginning of this journey come back to me. Am I supposed to claim this life by touching her? Could it be so simple?

I clamp my hand around her forearm, willing any fight in me to flow into her body. An ice cold current flows up my arm and straight to my heart. I try to pull back, but for several seconds, we are bound together. Her amber eyes lock on mine.

"I'm here," I whisper, tightening my grip as the electric sensation fades. I don't want to let her go.

The cacophony of shouting becomes more distinct, and within seconds, whatever language they speak here is now familiar and natural in my frazzled brain.

"She killed my son!" a woman shouts.

"She must be possessed by a demon! No small girl could have thrown someone twice her size over a cliff without the devil's help!" a man adds.

They must think she killed the boy who fell into the canyon.

I stand, glaring, adrenaline charging through me as I prepare to shout in her defense about what I saw. Spera's mother lets out a plea as another angry chant ripples through the mob, making me regret being able to understand.

"Wait," Asher's familiar voice commands from somewhere behind me. Instinct creeps up my spine. Everyone falls silent. As I turn around, everyone else in the courtyard drops into a deep bow. The only two left standing are Asher and me.

In the daylight, he is breathtaking and horrifying, his eyes the same silvery white. He runs one pale hand down the length of his black cloak and draws the hood over his black hair before he steps from the shadows and into the afternoon sun. Panic floods my veins as he glides toward us, but his white eyes are locked on Spera.

"These people worship Asher?" I whisper.

"They think he is a prophet," my guide answers. She raises her chin in a salute of defiance. I turn my attention back to Asher. He towers over Spera. His long shadow covers her completely.

"Have mercy, I beg of you! She is just a girl. She didn't do this. I know my daughter," her mother pleads with him.

"I will do as you have asked, good woman, as your spirit is clean of sins against the gods." His deep voice reverberates throughout the courtyard. He closes his eyes and tilts his face skyward. Bathed in sunlight, his face is white as snow. I don't know whether it's seeing Spera's mother or Asher's physical similarities to my mother, but in this moment, I wish she was here with me.

"Show me what lies within the girl," he commands to the sky. I draw in a breath as he lifts Spera's dirty chin with his hands. Her eyes stare straight into his. The fear coiled within my belly now seems to belong to me alone.

"This girl's soul is struggling against a most vicious demon, but she is strong. I can force the darkness out," Asher bellows, and turns to face the silenced mass. "There is no need to end her life this day." The crowd roars in celebration. The satisfied twitch in Asher's mouth makes me feel sick.

"What did he see?" I whisper to my guide.

"Nothing," she bares her teeth around the word. I move my focus back to Asher, studying everything about him: the marbled smoothness of his skin, the lean muscles that rope his forearms, the way his fingers curl when he speaks.

"Thank you for your mercy," her parents sob, collapsing against their restraints.

"She must come with me so I may cleanse her spirit." He bows his head in a show of sympathy.

"Whatever it takes, please!" They answer. Even though I stand a few feet from Spera, her contempt for Asher rolls off in waves of heat. Her eyes plead with her parents, but they look only at Asher. I see what she's trying to tell them: she would rather die. Why won't she just tell them?

"I must take her this very moment," Asher says, as if he's offering them a choice.

"Anything," her father agrees. "Anything to save her."

"I will send word of her progress. I will keep her safe," Asher says with a sad smile. "But she can never return."

"We know," her mother says, fighting to keep the devastation from her voice. "May we say good-bye?"

"Of course." Asher gestures to two men standing guard. They pull daggers from their belts and cut Spera's parents from their restraints. They rush to their daughter's side and cover her with their arms and tears. She stares vacantly over their shoulders.

"Take this, dear Spera," her mother says as she fumbles at the back of her neck. She straightens and holds her hand out. A silver horseshoe dangles from a leather cord. She fastens it around Spera's neck and puts a trembling palm over it.

"This is my most precious possession. Keep it with you and you will never be alone."

I choke back a sob. The necklace Lucas gave me belonged to Spera. The kiss he gave me belonged to her, too. I see now that I have her eyes, and more of her features have claimed my face since I was struck by lightning. So why does she still feel like a completely separate person from me?

"This choice is complete," my guide says as we watch them prepare Spera for transport. I long to stay here and show Spera some measure of support, even though she can't see me, but the scene begins to blur as my guide moves on.

SELECTION

The sounds of hundreds of people shouting and cheering flood my ears before the black of transition scatters. My pulse accelerates, sending a prick of adrenaline through my limbs. I'm standing in the middle of an empty sand stadium. The floor is rung in a stone wall, probably six feet high. The stands are packed with men who have plates covering their chests, and swords slung across their backs. The men in the first two rows also hold shields at their fronts. When they stand together, they form a second and third wall. A throne is carved into the first row at one narrow end. Asher stands in front of it. His arms are folded at his front. Boredom adorns his face.

"Soldiers, greet your commanding officers," Asher barks. The clatter of a door opening spins me around. A group of ten men, dressed identically in armor, walk onto the arena floor. The first in line is Lucas. The rest of Asher's army erupts in cheers. I remember what Vanessa said about Lucas, and my stomach knots. What will it be like to see him as Asher's right hand? Will I be able to look at him the same way after this?

"Now, welcome the new candidates," Asher orders. Another door on the opposite end of the stadium opens. A handful of girls stumble onto the sand. There are ten in all. They blink in the bright light of the open stadium, as if they just stepped out of the dark. They're wearing brown burlap knee-length dresses. A blonde girl walks away from the others. She narrows her eyes and circles the group, her expression hard and discerning. A flash of long black hair catches my eye. The girl turns, and I lock eyes with Spera. She's taller than she was the day I saw her in the village. She's leaner, too. Purple half-moons ring the underside of her golden eyes. Her skin is chaffed around her wrists, and her lips are cracked and peeling.

"Candidates, welcome to your matching ceremony," Asher says, the first note of excitement touching his voice. "Your first goal is to not be one of the first four mauled to death or eaten. I only need six of you to survive. Your second goal is to gain control over one of the match beasts. It's seldom accomplished, but you're welcome to give it a try. Anyone who does so will receive my favor in the days to come. Make no mistake of it, this is the easiest day you will have in this process. You may use swords provided to you by my officers. I warn you, they're a touch heavy. Officers, drop your weapons, and take your position."

My gaze flies around the arena as the officers withdraw their swords and lay them on the ground. The girls eye the weapons, and then the officers. Several of them back away, staring up at the legions of soldiers in the stands.

"Officers, observe the candidates—how they fight, how they survive. During the selection ceremony tonight, you will be able to choose a surviving candidate to dedicate yourself to for the duration of the Vessel process. Lucas, as my most trusted officer, you will, as usual, choose first." The crowd roars again, chanting Lucas's name. Dread forms a pit in my middle.

"Release the matches," Asher orders, smiling. "For the Novus!"

"For the Novus!" the soldiers echo him in unison, and remain standing while Asher takes a seat at his throne. A guard steps forward on the first row, claiming a post over a door. Another guard does the same on the opposite side. Together, they crank a lever from right to left, and both doors raise at once. Predators race out of the openings and onto the floor. The animals are just as thin as the girls. I can count ribs on all of them. Once ten predators have entered the arena, the gates drop closed again, and the sound of drumming fills the stadium as the soldiers fall eerily silent.

A tiger trots a loop around the group of girls, tail swishing, ears flat back. It lowers itself and moves forward, leaping once it comes within ten feet of a girl who's watching a male lion stalk her from the front.

She screams once, but it only lasts a little over a second. I swallow down a burning wave of nausea and turn away. No one cheers. The soldiers watch the floor with the seriousness of a surgeon. I peer at Lucas, feeling sick. He rocks his weight back on his heels and stretches his back, then cocks his head, studying the candidates. A blonde girl picks up the handle of a sword. She can barely lift it off the ground.

One of the girls takes off across the floor at a sprint. It's a mistake. Two wolves take off after her, their strides long and loping. I shake my head, trying to clear the image, and clamp my hands over my ears so I won't hear it when the wolves catch her. Spera stands in the center of the chaos, completely motionless, her feet shoulder width apart, her fingers relaxed at her sides. She's trying not to draw attention. Fear and anger swirl inside of me, and while I know I must watch, I wish it would all end.

Two more girls make a break for the barrier. One lifts the other one up, and she throws her leg over the top of the wall. The guards push forward as a single unit, and knock her back into the ring. She hits the sand on her side and gasps for air. A black panther has caught sight of the prey on the ground. The girl can't scramble to her feet in time. The panther pounces on her side, and takes a kill hold of her throat.

"I want to move on," I say, covering my face with my hand.

"It's not time yet," my guide responds. "Asher is right. This is one of the easiest tests the girls will face. And at least those who perish here die quickly. Not every candidate is afforded that kindness."

I drop my hands, even though my eyes are still closed, and inhale deep. Spera went through this. I owe it to her and to myself to watch. I open my eyes, and resolve not to close them again.

Spera has twisted to see the girl who fell from the wall. The girl is fighting hard against the panther, scratching at its eyes, and bringing her knees up against the cat's belly, but she can't shake it loose.

Spera's fingers curl. She watches the black cat, which has its back to her, and then looks up at the closed gate a few feet in front of it. *She's going to try to leap out, too.* She bolts for the cat, who's too focused on its prey to notice someone charging. Spera punches off the ground, and uses the flat place between the cat's shoulder blades to spring into the air. Her hands are outstretched, and her eyes are fixed on something above the gate. She wraps her fingers around the lever the guards used to control the door. She maintains her grip as the guards shove her back into the ring, and their force helps Spera crank the lever. The gate rolls open. The panther looks up, releasing the girl. So do the wolves at the far end, and the lion in the middle of the floor. Even though they're clearly starving, they all run for the opening, leaving their prey behind.

There's only one predator left in the arena, and the blonde girl is standing in front of it, arms spread wide, not allowing it to pass. She bares her teeth, hissing, and swings the sword in a low arch each time the cat flinches left or right. Even though the sight of it is mesmerizing, I tear my eyes away in search of Spera. She's kneeling over the girl attacked by the panther. Blood leaks from the girl's throat. Her body vibrates. Her eyes dart back and forth in terror, and a gurgling sound comes from her open mouth.

Spera wipes the hair from her face, and whispers something. The girl makes a tiny nod. Spera pinches the girl's nose closed and covers her mouth with her other hand. I gasp, my eyes wide and disbelieving. *What is she doing?* The girl's convulsions intensify, and her fingers grip Spera's dress, but she doesn't try to pry her arms away. I recall the way she nodded at Spera. Spera must have asked her if she wanted to die.

The girl's hands go slack, and slip to the sand. A sob escapes me, and I press my palm against my mark. In Asher's first attempt to eradicate humanity from these girls, Spera has demonstrated unequivocal mercy.

"What have you done?" Asher bellows from his throne. "The animals' blood was to make these first choices, not you!"

"You only said four of us had to die. You never said how."

"I will have you put to the fire for this," he seethes.

"I will gladly go." She glares up at him.

"Sire," a guard interjects from beside him, and points across the ring, where the blonde girl stands next to the snow leopard, petting its head, the sword at her feet. Every soldier shouts in triumph, and begins to chant a name.

"Lenya! Lenya!"

Asher purses his lips, stealing a last glimpse of Spera before refocusing on Lenya. Lucas turns away from Lenya, his black eyes narrow, and watches Spera as she walks across the ring to stand beside the gate they came through. Blood drips from her fingers, and more is smeared on the front of her dress. I catch myself reaching for where her horseshoe charm should hang from my neck. I couldn't have done what she just did. I'm not a thousand years ahead of her—I'm a thousand years behind, maybe more. How will I begin to catch up to who she was?

"Come," my guide says, stretching out a hand.
"Where are we going?" I ask, my throat raw with emotion.
"Don't you want to see who chooses Spera?"
"Yes," I say, and the arena falls away.

I Choose Spera

The room that solidifies around us is a polar opposite to the rough, dusty, sand arena. A long white marble table runs the length of a black stone floor. Five of the candidates, still in their dresses from the arena and covered in grit, stand on top of the table at its center, surrounded by food. Their hands are bound behind their backs.

Lenya sits next to Asher. She's in a new dress, and her arms and face have been scrubbed clean. A plate of food sits in front of her. She picks at it with her fingers. The side of her face twitches with the control it takes not to devour everything at once. Asher fills his fork with slices of meat, and feeds it to Lenya, but his eyes set on Spera, and he glowers.

"One of you could dine by my side for all of time. I would see every wish fulfilled, every desire. In my world, where nothing changes, you alone would forget what it is to want, because you will have it all," Asher says with a growl.

Beside him, Lenya licks her lips. She follows his stare to Spera, and her eyes narrow. Suddenly, she drops her food. Her eyes roll in her head, and she collapses to her side.

The guards advance, swords drawn.

"At ease." Asher raises a hand. "Lenya has visions of the future," he explains. "Didn't I tell you this group of candidates is the most extraordinary yet? Someone in these six holds the key to destroying the veil and delivering the Novus. I can feel it." He turns his attention to Lenya. "What did you see, girl?"

"That one." Lenya points at Spera without sitting up right. "She's black as night inside. She doesn't want the throne. She never will. Nothing that you can do will change her mind."

"We'll see about that." Asher pets her head like he might a cat in his lap.

"You will," Lenya whispers.

I smother a gasp, Lenya's sideways face so strikingly similar to Vanessa's that it takes my breath away. Her hair is silvery blonde, where Vanessa's is more the color of honey, but both their eyes are emerald green. Lenya moves her hand to her face. Vanessa's ring gleams from her finger. Lenya and Vanessa must be one in the same. If I can tell Vanessa who she was, maybe Maris can send her back, and she can see this for herself. She'll have so many answers, so much more information.

"Is it possible for someone I know in my life to be here in a previous incarnation, too?" I ask my guide.

"Why wouldn't it be?" She raises an eyebrow.

The sudden swell of wonder bursts: Spera becomes queen, and Lenya had a vision of dying at her hands. Spera will kill Lenya to become queen. I think back to Spera's defiance in the arena. That was not a girl who wanted to become queen. Does she fight for the title so she has a chance to affect the veil?

"Now, as is custom in these ceremonies, Lucas will read the prophecy of the Vessel and Novus, and will tell you what you're fighting for, so heed his voice," Asher orders. Lenya straightens beside him. Several of the other girls turn to face Lucas. Spera doesn't move at all.

"A sire's blood in a Vessel's heart, the first step for Unseen life to start," Lucas begins, clasping his hands behind his back. "The door and vessel, Vires blood and Vires soul, all must be willing to pay the toll. Only then may the Novus take form, or be lost forevermore. The Vessel first must face the veil. Her heart will choose which world will prevail. Should the Novus come to be, first breath must be drawn among the Seen. Light and dark, their balance the key, their matches kept a mystery. Six pieces show the story's core, the final piece will change the score." Lucas pauses, and looks at every candidate individually. Only Spera refuses to meet his eye. My mind whirls, trying to catch pieces of the prophecy so I can relay them to Vanessa.

"What does Vires blood and Vires soul mean?" I ask my guide.

"Vires is Latin for strength. A human body is weak compared to most other animals, but your souls show incredible resilience and determination, often to the point of madness. Asher believes that in order to deliver and protect the Novus, the Vessel must be stronger than any human is capable of being naturally. He will introduce the stronger blood from the animals the girls survived in the arena, in hopes that strength will manifest in their bodies."

"What if he's wrong?" I whisper.

"That's not a possibility anyone has been willing to offer to him yet," she replies.

"This prophecy, carved into diamond by forces unknown, may be speaking about one of you," Lucas continues. "Our world rests in the Vessel's hands, the gift of the only Unseen life in all time in her belly. This kingdom will honor you, rejoice in your name. You alone will be able to decide the fate of the veil. You alone will sit at Asher's side as the true and permanent queen of our world. You can destroy the veil separating our world from yours, and live forever. You will fear nothing. You will want for nothing."

Spera snorts.

"Is this funny to you?" Lucas approaches her.

"Nothing about this is funny. I will want for nothing? I want to go home. I want Asher dead." The crowded room breaks into murmurs and chatter. I look to Lenya, wondering at the prophecy she'd just spoken. Had she foreseen Spera's outburst?

"The Vessel will want for nothing. You will probably be dead by sunrise," Lucas argues, and the other soldiers fall to silence.

"Asher needs six of us, right? It looks to me like I at least have until the next stage of this process before you can kill me." She glowers at him. He steps up on the bench, and then to the table top, towering over her.

"Don't speak of the process as if you respect it, as if you respect anything. You owe everyone in this room an explanation for why you desecrated the Blood choices today," he orders.

"Asher owes us his definition of the word 'choice,'" she counters. "You can't starve wild predators and then act like it's some divine providence when they chase down the first sight of food, especially when we're all trapped in a ring together." Spera cuts her eyes at Asher. "I wanted to see what the animals would choose if they truly had two options to decide between—freedom, or starving girls who would be little more than bones to chew on."

"I found my match," Lenya counters, and smirks.

"You subdued a starving, scared animal with a sword. That cat was smaller than the rest, and at the far end of the ring. It chose to pacify you, as you choose to pacify Asher now."

"Do not speak so boldly of your king," Lucas growls at Spera.

"He is not my king." Spera glares up at Lucas. "He is a fool."

"And I am a fool. Because I choose you," Lucas says. "You are like a wild colt, disrespectful and full of pride. I will make it my mission to break you. You are my candidate. Until you belong to Asher or die in the process, you will belong to me."

"I belong to no one," Spera says through her teeth.

"Careful, Lucas," Asher says, a note of jest in his voice. "That could be your future queen."

"I highly doubt it," he says without taking his eyes off Spera.

"Then why choose her?" Asher asks, genuinely curious.

"She is the biggest threat to a sacred process that you created. I would rather show my loyalty to you and the Novus than choose the strongest candidate, who is Lenya, by far."

"I choose Lenya," another officer chimes in, stepping forward.

"Calen, as second to Lucas, you may do so as long as Lucas is sure of his choice." Asher stares at him quizzically.

"I am sure. Maybe she'll surprise us all," Lucas states.

"Yes," Asher muses. "Maybe she will."

The four remaining officers select from the four remaining candidates. Each guard ushers his candidate off the table. Shackles are locked around their wrists, and they are stood in a circle at the end of the room. Asher follows them, towing Lenya by the arm, and gives her to Calen.

"Let's discuss the next step in the process. Your blood will be replaced with superior Vires blood. This process is slow and painful at first, but most of you will come to enjoy it. Even . . . crave it." His words send up a flare in my memory. Asher said something similar to me before he gave me what he claimed was medicine. He said it will help my body produce more red blood cells. There's a very good chance he gave me then the same thing he's referring to now. Dread prickles across my scalp. Asher has already begun my candidate process. "Still, it can be a struggle for the body to accept, so be prepared for extreme measures to be taken, such as withholding food and bloodletting, should it appear your body is rejecting what's good for it."

"Sounds like more choices to me," Spera mutters.

"Silence," Lucas growls in her ear.

"Once the blood exchange is complete, the battles for the throne will begin. You will fight each other one on one. One candidate will leave the ring alive. The defeated candidate will be branded with my mark, and cast to the flame, releasing your soul whole so that you may return to me in another life should the prophecy fail again in this cycle, and I deem you worthy of a second chance," Asher explains, striding around the outside of the circle.

"Look around this circle at the five other human faces staring back at you. Humanity is what makes you weak, it's what binds you to the ideas of your mortal world, believing your short lives precious and sacred. That humanity must be eradicated if you are to survive as a queen in the Unseen realm. When you live thousands upon thousands of years, you will lose count of how many times and ways other creatures will attempt to end your reign, your life. There will only be one queen. Only one of you will survive to the end. But each of you is important, because each of you will help eradicate that humanity in the future queen, and elevate her above mortality. This may seem cruel and unnecessary, but I am a results man, and this is how I have been able to create my best results thus far. We haven't uncovered the true Vessel, but each time, we grow closer. Something in you six is unique. I can feel it."

My blood runs cold. *I'm a results man*. I've heard that before, too. Asher had gained such easy access to my room, my chart. He was never in the room when Dr. Andrews was present. Could they be one in the same? My mother often said there's no such thing as a coincidence.

"The Vessel, the true queen, must be a warrior," Asher begins again. "Fierce, loyal, brilliant. She will answer to no one, not even me. The veil itself will answer to the queen. I cannot choose which one of you will wear the crown. I cannot choose who will deliver my child. You alone hold that choice in your hands. It is the law of balance, a law we must all respect and cherish, no matter how high the price balance sometimes forces us to pay. Our homes, our families." Asher casts his gaze at Spera.

"Your destinies are far greater than you could ever have imagined before coming to me. Lightning chose you. I will craft you. You will set yourself free of all the expectations you ever had for yourself, and become more," Asher finishes. Lenya lifts her chin.

"For the Novus," she says, and the guards repeat her in echo.

A shudder passes through me. Maybe Vanessa shouldn't come to see this. She'll be horrified to witness how brainwashed Lenya became, and how quickly. I study Lenya. Then again, Vanessa is one of the smartest people I've met. Could she be playing into Asher's hand as a means of survival?

"Come, Spera," my guide says to me. "You have much to remember, yet."

SCARS

The darkness of this transition begins to lighten, but not by much. The ground beneath my feet is cold and wet. Collecting moisture drips from a gray, rounded ceiling. We must be in some kind of tunnel or cave. It's obviously man-made. The edges are too smooth, too deliberate. A rotten odor makes me reluctant to breathe the damp air as we walk through shallow mud along a stream.

The cylindrical hallway opens ahead. We step down into a dank cellar. The floors are still muddy and the stone roof hangs even closer to our heads.

"What is this place?" I ask, failing to stop the shudder that forces its way through me.

"Asher had a holding chamber carved in the base of a mountain," my guide says. The sound of something stirring on the wet floor draws my eye farther down the hall. A few feet ahead of us, the stone wall recedes. The opening is striped with thick metal bars. A tiger turns tight circles in the small enclosure. It hisses in frustration and wheels again. The next five cages are filled with five of the other animals from the match fight in the arena:

a lioness, a panther, Lenya's snow leopard, a tiger, and a male lion. The rage and confusion flashing in their wild eyes is identical. Part of me wants to walk as close as possible to the opposite wall. The other part is searching for something to pick their locks. These must be the animals he's drawing the stronger blood from. I wonder which cat he chose for Spera, and then blanch at the curiosity.

Human fingers wrap around the next set of cold bars. They're so thin the only thing left between the dank air and the bones is a layer of droopy skin. I step to the front of the cage. A girl's head hangs low between her skeletal arms. Her back rises and falls in shallow quivers that barely disturb the thin fabric of her dress. A row of dying girls stretches down the hall, the walls between them made of bars, all of them visible to each other.

"Is he starving them?" I ask quietly, remembering the measures Asher cautioned he would take should the girls' bodies refuse the foreign blood.

"Yes. The body must be truly hungry or it will reject the transformation," she explains. "The physical body of the Vessel will be turned into an Unseen. Replacing the candidates' blood is the first step."

"It's ready," Calen calls to the others. "Lucas, we'll dose the first five, throw feed, and then help you with Spera. Maybe we'll get more down here today."

All doubts that Asher dosed me with the same blood in the hospital evaporate. I clutch my stomach and stare at Spera as a new round of snarls echo throughout the tunnel. Spera curls herself into a ball in the far corner as the other five candidates lunge at their cage doors.

"Are they trying to scare off the guards?" I ask, watching as a girl two cages down from Spera reaches between the bars and makes a swipe at the girl next to her. For the first time since seeing the girls in cages, I'm glad they're in them. They'd tear each other to pieces given the chance.

"That's not resistance you're seeing. It's impatience. The strength of the new blood is like a high for them. They become addicted to it," she says. A dark thought brews in my mind, a wish I can't admit out loud. I want Spera to drink every last drop. She needs to be strong.

"Why doesn't Spera want it?" I ask shifting where I stand.

"Nothing comes without a cost. When the predator's blood takes over, so does its nature. As you heard before, Asher is not only trying to rid the candidates of their weaker blood, he's trying to rid them of their humanity. In all the centuries Asher has done this, Spera has been the only one to refuse," she replies. The cavern becomes eerily quiet as the other candidates receive their transfusions.

"Why doesn't he just let her go?" I ask.

"Her choice to refuse him has had the opposite effect. It makes her all the more special to him," she explains. "Watch now, they're about to feed them." She points at an arched opening at the other end of the aisle.

The six officers enter through the doorway. As they walk in single file, my attention is deviated to their hands, which are holding different pieces of some kind of deer. Blood drips from the severed ends of the obviously fresh kill. I turn away as they begin heaving body parts into each cage.

The first girl pounces on a severed hindquarter and glowers unknowingly at me as she guards her bloody meal. She bares her teeth and snarls a warning before tearing a piece of skin off. My stomach heaves in protest, making me gag on my own bile. The sounds grow louder and more intense as the others begin to gorge themselves. The tearing of flesh and meat turns into smacking and crunching, which is by far the worst. I hear the bones crack between their famished jaws.

Calen and Lucas pause outside Spera's cage, staring at her.

"She still won't eat?" Calen asks Lucas.

"No." He frowns and crosses his arm. "We've done this hundreds of times, and I've never had one flat out refuse. Her body isn't taking well to the blood we're able to force into her, either."

"Should we find a new match?" Calen suggests.

"I think it's too late for that."

"So we just let her die? That hasn't happened before, has it? Don't we need six?" Calen ends in a whisper.

"If not for Lenya, Asher would probably advise we release all of these souls and start again. But she's had several visions that have proven true. Asher will not let this process fail."

"Maybe if an animal actually chose to give me its blood, I would choose to drink it, and my body would accept it," Spera rasps from her cage.

"If a wild animal knocks on the door to the Kingdom, we'll be sure you're the first to know," Lucas says.

"Well, she still has her sense of humor, now doesn't she?" Calen says, and punches Lucas in the arm.

"That she does." They turn and walk down the hall, and disappear through a door in the opposite wall. Spera rests her knees on her head. Through her cage bars, I spy Lenya gnawing on a bone. Her face is smeared with crimson. She looks at Spera, opens her mouth, and begins to seize.

She falls to her side, trembling. Her eyes roll. Spera crawls away from the wall she shares with Lenya, coming to a rest at the front of her cage merely inches from where I stand. Up close, she looks much older than she did in the village courtyard.

"How long has she been here?" I ask my guide.

"Nearly a year. Asher's process is very hard on the body, and Spera's rejection of food is taking its toll as well."

"Spera," Lenya hisses at her. Spera doesn't respond. "Spera, if your door were to be left open, what would you choose?"

Spera lifts her chin briefly over her shoulder, then resettles without answering.

"Make up your mind now, Spera. I saw a choice is coming for you. You say you understand choice and balance better than Asher. Perhaps the stars above agree with you. Know what choice you'd make between running and staying, Spera."

"What are you babbling about?" Spera snaps.

"You'll see," Lenya answers. The officers return, and neither girl speaks again. Spera rests the side of her face on the bars, staring at the lock on her door, no doubt imagining it open. Each officer moves toward his candidate's door, leather pouches in their hands. Lucas pulls a key from his belt and unlocks Spera's door.

"Not sulking in the back today?" he asks. She watches him, unblinking.

In a cage a little farther down, a candidate giggles to herself as she licks a bone clean.

"Spera," she calls in a singsong voice and drags the bone along the bars of her cage. "Spera. Can you hear me? I'm coming for you." A delirious grin cuts her face in half. She lets out a challenging hiss. Her black hair falls across her gaunt face, leaving only her teeth exposed. The shape of them draws my eye, her incisors longer and sharper than normal. The skin on her face and arms is striped in a tiger pattern.

"Go for Spera all you want," Lenya says, and saunters to the wall between them. She rubs her cheeks along the bars, the way a cat does to claim territory. "And when you're done I'll tear out your throat."

I cringe, wide-eyed, at the words coming out of Lenya's mouth and the malice in them. I can't imagine Vanessa saying something like this. The other girl launches herself at Lenya, swiping through the bars. Lenya grabs the girl's arm and bites down. The bones in her forearm cave under the pressure of the bite, emitting a muted popping sound, and the girl lets out a blood-curdling scream.

"Lucas!" one of the officers shouts. Lucas jumps toward the wall between their cages, shouting and banging his hands on the walls. Calen fumbles the keys to Lenya's cage. Lenya digs her fingers into the girl's arm and twists it too far. Her elbow disjoints, and she screams again. Lenya licks the blood dribbling from her bite mark.

"Lenya, release her!" Calen shouts, searching for the key that is buried in the dust. "Lenya!" Lucas pulls out a ring full of keys, and begins trying them one at a time in Lenya's lock as the other girl's officer jerks her door open. Lenya's lock finally clicks with release. Lucas shoves her door open and rushes inside. Lenya releases the girl's arm, and swipes at Lucas, her teeth bared. Lucas grabs his face and twists away. Blood gushes through his fingers. He pulls his hand away from his face. I gasp in horror, his teeth visible through the tears in his cheek. Even the other officers seem distracted by the extent of Lucas's injury.

Two officers slide into the wounded candidate's cell. I spy a bottle of Tenix in one of their hands. Calen approaches Lenya slowly, his hands lifted a little way from his legs, his face round and soft.

"My queen," he says softly.

"She's no queen," the wounded girl snaps.

"She is, though," Calen replies, admiration in his voice. "She's my queen." Lenya relaxes. She tosses her blood-spattered hair behind her shoulder. "You're more than a queen. You're a goddess," he whispers, and he waves his hand to Lucas, signaling him to leave. Lucas slips through the door. "Are you alright, my queen?"

"I'm perfect," she says. She drops down to all fours, curls into a ball, and nestles her head into the crook of her arm.

"Well, she cooled off quickly," Calen says, backing out of her cage.

"Lucas, we only have enough Tenix for you or her. Who should we heal?" an officer asks.

"That's no question. Heal the candidate," Lucas says, and presses a cloth from his belt against his face.

A sudden chill floods the cavern. I hug my arms around my front, and peer over my shoulder. Asher stands in the archway dividing the predator cages from the human cages. His face twists in fury. I follow his gaze to Spera's cage. The door is open, and the cell is empty. My heart leaps. Lenya told Spera the opportunity to run was coming. She's the reason Spera stayed toward the front of her cage. She knew Cavilla would instigate a fight, and she used it to help set Spera free.

"What has happened here? Where is Spera?" Asher demands.

"She was just here," Lucas says, turning to stare at her door. Blood flows down his cheek and drips from his jaw. Clarity strikes me center: this is how he came to have those scars I saw. This is why he couldn't tell me.

"Cavilla attacked Lenya," Calen points to Cavilla's arm. "Lucas went in to pull them apart, and Lenya turned on him. Her door must have been open. We didn't hear her leave."

"How could you let her escape? Do you have any idea how important she is? In thousands of years we have never seen anyone like her," Asher growls, advancing toward Lucas. I can't help noticing Lenya sit up from her cat-like position, her green eyes darkening.

"Sire, we made every effort to—" Calen starts to explain, stepping between them. Asher cuts him off.

"Find her," Asher demands, pointing at Lucas. "Your life depends on it. All of your lives depend on it!" His officers move to the armory room in a charged silence.

"Do their lives really depend on it? I heard Unseens can't die on your side of the veil," I ask my guide.

"This is all happening on your side of the veil, where mortal limitations apply."

"What happens if an Unseen dies? Do Unseen souls reincarnate, too?"

"No. We are immortal, but we are only immortal once. We are given everlasting life or we are given no life at all," she explains. *So, if Lucas dies, it's forever.* The thought hits me harder than I expect it to.

"Are you as slow as you are foolish? Must I do this myself?" Asher's voice splits the thick air. Fissures glow across his broad body. I flatten myself against Spera's cage as he springs forward and lands on all fours. Standing just a few feet from me, I recognize the creature that chased me through the fields at Wildwood.

Asher's new form takes off downstream, swinging his yellow-eyed, saber head from side to side to pick up any traces of her scent. Lucas leaps into the air, transforming into an identical creature by the time he hits the ground. Panic shoots through my core. Spera doesn't stand a chance. No sooner has the thought echoed across my brain, the underground cellar instantaneously falls away.

FREEDOM

The void of transition is over quickly. Wherever we are now feels painfully bright, and the dry air that fills my lungs leaves familiar grit in my throat. We're back in the desert.

"Where's Spera?" I ask as I shield my eyes with my hand. My guide points in the opposite direction. The instant I see her, I wish she'd died in that cellar. At least she'd be at peace, resting. She'd be free.

Instead, I see Spera dragging herself across the sand, her movements so weak that no dust rises from what little progress she's making. She crawls a few feet more and collapses. Her lips are cracked and bleeding. She brings a clenched fist to her face. Her fingers shake as she opens them. The silver horseshoe gleams in her dirty palm. She squeezes her hand shut and lets out a desperate cry. I close the distance between us, reaching out for her skeletal shoulder when I hear the sudden muffled crunch of paws on sand.

Asher and Lucas approach in their beastly forms. Spera barely stirs. I take a defiant, futile step between them. They might not be able to see me, but they're going to have to go through me first.

The ground quakes beneath my feet, and I brace myself for the transition. The barren surroundings do not fall away. A familiar rhythm in the rumble makes my heart pound in my chest: one-two three, one-two three, it's the cadence of running horses. Their approaching forms shimmer on the horizon, distorting in the heat radiating from the ground. Asher pauses, baring his teeth at the coming herd. He flattens his black body against the ground and waits, his long tail swishing in agitation. Lucas, the smaller of the two, stays behind him.

"Is Asher afraid?" I whisper, assessing his body language.

"As afraid as an Unseen can be," she says, clearly amused. I nearly laugh.

"Why?" I ask.

"Horses are the only mortal creatures that can cross to our side of the veil, as their elemental balance is perfect, and requires no Tenix to bind them together. The veil allows them passage in their true forms," she says as they roar toward us without a hint of slowing down.

This feels familiar. They gallop in tight formation and make an impenetrable circle around us. As soon as the circle is sealed, they slow to a walk and turn in to face the center.

A black horse steps out from the solid wall and takes a guarding position between Asher and Spera's failing body. He unknowingly stands so close to me that I can hear his heartbeat. Wind whips his wild mane across my face. He smells like the ocean: salty and powerful. I've seen hundreds of horses in my lifetime, and none compare to the majesty of this creature.

His deep eyes lock on Asher. His muscled body quivers with readiness and he issues a shrill challenge. Asher's saber disguise dissolves and he climbs to his human feet. As if testing the horse's commitment, he takes a quick step toward Spera. The horse strikes his perfect head like a snake at Asher. To my surprise, Asher jumps back. Lucas transitions into human form, and draws a sword, but Asher signals for him to stand down. The horse moves toward Spera and lowers his muzzle to the ground, pawing at the sand by her face.

"What does that mean?" I ask, filling with nameless dread.

"The leader of the herd is giving his life for Spera. He is presenting himself to Asher for capture," she responds. "The horse has chosen Spera over himself."

My guide touches my palm with her finger, and I watch as she traces over an invisible design.

"You didn't think you had a hoofprint in your hand because you love horses, did you? This choice was not up to you. The horse marked you."

I look back to the black horse in disbelief. His eyes still smolder with freedom, but his tail has dropped from its arched, defiant display and his weight is evenly distributed between his four legs, no longer coiled in his hindquarters.

"How does that help Spera?" I whisper. The thought of watching Asher kill the horse is almost as gut-wrenching as the idea of Spera's inevitable death.

"Only a horse's blood is strong enough to save her now. It is the strongest kind of mortal blood. This prey animal fears no predator. They will attack anything that threatens their safety or the safety of their herd, from lions to wolves to alligators. When the instinct to fight is triggered, they will challenge any opponent. This stallion is willing to let Asher use this will to fight in his blood to save Spera."

"But why would the horse offer his life to save Spera?" I ask, glancing at her ethereal face.

"Have you already forgotten? Spera laid down her life for him and some of his herd when the young man tried to drive them off a cliff. There is only one way to repay that kind of gift," she replies.

A life for a life—a cycle that can't possibly save anyone at all. Spera wouldn't have wanted this. I stare at the horse, aghast and humbled. He stands like a stone. *Like a statue.*

The thought makes the desert fall away as my mind races a thousand years into the future—into Vanessa's monstrous home—where the statue of a black horse stands, his mane still blowing in the desert wind. How is that possible? If it was true, and it really was him, then he's safe and protected. Vanessa would never let anyone take it. She wouldn't even let me touch it.

"This I did not expect," Asher muses, derailing my train of thought.

"What did you not expect, sire?" Lucas asks.

"This horse has chosen to volunteer its blood for Spera." Asher smiles to himself.

"That's impossible," Lucas says, scoffing.

"I think it's quite possible. Spera defended this horse from a vicious brute of a boy the day before her parents gave her to me. I don't like to make a habit of searching for candidates so close to home, but then I heard her screaming. I looked through the veil in time to see her throw a rock at him. It hit him in the face. Blood went everywhere." Asher chuckles to himself. "They fought for a second. Then the boy fell over the edge of a cliff, and you know what Spera did?"

"What?"

"She tried to catch him," Asher says, his voice trailing off. "But he was twice her size. He dragged her over the edge, too."

"And she lives?" Lucas says, furrowing his brow.

"She lives." Asher drops his chin. "A soul like that, I couldn't let it fall to ruin at the bottom of a canyon."

"You saved her," Lucas murmurs.

"I caught her with a bolt of lightning. And at last, I think the stars are showing their gratitude," he says. The breath stills in my chest. If Asher saved Spera with a bolt of lightning, did he also save me the night I was attacked at Wildwood? If he was the lightning, which Unseens were inside the beasts that chased us down?

Asher sweeps Spera off the ground and places her limp body across the horse's broad back. Spera's hand falls away from her necklace. Asher jerks the chain hard enough to break it and tosses it to the ground. "You should really be the one lifting your candidate, Lucas," Asher grumbles. "She's light as a feather, but it's a matter of principle." He turns, and his face knits with confusion. Lucas is kneeling, his head bowed, his hands flat in the sand.

"What are you doing?" Asher asks.

"She's the one, sire. You'll see. She's the Vessel. The blood chose her. It truly chose her. She was right about everything."

"I think you've been too long in the heat, Lucas," Asher says, and they begin the trek back the way they came. The black horse makes one last trumpeting call to his herd, and then he doesn't look back again. Before he stands, Lucas grabs the little necklace, and tucks it into his belt. He wipes his face, his eyes wide as if he's seeing for the first time, and follows behind the horse.

REVELATION

My heart fills with dread as a familiar setting takes shape around me: we're back in the cellar. Lucas sits on the ground outside Spera's cage front, leaning his back against the door. His cheek is bandaged. A small burlap bag rests against his hip.

He peeks over his shoulder, taking caution not to make a sound. Spera is lying on her side, covered in a blanket, which I don't remember seeing the first time we were here. Another blanket is rolled under her head for a pillow. Her hair is smoother and shinier than I remember. She rolls over. Her face is still lean and sharp, but the hollowness has left somewhat. She stirs to waking, and her eyes flicker open.

She pushes off the ground, surprise lining her face.

"We found you," Lucas says softly. "I'm sorry you're in there."

"What happened?" she asks groggily.

"There was a black horse in the desert. He found you the same time we did. I thought we were in for a fight. Instead, he came back with us. He . . . he lives in you now."

"Did Asher kill him?" Spera asks, her voice high with panic.

"No. He only took enough blood from the horse to complete your transformation. In case anything goes wrong, Asher has ensured he will have access to him for the rest of time, but he's not dead."

I know exactly where he is—in the study at Vanessa's house. It's one more piece of evidence pointing to David Andrews knowing way more about the world in the clear than he let on. Something tells me Asher wouldn't let the source of Spera's match blood out of his sight. Could David Andrews truly be another face for Asher?

"When you choose a form to take on this side, do you always have to take the same form?" I ask my guide.

"No, not necessarily. We tend to outwardly reflect our inner traits that transcend whatever body or face we take. I am not a physical threat, so I'm not going to be bulky and large like Asher's officers and soldiers."

"But you're kind of magical so you . . . glitter?" I peer at her pearly skin. She cracks a smile.

"That's certainly one way to look at it. But I imagine with practice and Tenix, we can take any shape or face we would want to."

"I brought you something," Lucas says. He pulls open the burlap sack, and retrieves several pieces of fruit. "Does any of this appeal to you?"

"Yes," Spera answers quietly. Lucas reaches through the bars to hand her the fruit. "So, the horse was my match?"

"Yes."

"And he delivered himself to Asher."

"Yes."

Spera bites into an apple. The first smile I've seen her make curls up the corners of her mouth.

"How did you know that would happen?"

"I didn't."

"But you must have," Lucas counters. "How else would you have known to wait for it?"

"I wasn't waiting for the horse. I was waiting to die."

"That's not fair to the process," Lucas says, becoming flustered. "Asher respects the honor of choice, the law of balance."

"What honor or balance do you see in this? I am locked in a cage. A horse's blood has been forced into my veins while I was unconscious. What choice is that?" she cries out.

"You have a choice of pursuing the most precious position of all time, the Vessel, the mother of the Novus."

"The Vessel has no choice! I would not choose this for myself! I did not choose to come here and fight to become Asher's queen. I chose to not die in front of my parents."

"I'm sorry." Lucas exhales. "Asher told me about the day you saved the horses, and how you fell off the cliff. I'm trying to understand the choice you made."

"When I grabbed the boy, Efran?"

"No. When you defended the horses."

"They needed help. There was no choice to make."

"There's no way for them to repay you, to balance the scales."

"Running free. Living. That's how they repay me. There was never a debt to balance."

"But you're here because of it. Maybe this is your repayment. Asher forced you here, yes, but do you see the opportunity the horse's blood has given you? In all the centuries we've done this, an animal has never presented itself for capture. What if this is fate's way of paying you back for risking your life by giving you an opportunity to become immortal?"

"You think freedom and Asher's queen are the same thing? A balanced scale? Are you free, Lucas? What drives the choices you make? What does your heart beat for?"

"The Novus."

"You mean Asher," she counters.

"No, the decisions we make are for the good of the Novus."

"That Asher is going to give birth to all by himself?"

"Hold your tongue!" Lucas's temper flares, and color touches his cheeks.

"Think about it, Lucas. What decisions have you made to protect the potential mother of the Novus? To honor her? Do you really think this one woman in all of time would have to be caged, starved, manipulated, coerced, made into a murderer? These things will honor her? Make her better?"

"It will be her choice!" Lucas chokes on the last word. His eyes dart back and forth, assessing Spera.

"Yes, a choice. Asher will allow for a choice, won't he? What if it's not the Vessel you need to create, but the sire? His blood exchanged, his body starved, his will broken and manipulated, and then his life pitted against anyone else who wanted to challenge him for the position? What makes Asher so sure he's the sire? Because he wears a crown when he sits down for dinner?"

"This isn't about a sire! This is about the Vessel!"

"Exactly," Spera whispers. "What if I am the Vessel, Lucas? What if I am the mother of your Novus? Is this what you would want for me? Is this how we honor what I will do for your world? Is this the choice you would make in how I am treated?"

"No," Lucas says. A tear leaks from his eye. He scoots the rest of the bag where she can reach it through the bars. Then he stands and walks down the hall. He doesn't look back. I am still spellbound, pressing my hand against my racing heart, when the world around me blurs to nothing.

HONOR

The twinkling black lightens to dusty yellow. A new hallway solidifies around us. The length of it is lit every four feet by a lantern, and circular windows are cut into the stone. One is right behind me. I reach for it, suddenly desperate for fresh air and open space. My fingertips collide with the clear area in the window. It's filled with translucent crystal.

Footsteps draw my ear up the hallway. Lucas leads Spera toward me. He opens a door across the hall from me, and steps aside to let her in ahead of him. My guide and I slip inside the room before he closes the door. The high walls are made of coarse black rock, which glitters despite its unfinished surface. A column of translucent stone stripes the back wall and allows a bit of dusk's weak orange light to filter through from outside. A heavy blanket lies rumpled in one corner. The rest of the room is bare.

"I'm sorry it's not more. But at least you can see outside." Lucas gestures to the window.

"Thank you," Spera says, and casts her gaze at the setting sun. "This is better." She clasps her hands around her elbows, keeping her back to him.

"I choose you," Lucas whispers.

"I know you did," Spera counters. "I belong to you until I belong to Asher, remember."

"No. You belong to no one. You are the Vessel. I can feel it. And I choose you, Spera. I choose to honor you." He drops to his knees. "I am loyal to the Novus cause. I am loyal to you."

"Get up." Spera rasps, watching him from the corners of her eyes. Lucas stands. "There's nothing you can do to change this, Lucas. You didn't bring me here. You're a pawn just as much as I am."

"You are not a pawn. You are the queen."

"I am no one's queen," Spera says, her words succinct.

"You have turned my heart. You have set it right. What if you could do that for the kingdom?"

"Do you think Asher would allow it? Have you told him of your changing heart?" Spera asks.

"No," Lucas says quietly. Spera turns back to the window.

"I will survive as long as I can in this place, Lucas. But I am not your queen. I am not your savior. I long to be out there, free, running with the wind, swimming in the sea. The horse's blood in my body only makes it worse. I ache on the inside."

"You would not choose to be here, even if you knew beyond all doubt you were the Vessel?"

"No." Spera shakes her head. "If I thought for one moment I could escape and no harm would come to me or my family, I would run and never stop."

"Is there no way to honor you, then?" Lucas asks.

"You asked what I wanted," Spera says, a bittersweet smile on her face. "That's a start."

Lucas steps forward. He takes Spera's hand in his, and presses something into her palm.

"The battles are tomorrow. This next phase will change you. It has to. Remember who you are," he says. He closes her fingers around something in her hand. "And if you forget, I will remind you. That is how I will honor the Vessel. Good night, Spera," Lucas says. He bows, and leaves the room. The bolt slides in place behind him. Spera opens her hand. Her mother's horseshoe necklace twinkles from her palm. She squeezes her hand into a fist, and brings it to her mouth. Her shoulders shake. She crushes her eyelids shut. Her chin trembles, and tears come rolling down.

I want to touch her, to show her someone is here. She's not alone. But her words to Lucas are true. There's no way out but through.

My guide takes my hands, signaling another transition. This time, we stay where we are, and the world around us blurs with speed. Spera lies down. Darkness falls outside her window. The stars track an arch across the sky. The sun rises, and with it, Spera stands, and my guide releases my hands. Spera's door opens. Lucas walks in, and time regains its natural passing.

Spera presents her wrists, eyeing the shackles on his belt.

"No." Lucas casts them into the corner of her room. "You will not wear those again when I have a say in it."

"Asher will notice."

"I don't care. This is my choice. I am making my own choice to honor the Vessel."

"Your heart *has* turned." Spera narrows her eyes. "Why?"

"I cannot hold hate for this process in my heart, because it's how Asher found you," Lucas begins. "But I see now how Asher's process honors him, not the true Vessel who will sit at his side. He honors himself. As you said, he can't give birth to the Novus all by himself." A guarded smile passes between them. "I shouldn't jest today, though. What you are about to face will change everything. You might not return to this room. If you do, you won't be the same."

"I don't expect to be."

"Is it so wrong that I want you to win?" he murmurs.

"You believe me the Vessel, and you are loyal to the Novus. I would expect you to want me to win."

"I think . . . I think it's more than that, though," he says softly. "I have been in your presence for a year, but I am only now beginning to know you. I want to know the girl who saved the black horse, and who tried to catch an enemy by the cloak to keep him from falling. Even more so, I want to know the woman who stands up to Asher at every turn. I've lived since the dawn of time, and I have never met anyone like you. I want to know you."

"What if I'm not the Vessel?" Spera asks, surprise alighting on her face.

"You are. I know you are."

"What if I'm not?" she insists.

"I'd want to know you anyway," Lucas says, his gaze dropping to the ground. Spera's eyes widen, and she scans the length of him. Before she can respond, the distant rumble of drums fills the silence. "It's time," Lucas says. He turns for the door, waiting for her to step to his side. I watch as she hesitantly raises her hand to his, squeezes two of his fingers, and then lets them drop. Lucas stares down at her, his mouth parting. She pulls her door open, and strides out.

I stare down at her mark on my chest. Three rings, three kills. I know Spera becomes queen. She will win all three battles. How many pieces of who she was die in the process?

We follow Spera and Lucas down the hall. Five more doors identical to hers line the stark wall. Two of them are swung all the way open. I peek inside the cells as we walk by. They are empty. Wild shrieks draw my attention further down the dimly lit hall. The last door shakes on its frame as whatever is behind it throws itself against the solid barrier.

"Sounds like she's ready for you, Spera," a soldier calls from beside a closed door.

"That's a girl in there?" I ask, looking to my guide.

"Do you remember the candidate who called out to Spera in the underground chamber? They call her Cavilla. Spera will face her next."

Of course I remember. How could I forget the sight of the dark-haired girl raking a bloody bone across the metal bars? The Tenix must have healed her arm in the same way Vanessa used it to heal my leg. She doesn't sound reluctant to fight. I watch Spera for any reaction, but she doesn't acknowledge the snarls coming from the closed door. The hallway widens, and descends to a sandy floor.

"They're about to start," she says. We make our way up a narrow ramp, which opens to the arena floor. The sand is stained with blood in one place. Thousands of soldiers are on their feet. They roar louder and louder, the calls for battle blending into one ominous sound. As the cries organize into a chant, they raise their spears in salute and stare toward one end of the stadium.

The hair on the back of my neck stands on end as Asher glides across a balconied ledge, Lenya trailing him. I frown at the sight, wishing she would stand up to him the way Spera does. Then again, there's more than one way to work against Asher. Lenya has proven her ability to outsmart his army.

"Has Lenya fought yet?" I ask my guide.

"Yes. There have been two battles already this morning. Lenya fought first. Since she gained favor with Asher, she was allowed to choose her opponent. She will also be allowed to skip the second round, and won't fight again until the final round. The winner here will fight the winner from the second battle immediately after this concludes. Once Lenya's opponent is decided, we will recess. The final two candidates will be marked, and the third battle will begin at sundown."

I close my eyes against the weight of this truth: Spera will kill Lenya and become queen. For the first time, I'm grateful Spera feels wholly separate from me.

The metal gates on the long end of the arena swing open, and Spera and Cavilla are led by their officers into the center of the arena. Another candidate is brought in and made to stand against the wall, waiting her turn to fight the victor here. Her skin is so black she's nearly blue, and she shines where the light touches her. Her eyes are bright yellow, and her face is perfectly heart shaped. She must be matched with the panther. Without warning, Cavilla lunges at Spera, nearly toppling the officer holding her restraints. A hiss escapes her bared teeth.

"Be still!" Asher calls smoothly to Cavilla. "Soon you will have nothing holding you back."

The officer removes Cavilla's shackles. I glance at her arm. There's a crescent-shaped scar where Lenya tore the skin with her teeth. The rest of Asher's army begins to pound their spears against their shields in a horrific, hypnotic rhythm and I have to remind myself this has already happened. There's nothing I can do to change what I'm about to see.

Asher raises his hands. "Let the third battle of the day begin!" he calls.

The stadium erupts with cheers and shouts. The two girls circle one another. Even though every eye in the arena is trained on them, my attention is drawn to Asher's throne. He leans forward on his marbled chair, staring hungrily at Spera. He hasn't glanced once at Cavilla. Lenya sits to his left. She isn't watching the fight either. Her green eyes gaze unwaveringly at his cold face. I wonder when she dies, and if I'll have to see it.

"Are you ready, Spera?" Cavilla warns, weaving her head back and forth. Spera waits, her stance unchanging, as Cavilla circles to her left.

"Don't you know better than to leave your back unguarded?" she hisses from directly behind her. Cavilla pauses, no doubt expecting Spera to move or turn or run. Spera stands still. Cavilla sinks down on the balls of her feet and then sprints for Spera. She closes the distance between them inside of a single heartbeat, Spera unmoving.

Cavilla punches the final step off the ground, soaring toward Spera's back. Spera turns and lifts her hands toward Cavilla's head as Cavilla reaches for her throat, claws outstretched. Spera is faster, planting her palms on either side of Cavilla's face. The crack of Cavilla's neck echoes in the stadium. Cavilla goes ragdoll limp in Spera's hands. Spera lays her fallen competitor down on the sandy floor.

The audience explodes into a thunderous roar. Spera does not acknowledge their cheers. She kneels beside her enemy's body and closes Cavilla's eyelids with her fingers. Her lips move quickly in a silent prayer. Without a single glance at the audience, she stands and walks quickly to the towering gates. Asher's stare never leaves her back.

I pant with shock and relief. Even though I knew she would win, she made it fast. I wish it would mean less of her humanity was lost in that fight. But the fact that she ended a life in any way would have to steal a piece of her soul. What other choice did she have? Allow Cavilla to kill her?

"Spera, look out!" Lenya shouts, pointing across the arena. The waiting candidate has broken free from her officer. She rushes Spera now, who must not have realized the second battle would begin immediately after a victor was determined from her first.

Lucas's expression is a portrait of dread. His fingers clamp around his spear. Indecision passes across his face: to save the human he wants to learn more about, or to refuse to interfere with the Vessel process.

The other candidate slips a wrist from her shackles, and slings the chain like a lasso. Spera spins around, and leaps sideways, out of reach. The girl closes again. Spera is still on the defensive, the other opponent too fast. She pulls her other wrist from the shackles, and flings them at Spera's legs. They crack against her shins, and Spera falls to her hands. The girl advances. Spera is slow to stand. The skin on her legs has broken open from impact, and an ankle is tangled in the chain.

Dread fills me. I didn't expect to see Spera come so close to defeat. Out of the corner of my eye, I see a flash of movement near Asher's throne. Lenya has grabbed a spear from a soldier. She slides her arm back, taking aim, and then hurls it into the arena. The spear head buries itself in the girl's spine. Her arms shoot out at their sides, and she drops to her knees, then falls face down in the arena sand. Spera heaves in the middle of the arena, shock rounding her angular face, blood dribbling down her shins.

"What have you done?" Asher asks, mouth agape.

"You said I *could* skip the second battle. You didn't say I *had* to," Lenya quips. "And that I could choose my opponent. I want to fight her, the girl with the blood gift." Lenya glowers at Spera. The stadium falls to silence. Asher stares from Lenya to the dead girl and then to Spera. His mouth opens. He stands. And he begins to laugh. His laughter echoes across the arena. The soldiers look around at each other, and an uneasy laughter grows in the stands. My insides twist and my mind whirls. What the hell just happened? Does it interfere with the process? Do I care? I can't imagine how Vanessa will feel about her previous incarnation if she gets to witness the same things I do here.

"Didn't I tell you these six would be extraordinary?" Asher says, and his army begins to cheer. "Come, we have much to celebrate."

Spera limps toward Lucas. He jogs to her and slides an arm around her back, then lifts her off her feet. Asher pauses where he stands, and turns to watch Lucas carry Spera off the arena floor. He raises his chin, and suspicion flashes in his white eyes. Lenya tugs at his forearm. He pulls his arm out of her grip, but follows her out of the stadium. Nervousness makes a home in me. Lucas is wearing his turning heart on his sleeve. Will he be able to recognize the feelings he's developing for Spera before Asher does?

SING FOR ME

Instead of using a transition, my guide and I follow Asher's processional to a large ballroom, which is already filled with soldiers from the arena. The high walls are made of translucent quartz. Flames dance behind the clear stone from floor to ceiling. Silver platters stacked high with meat blanket a long marble table. Asher takes a seat at the center on an onyx throne. Lenya and Spera are led to him, and chained on either side of him. Their shackles are only long enough for them to reach from the table to Asher's mouth. Lenya feeds him each time he sets his eyes on her.

Spera stares straight ahead, holding her chin high in defiance. I catch myself mimicking her. Lucas glares at her arms from across the room, no doubt resenting seeing the shackles back on her wrists.

"Are you not hungry, my dear?" Asher asks Spera. His smooth voice makes me dizzy with resentment. I clench and flex my hands at my sides.

"No," Spera answers without facing him.

"But you must have worked up such an appetite," he croons.

"You eat although you do not hunger," she counters.

"Lenya, you are certainly the more enjoyable company. I do wish you well this evening," Asher says without taking his menacing eyes off Spera's stony profile.

Lenya's gray eyes flicker briefly to Spera. A moan escapes her lips and her body begins to seize with a vision. Spera jumps to her feet, but her chained arm yanks her sideways and she falls into the side of Asher's throne. She grits her teeth and stares across the lofty room. I follow her gaze to Lucas's face. His body tenses with helplessness.

Lenya whimpers face down on the marble table. No one moves to help her.

"Lenya, darling. Tell me what you see. What does the future hold?" Asher asks, his voice too loud to be meant for only her. Lenya collapses across Asher's lap. He strokes her hair with his hand like a pet.

"Of my victory, my beloved. And of your victory. You have given every effort to this cause. And finally, your true queen is in your home. A new life will follow, if you are humble enough to listen when the stars cry out for you in guidance," she purrs. Spera's horrified, amber eyes are hard and fast on Lenya's face. As are mine. I know she's lying. Spera doesn't. Why would she lie? What did she really see?

"Is that so? Humbleness is a thief in reverse. I am king. I am pure. I have defied death, and will soon defy one of two laws placed on my kind." His jaw sets and his white eyes flash. Then he exhales, and blinks away the intensity from his face. "Humble just isn't a good look for me." Asher casts his gaze from Lenya to Spera and traces their throats with his thumb. Lenya moves into his touch. Spera pretends she doesn't feel it. A moment of conflict creases his face and then vanishes. He appears aggravated in the lack of her reaction.

"I must ensure both these souls return to me, regardless of tonight's outcome. You've each earned the first two rings of the Kingdom's brand."

"I would say only Lenya earned two," Spera counters.

"Would you like to kill something else?" Asher quips. "I'm happy to round something else up for you." Spera's body deflates, her spirit with it.

"No. That won't be necessary," she says quietly.

"Good, then we're all in agreement." Asher flashes a hostile grin. Spera shudders, and the same shiver finds my back. We both keep our eyes trained on Lucas as he steps to her side with another guard and shackles her arms and legs. Calen and another guard fit Lenya with her restraints.

"Apologies, Lenya. You travel with excellent manners, but your little stunt in the arena today makes me worried you won't wait for the fight to make a move on Spera. That's not something I'm willing to risk," Asher explains.

Once both Spera and Lenya are secure, Asher leads the way across the great hall to a pair of double doors made of solid iron. My guide and I blend into the small processional and follow them into the next room. The round wall is made of a blue-black stone that glitters like a clear night. The circular ceiling and floor are mirrors, and reflect the tiny sparkles over and over.

Guards usher Lenya and Spera into the center of the floor and step away. Asher walks a circle around the two, leaving a crackling trail of electricity behind him. White flames rise from his path. As he closes the ring, the fire seals the three of them inside. I watch on, horrified and spellbound. Lenya bows in front of him. He brings a finger to her bare back. Her skin sizzles under his touch as he draws two perfect circles in the center of her back. She does not wince, even though smoke and blood trickle from her skin. I wonder if Vanessa knows she's marked, or if her own lightning strike burn didn't recreate the rings the way mine did.

I watch, disgust rising in me, as Lenya thanks Asher before standing. He moves in front of Spera, who stares unwaveringly at his face.

"Bow," he commands.

"No."

Anger twists Asher's face, and his white eyes grow dark. "You will kneel before your king."

"You are not my king."

Asher presses his finger against her chest. Spera is a statue under his touch. My gaze falls to the identical symbol burned into my chest. A new pain throbs from the mark.

"Every time you look at your reflection, you will always see me," he says, and begins to draw the first circle.

"We are moving on," my guide says. I watch Spera and Lenya standing together in a ring of white flames until they have completely faded from view.

A DIMLY LIT ROOM WITH A DIRT FLOOR solidifies around us. Spera and Lenya sit side by side in separate cages, each dressed in identical, white linen shifts. Lenya leans against the wall between them, her gray eyes trained on Spera.

"Where are we?" I ask, keeping my voice as low as possible.

"Beneath the arena. This is the final holding chamber. Asher makes the last candidates spend time together before they fight," my guide answers.

"Why?"

"Any bond formed between the two of them will make their deaths more of a betrayal of humanity. Asher is closer to his goal now than he has ever been before. He will not leave anything to chance," she explains.

"I have something for you," Lenya whispers suddenly, drawing my attention to the two of them. Spera doesn't move a muscle. "Spera, please. It's meant in peace."

"Was throwing a spear through Nolie's back also meant in peace?" she scoffs.

Please, Spera, I silently beg. *Just give her a chance.*

"It is. I promise you," Lenya says. Spera glances at her over her bare shoulder.

"I'm listening," she says. A guard I hadn't yet noticed shifts his weight in the shadowed far corner. As he repositions, Lucas's face is revealed in the glow of the closest lantern. I feel a comfort in knowing he's not far.

"I know about Lucas's turning heart," Lenya whispers quietly.

"So?" Spera replies. Her eyes lift to Lucas.

"Your heart is turning too, is it not?"

"I don't know what you're talking about," Spera growls.

"Even if you don't care for him, I'm certain you don't want him replaced with another officer. Some of them can be quite . . . cruel. I don't mean you any malice," Lenya adds quickly.

"I have seen the way you behave with Asher. You love him," Spera argues.

"We do what we have to in order to protect our interests, don't we?" Lenya says and glances in Lucas's direction.

"Why did you kill Nolie?" Spera asks in a whisper. "What interest of yours did that protect?"

"Because my vision was this: our fates are intertwined. If you die, I die."

"Why?"

"I don't yet understand it. But I also witnessed a way we can both survive this night." Lenya twists a ring off her finger and hands it to Spera. "Take this. I have another one. If we each wear them, we can speak without voices." She shows Spera the identical ring on her other hand. "Do as I tell you once the battle begins and I will do my best to make sure we both survive."

"Why should I trust you?" Spera asks. "How do you know this will work?"

"Because this is what I saw during the banquet," she confesses. "What I told Asher was a lie."

Spera studies her face with skepticism.

Do you hear me? Lenya's mind calls out, filling my mind. Spera's lips crack with disbelief. She must've heard her, too. I crawl beside them and press my own hands against the front of their cages. I wrap my fingers around the bars, so close to them I could reach out and touch them. I don't know why I'm able to hear this, but for the first time, I feel a deep connection to Spera. I wish I could be inside her mind and show her what I've seen in this life, in hopes it could bring her peace, and a sense of trust for Lenya.

"What else have your visions revealed to you?" Spera presses, edging toward her with new interest.

"I have seen Asher's greed. He fantasizes about having us both. I think we can use that to our advantage." The grinding sounds of moving metal screech from somewhere above the holding chamber.

"It's almost time," Lenya says, flitting her eyes to the ceiling. "You must trust me, Spera. Follow my lead once we're in there. We can both survive this, and then I will help you escape. I have seen that it is possible." She brings her pointer finger to her temple.

"Why would you help me?" Spera asks, her face lining with suspicion.

"I have done some dark things here," Lenya answers softly. "My soul is desperate for a way to set something right."

"If you truly think you can help me escape, why not leave with me?" Spera asks, and my soul lifts at the idea of them both alive and free.

"My parents are dead, and my first battle was against my sister. I have nothing to go back to," Lenya answers bitterly.

"Asher's cruelty is not a reason to stay. I won't leave you here," Spera insists through clenched teeth. The sound of marching footsteps grows louder as guards approach the little room.

"Focus, Spera. We must both live first, and only then will we have our chance," Lenya whispers. "Let us get through this and then we can discuss what lies ahead."

Spera turns a tense eye to the main door as it swings open. Calen leads two fellow guards into the holding chamber. Lenya growls and lunges at Spera, swiping at her face through the gaps in the bars. She bares her teeth, shrieking angrily.

Follow my lead. Lenya's silent words echo in my mind. Spera glowers at Lenya and throws her lean body against the metal bars.

"This is going to be something to see! Your Spera versus my Lenya." Calen says and claps Lucas on the back. "Everyone is whispering that Asher has truly succeeded this time. The whole Unseen realm has its ear turned to us this day."

Spera dutifully slides her forearms between the metal bars and Lenya does the same for Calen. Their hands are shackled with thick metal cuffs before they are allowed from their cages. As soon as she steps through the cage door, Lenya makes a show of throwing herself once more at Spera.

"Yes, this will be something to see," Lucas says, mustering up a fake, cruel laugh while they lock another set of restraints around their ankles.

Spera looks unsettled as we follow them into the arena and onto the battlefield. She knew what she had to do before she sat side by side with Lenya. Now, uncertainty is etched on her hard face. If Spera wants to win, she will. Even Lenya seems resigned to that fact.

Lenya and Spera are led to separate ends of the ring. The soldiers chant and raise their spears. Even Lucas seems lost in the finality of the moment at hand. He absently runs his hand across Spera's in a subconscious offer of comfort.

Careless! Lucas is drawing Asher's eye, Spera, Lenya's frantic voice calls out in my mind. I throw a worried glance at Asher's throne. Lenya is right. Asher narrows his eyes as he stares hard at the pair. Spera reacts instantaneously and lunges at Lucas as he kneels to remove the cuffs around her slender legs.

"Enough," Asher bellows from his high throne. "My dear Spera, save your strength for the battle at hand. This is, after all, the beginning or end of your life. Treat this moment with respect." Prickly relief washes over my skin as a thunderclap of cheering begins again, distracting Asher from Lucas and Spera.

Thank you, Lenya. I will trust you in this, Spera's mind whispers. Lenya locks eyes with her for a fraction of a second. My insides release and then knot again. Spera chose as I would have. There's no way I could kill Vanessa to save myself. Now both of their fates are uncertain.

"Finally, this day has come, this splendid moment," Asher announces as the soldiers quiet down. "We have waited long enough, my brothers. Let it begin," he growls and eases back onto his black throne.

Lenya charges across the sandy pit and launches herself at Spera. Spera knocks her off easily and spins to face her, ready for another attack. Lenya comes again. They claw at each other's throats, feigning a desperate fight for a fatal hold. Lenya suddenly cries out and stumbles. Her palms clamp on either side of her head as she drops to her knees.

Come for me, Spera. Make it look good, Lenya's voice echoes in my mind. Spera rushes for Lenya's seizing body.

"Stop! Spera, I command you to stop!" Asher shouts, leaping to his feet. Lenya collapses, lying face down in the sand. Spera circles her limp opponent, lunging and snapping as she inches closer. "Lucas, restrain Spera! Lenya's visions cannot be interrupted."

Spera bares her teeth at Lucas as he moves to her with faked caution. He cuffs her arms and holds the head of the spear to her back. Lenya moans, and rolls to her side.

"Asher," Lenya whimpers and climbs weakly to her knees.

"What did you see?" Asher calls out, sounding irritated. "What must have been so important that the stars decided to reveal it to you at this most crucial moment?"

"My love, please do not make me repeat what I have seen," she pleads.

"You must, my dear one," he croons, his curiosity blatant in the way his fingers tense over the arms of his throne.

"I do not want it to be so. I want you all to myself! Please tell me there's another way," Lenya babbles, her eyes rolling in her head.

"Tell me what you have seen!" Asher commands.

"I have seen that neither of us are enough power on our own. My Vires blood was not a true gift from a wild-born creature, and she cannot see what is to come. To throw away either gift will bring a plague of ill fortune and low morale—the stars themselves would take offense. The resistance we will face is great, the risks to your Novus more deadly than anything you've ever faced. If you are to be successful, I must share you with that wretched girl," she cries, spitting her last words in Spera's direction.

"Do you see now, my brothers? Do you see how blessed our goal has become?" Asher shouts. Every soldier punches his spear into the air and shouts in celebration. Spera stares at the roaring crowd, shock rounding her haggard face. "We shall have them both!"

We've done it, Spera, Lenya's voice rejoices in my head. If Spera answers her, I don't hear it.

"Officers, prepare two rooms fit for my queens," Asher calls down to the arena floor. "We must keep them separate until they learn to tolerate one another."

I let out the breath I didn't know I've been holding as Calen and Lucas escort their new queens from the arena.

"We are done here," my guide announces. "It's time to move on."

"What could possibly kill Spera if she survived that?" I ask her. She doesn't answer me, but there's a darkness brewing deep within her frigid eyes that chills me to the core.

CHAINS AND CROWNS

A sher sits high on a throne made from the white quartz a guard at each side. Several more guards arm an arched doorway on the opposite side of the grand room. I spot Lucas among them and follow his gaze across the floor. Spera stares vacantly out of a circular window pointing to the afternoon sun. A breeze whistles by the opening, and her silky white dress ripples in the free air. She hugs her arms to her chest. A golden snake cuffs each wrist. Spera's long black hair is pulled back in a single thick braid. Precious stones glitter in each ear. Coils of gilded metal adorn her slender throat.

Is she wearing the ring? I step beside her to get a closer look. Her hands are bare. I swallow my disappointment and peer out the window at the vast nothingness surrounding Asher's castle. Red, flat earth stretches for miles. A darker blue streak acts as a border between the desert and the sapphire sky. The faintest salty scent of ocean surf rides the current of air that blows steadily past the opening. I glance through each of the other three windows, which are carved into the rounded stone wall like the points on a compass. The same navy barrier divides the land from the sky all the way around the tower. They're on an island. There's no way Spera can escape. I study her motionless profile. Even though she drips in gold and jewels she wears the face of a prisoner.

"Where are we?" I ask my guide.

"On a small island between Egypt and Saudi Arabia. Asher moved his queens and his legions here following the branding ceremony where he gave them both their third rings."

"We're not on the Unseen side?"

"No. And because Asher marked their rings without a third kill, Spera will never be able to cross to the Unseen side in her mortal lifetime."

"What will he do? Is there no way for her to affect the veil?" I ask, Spera's reason for not making her choice becoming clearer.

"They still have yet to find the door," she answers. "But be warned it is not a mistake he will repeat."

"How long has it been since the battle between Lenya and Spera?" I close my eyes and try to piece together an outline of what I know so far.

"Nearly two years," she answers. I shudder at the thought of two years as Asher's captive queen.

Lenya glides into the room. Her long dress is a black replica of Spera's. She gingerly carries a silver tray to Asher's throne, offering him an assortment of food. As she passes me, I glance at her back and catch sight of her completed brand.

"You are so caring, sweet Lenya," he croons without taking his eyes off Spera's bare back. "My vizier is on his way. He has sent word he may have found the door to the veil, and that the journey ahead will be long and difficult. Are you ready to earn the crown you wear, Spera?"

"I'd rather you just take the crown back," Spera says without looking at him. Lenya scoffs and places a hand on Asher's arm. He absently brushes it off. Her whole face falls in response. She seems genuinely hurt. I study her clouded eyes, watching for any familiar defiance to shine through. She remains completely in character, obviously determined to secure her position in Asher's deadly palm.

A pair of heavy doors swings open and a thin, older man enters the round room. He is nearly identical to my own guide, and moves with the same otherworldly grace. Where my guide looks like she was carved from a pearl, this Unseen is the color of charcoal.

"And here he is," Asher eagerly greets the new arrival. "Raffin, punctual as always." They clasp their hands around each other's forearms. My eyes move from Raffin to my guide.

"Do you know him?" I whisper.

"I do," she says, her resentment of him too fierce a thing to come from anger alone. Whoever he is to her now, I can tell he used to be something much different. She fixes her icy stare on his charcoal face. "We are done here," she says flatly as Asher and Raffin stride to the open doors.

The last thing I see before the scene dissolves is Spera leaning ever so slightly out the window, closing her eyes as the wind catches her hair and angrily snaps it free from its braid like the crack of a whip.

AN OFFER

This new memory could be a tropical paradise, unless you factor in the armed guards and the pair of locked doors fit for a maximum-security prison. The walls and ceiling are the same incredible, bewildering crystal as the high tower we just left. Sunset makes the clear stone glow blood red, and casts deep shadows over the two guards standing at attention by the side of a circular pool. I immediately recognize Lucas's backlit outline, and assume the other guard is Calen.

Spera sits opposite Lenya, submerged to her bare shoulders in water hazy with heat. This is the most relaxed I've seen her yet. She still won't close her eyes. Lenya plucks an orange blossom from the rainbow of flowering lily pads adrift in the pool, and pulls the petals off one at a time. Spera slides her fingers toward the water, tumbling freely down a cascade of unfinished white rocks. She's wearing Lenya's ring. I press my lips together in anticipation as I catch sight of it.

I am thoroughly enjoying Asher's absence, Spera calls out silently to Lenya. *Do you know how long he and Raffin will be gone?*

A little smile tugs at the corners of Lenya's mouth as she pretends to glower at her fellow queen. *At least a couple of days more. He said the journey is very far. He once told me that he has tried opening the veil in nearly ten thousand places, but none of his attempts have made a dent,* she snickers.

I smile at their playful exchange, grateful to see some of Lenya's true self make a return appearance. She reminds me so much of Vanessa when she's not fawning all over Asher.

Do you think he's right this time? Do you think we will be asked to open the veil? Spera asks.

Who knows? Lenya rolls her eyes. *I don't think Asher ever believes himself to be wrong. There are whispers that Raffin located an important piece of the ritual scroll. Something about the elements.*

I only wish there was a way to be certain. Spera lets out a frustrated sigh and drags her fingers across the milky surface.

"Are you weary, my queen? Shall I escort you to your quarters?" Lucas calls out, maintaining reverence in his voice.

"Not yet Lucas," Spera answers without turning her face. "A few minutes more."

Have you had any visions? Seen any way to escape yet? Spera asks Lenya tentatively.

No. Asher has doubled the guards surrounding the exterior of the fortress. Unless you plan on tunneling to the sea, there's no way to get out undetected. Lenya's eyes flit to Lucas. *Perhaps you could have a little escape of your own.*

What do you mean? Spera ceases all motion.

You and Lucas should spend some time alone while Asher is gone. He's certainly not hard to look at, and he would do anything you ask of him. What do you want, Spera? A girl has needs. Lenya leans back and glides a short distance further away.

I don't want anything in this place. She bites down on her lip and stares at the water.

Now that's not true, Lenya responds, and a coy smile curls her features.

I don't feel anything for anyone. I am dead inside.

I'm not sure that's true either. But I'm not talking about warm and fuzzy feelings. I'm talking about feeling things like his abs and whatever those muscles are called that make his shoulders all broad and round. Feel those. Lenya winks. Pink blooms on Spera's cheeks, and her golden eyes flash with amusement. *Are you really telling me you're surrounded by all these men all the time, and you aren't the least bit curious? Lenya asks. Do you prefer women?*

No. I prefer men. Spera flushes a deeper red. *I can't believe we're having this conversation.*

Wonderful. You should pick one. Or two. Hell, as many as you can keep up with. But start with at least one.

Lenya!

It's been two years, Spera! We're stuck here. Asher doesn't do it for you. Find someone who does. Lenya peers at Lucas. *Or if you aren't interested in seeing what he can do for you, maybe I will.*

No. If anyone in this place interests me, it's Lucas.

Hmm was that a little possessiveness I heard just then? Lenya smirks at her. That's good. You two should spend a little time alone. You can use the garden off my room. If Asher does come home early, I will make myself visible in the main area of the palace. He won't look for you in my quarters. You'll have plenty of opportunity to . . . untangle, Lenya suggests.

There will be no . . . tangling.

Sure. That's what they all say.

The two queens lock eyes over the top of the swirling water. *Calen is a lazy fool with Asher away,* Lenya says. *He leaves his post by my door soon after he escorts me from bathing, and doesn't come back again until well after sunrise. Spend the night with me tonight. Tell Lucas to come just before dawn when the guards' shifts are changing. You two can spend the whole day in my courtyard if you like. I will make sure you are undisturbed. Don't change your mind. This is exactly what you need.*

"I am finished here, Calen," Lenya says aloud quickly. He opens a length of plush fabric, and she wraps it around herself as she emerges from the water.

"Asher really ought to see that this pool is made bigger. I found it too crowded today," she jeers.

Calen casts an amused glance at Lucas and then follows Lenya out of the iron gates. Spera watches them leave before wading to the middle of the pool. Lucas follows her with his eyes as she reaches for a white blossom and plucks it from its floating pad. His hard face melts into adoration as she sweeps the flower behind her ear.

"They're alone now. Why are they still being so careful?" I whisper to my guide. Even though I know they can't hear me, it feels like a crime to disrupt the silent spell between Spera and Lucas. My guide nods at the crystal walls, which are as clear as glass now that the sun has set. Guards pass by on two sides. Their heads don't turn as they march down the hall on the other side of the translucent divide, but nothing out of the ordinary is happening to draw their eyes.

"You seem in good spirits, my queen," Lucas calls out softly to her.

"I am, Lucas," Spera replies without taking her eyes off the water. She turns her back to him so her face is shielded from the guards rounding the hall outside. "I wish you were in here with me."

"What . . . what did you just say?" Lucas leans forward.

"I have known you for three years now. I know what your touch feels like on my arm and against my back. I could pick your footsteps out of a thousand, your knock on my door out of any guard in this castle. But I don't know your heart outside of all this, what moves you if not the Novus. You once said you wanted to know the woman who would stand up to Asher at every turn. I want to know the man who defies him behind his back whenever the needs of his Vessel require it. I want to know what you want, who you are when neither Asher nor I am pulling your strings." Her hands absently skim the water's surface while she talks. I can't take my eyes off Lucas, mesmerized by the storm of want and fear clouding over his face.

"I am not a man," Lucas says quietly.

"You're in my world now. In my world, you are a man. Meet me in Lenya's garden tomorrow morning. Make sure no one else expects to see you. I want to get to know you. But Lucas, this is a choice. Come only if you want to. If you don't, I'll understand."

"I wish to be in there with you now. I will be there in the morning."

"It is time," my guide says. Her voice seems so out of place in this most tender moment. I resist the overwhelming impulse to argue with her. Instead, I let out a hard breath as conflicting emotions fill my chest to bursting. I long to be a part of what they have, to believe I am connected to the devotion I see on Lucas's face. Watching them together, the only thing I feel is distance. My grasp on where I belong in this is disintegrating to dust. One swipe across its surface and it scatters in the wind.

BURNED

Gray morning light dispels the dark of transition. Before my eyes, a two-acre garden takes shape. Every inch is covered with something blooming. For just a moment I can't imagine why anyone would ever want to leave. I reach for the closest thing to me—an arbor made out of thousands of braided morning glory vines nearly ready to open their petals to the new day. Shimmering flower dust leaves a silver streak on the tip of my finger.

Asher's tendency to cage everything has added more surfaces for plants to climb. Blossoming white vines stretch skyward along the crystal walls, giving the effect of a flowering spider web. The first light of dawn filters through the uncovered spaces of the crystal barrier, and makes the mossy ground shimmer with a blanket of faint rainbows. I stretch my arms in front of me and marvel at the same effect the refracted light has on my bare skin.

The sound of moving water draws my ear. A cluster of weeping willows leans toward a pond nestled in the far corner of the garden. The crystal wall behind the pool appears to melt like ice into a steady stream of water that tumbles down the face of a white stone and into the pond. I draw a deep breath, anticipating the cool, lingering scent of wild water to fill me with a sense of freedom, no matter how false. I wrinkle my nose at a sour tinge in the air.

Suddenly, just loud enough to be audible over the cadence of the little waterfall, comes a sound I've never heard before: Spera's laughter. And then a familiar chuckle—Lucas. I am torn between giving them a moment alone and wanting to be a part of it. In a matter of seconds, I'm halfway down the length of the garden, just in time to see Spera throw her head back in a genuine smile, her hand covered by Lucas's.

They sit together on the far side of the pond, shielded by a dense grove of lilies and irises. Lucas says something that makes her laugh again. She reaches her other hand to her neck and plays with the silver horseshoe charm as she watches his happy face.

He reaches for a lock of her hair that hangs close to her eye. "May I brush your hair from your face?" he asks.

"Do you want to?" Spera asks.

"Yes."

"Then you should."

Lucas uses his finger tips to gently tame the runaway lock of hair. He doesn't let it go, spinning it between his fingers instead. "I love the way the sun catches in your hair. It turns some pieces red."

"Your eyes are lighter here. I don't know that I've ever seen you close up in the sun," Spera answers. Spera traces his brow, peering in his eyes. He takes her hands in his and kisses her knuckles.

"You aren't wearing your ring. You always wear it," he comments.

"Lenya said she didn't want to hear us in case we started having . . . too much fun." Spera blushes.

"I thought Lenya was the type who would definitely want to hear us having . . . too much fun."

"True." Spera breaks into a grin. "It's nice to be alone with you. Truly alone." She leans into him, her lips parting. "Can I kiss you, Lucas?" she whispers.

"Do you want to?" he murmurs, their lips an inch apart.

"Yes."

"Then you should," he says. He stays still, and waits for her to come to all the way to him. She gently kisses his mouth. His hands slowly encircle her waist and pull her closer. The muscles in his arms flex as he holds her tighter, breathing her in. Her body rises as she lifts herself onto her knees, pressing her body to his. Her hair cascades over her shoulders. He reaches up and brushes it back, tightening his hand to a fist. A moan stirs in Spera's throat, and Lucas turns his attention from her mouth to her neck. She digs her nails into his back, gasping, and then takes his face in her hands, and guides him back to her lips for another deep kiss.

"What else do you want?" Lucas asks as they pull slightly apart, their foreheads resting together.

"I want more," Spera says, Lucas pulls her to him in one swift motion, and lays her down in a cool patch of dew-soaked clover. He frames her head with his forearms, and peers down at her, his eyes roaming her face.

"I can't have this only today," he whispers. "I want this tomorrow. I want you to want this tomorrow, too."

"I do," Spera says. She wraps her hands under his arms and explores the muscles across his shoulders. "I promised Lenya I would tell her what this feels like." She bites her lip. "But I think I'm going to keep it for myself." She pulls Lucas down to her. He closes his eyes, and explores her mouth with his. My heart aches with grief and want. I want Lucas to call me Tanzy, to look at me and see me, and kiss me like that. But I also know their end is coming, and in this first happy moment, they have no idea.

"Asher, no. Wait, darling!" Lenya's frantic voice fractures the peace of morning, and makes all of us spin toward the top of the garden. "Don't go out there. I am keeping a surprise for you in the garden. Please don't ruin it," she begs.

"Asher," Spera says on a gasp.

"Lucas freezes. His jaw tightens as he tucks Spera behind him. She wraps a nervous hand around his arm and peers toward the blooming arbor.

Something too familiar about the way she's dressed makes me pause for a split second, paralyzed by the sensations of déjà vu. I scan the full length of Spera, and then down myself. We are wearing exactly the same thing, each of us standing barefoot in a simple white dress, loose black hair falling wild against our backs. To my horror, I realize there is no difference between us but the horseshoe charm resting above her mark—both of our hands are bare. Spera chose to take off her ring. Lenya couldn't send an early warning.

"Spera is here, I know she is. I can smell Lucas. What are they doing here?" Asher's voice carries across the enclosed courtyard as he storms down the sloped lawn. Lenya hangs back, watching his descent from the top of the hill.

"Asher, I am glad to see that your travels were safe," Spera calls, and steps from behind Lucas.

"What are you doing here?" Asher growls without slowing down.

"Lenya wanted to prove to me how superior her garden is to mine. I decided to come see for myself. I am reluctant to admit that she is right," Spera says, drifting farther from Lucas. Lenya cautiously makes her way toward them. "This place is beautiful," Spera adds. "I would be pleased to have one such as this."

"This place is worthless," Asher counters. His rage simmers to an angry pout. "I could create something truly spectacular for you, something equivalent to your beauty. This is no match."

"You still find her so much more beautiful than me? Even in commoner's attire?" Lenya interjects and crosses her jeweled arms. Asher's eyes flit to Lenya, temporarily distracted by her presence.

"I did not know you would be home or I would have made myself presentable," Spera says, following Lenya's diversion. "When you are gone there is no one to impress."

"You've never done anything to please me before," Asher muses.

"I find when you are pleased, you are more tolerable," Spera backtracks. Asher's face twists with rage. I see his eyes on the horseshoe charm around her neck. He moves within a hair's width of Spera in a single stride, snaps the leather cord from around her neck, and squeezes the silver charm in his big pale hand.

"There's only one way you came to possess this necklace again," he says, turning his stare to Lucas. "The necklace you claimed to have broken, you worthless thief. You know the punishment for stealing from me."

Asher stops midsentence, his white eyes moving from Lucas to Spera. He touches her swollen lips with his finger, and then moves to pluck a piece of grass from a twisted lock of her black hair. Disbelief flashes across his face, and the back of his hand makes contact with the side of Lucas's face.

"Are you courting my queen?" he spits, barely able to speak.

Before Lucas can right himself, Asher clamps a pale hand around his neck and lifts him from the ground. Lucas sputters, clawing at Asher's grip.

"Asher, please! Don't hurt him," Spera begs, and bows in front of Asher.

"Don't waste your breath, and don't you dare bow now," Asher snarls. His hand trembles with the amount of force he's using. Lucas's eyes roll back into his head.

"Asher, please! I'll do anything!" Spera begs.

"I can't watch this," I whisper to myself and start to turn away.

"You must. This is why you are here," my guide insists. She takes me by the shoulders and gives me a shake. "You must see this through. You are too close now to surrender. You will need to be brave in the days ahead."

I draw in a broken breath, and turn back to face the events unfolding.

"Asher, leave these two alone in their poor judgment," Lenya says, stepping to his side. "I can be enough for you. I want nothing more than to be your one true queen. If Spera is truly necessary to open the veil, then demand that she give you at least that measure of loyalty. Make her swear an oath that if she can open the veil, she will be your Vessel. It is in her best interest to deliver the Novus, is it not? Then we all get what we want."

"Spera, you do as I say or you will watch me gut him," Asher says evenly.

"Anything," Spera says, closing her eyes as a single tear slips out.

Asher tosses Lucas's limp body to the ground, and draws a small dagger from his leather belt. He holds the handle out for Spera.

"Make an oath to me. A blood vow that you will spill your blood on the door of the veil, and should it open, you will be my Vessel and deliver the Novus. Make this promise and I will allow Lucas to live despite the atrocities I have witnessed here."

"I have your word?" Spera asks, every inch of her rigid.

"You have my word," he says without moving his fiery stare from her face.

"Then you have mine." Spera plants her left hand into his open palm and shoves the dagger through both of their hands. Her eyes shine with pain and strength as their intermingled blood drips to the mossy ground.

Lucas begins to stir, moaning as he rolls to his side. The look on Lucas's bewildered face turns to agony.

"Seal your oath with a kiss. I desire a first taste of your lips, and only then will I consider Lucas's debt repaid," Asher wagers.

Spera closes her eyes and takes a measured breath before leaning into Asher. Watching them kiss is like seeing an explosion. I can hardly stomach it, but can't turn away. I can practically feel Asher's hot touch on my own skin as his hand moves from her jaw to her collarbone. Spera winces under his palm as he presses it flat against her mark.

"Don't!" Lucas rasps as he pushes up to his knees.

Spera throws her head back as a scream rips from her throat. Asher pulls the knife from their hands and watches her stumble backward, her mark glowing blood red. Before I can ask my guide what he's done to her, the three circles burst into black flames. Her charred skin peels back, curling against the heat as the exposed flesh smolders beneath.

"Asher," she manages to cry out, pain and disbelief making her voice crack.

"It's what you asked for," he states, his face emotionless. She flings herself face down into the tranquil pond. A scream of pure agony sounds from somewhere behind me as Spera meets the water, the surface erupting with fire. I stop breathing—shock and grief and terror making me too still to draw in air.

The luminous walls melting into the stream. The sour smell in the air. Whatever accelerant Asher uses to fuel the flames inside the fortress walls is cycled into the pool of water, and Spera's burning body disintegrates into ash.

ASHES TO ASHES

Lucas crawls to the fiery edge, and for a second I think he might reach through the flames to try to find her. A flash of silver sails past his face and drops to the ground by his outstretched hand. It's Spera's necklace.

"What were you thinking? Betraying me for a mortal girl," Asher growls at Lucas. Lucas doesn't acknowledge him, his wet eyes locked on the horseshoe charm. He plucks it from the earth and cradles it in his giant hands.

"Be grateful for my generosity. At least now you'll have something to remember her by while you wander this earth alone," Asher says menacingly. Lucas doesn't seem to hear him. He rises to his feet and staggers away from Spera's grave.

"Asher won't try to kill him?" I ask through jagged breaths.

"No. It is far greater a punishment to let him live without her."

He does have a reason to live. Me. I rush to his side, determined to let him know that Spera will return to him one day, even if in a different form. If there's any way I can give him any peace, I have to try. As I reach a hand for his trembling arm, he stands still and lifts his grieving face to the rising sun.

Dawn casts a single beam of light through the crystal ceiling and washes Lucas in its pale glow.

"I swear to you," he whispers through clenched teeth. "I swear if you let her return, I will guard her with my life. I will protect her from any threat. He will never possess her again. Please. Let me cross so I may pledge my life to keep her soul safe should she ever return." His voice cracks as he pleads with the sky.

I swallow the lump in my throat and step closer. Every inch of him shimmers. Then he's gone, his entire being dissolved into the beam of light. Frantically, I scan the ground for Spera's necklace, but it's gone too.

"At last, it is just you and me," Lenya says, and wraps an arm around Asher's bare back and reaches to tilt his face to hers.

I'm sure she's just trying to protect herself. Yet her affection for him feels deeply wrong. Spera's charred remains are still smoldering only a few feet from them.

"I told you I could be enough on my own," she croons. Asher slings her to the earth.

"You are not enough!" he barks. "Your blood cannot open the veil. You and I both know that. Spera is the only one that I need, the only rightful queen. She is my Vessel! Do not fool yourself into believing you are equal to her. I only let you live because you used to amuse me." He glares down at her stunned face before turning away from the burning lake and starting up the hill.

Lenya slowly climbs to her feet, the color drained from her porcelain skin.

"Asher, please! You are wrong!" she screams at his back. "The Novus can't return without me! Asher!" He doesn't turn around. Lenya clutches her hand to her stomach and stumbles backward as if she's been struck. Tears spill from her eyes. "The Novus can't return if you don't believe me. You were wrong, Asher. But you'll never hear it. My child . . . my child . . ." She gasps, choking on her tears. "This is how it ends, then. And you . . . you shall have neither of us," she whispers as she backs toward the fire, opens her arms wide, and lets herself fall.

"No!" I scream, rushing to the edge of the pond. The bright flames consume the pond. I can't see through them to the water beneath.

"No," I repeat, barely a whimper. I sit back on my heels and stare into the orange glow. My burning eyes sweep the length of the garden and lock onto Asher's retreating form.

"Asher!" I cry out, rage like I've never felt flooding through my veins.

"Tanzy, no," my guide pleads as she pulls on my elbow. I shake her off. I spring to my feet and race for my enemy, closing the distance in seconds.

"Tanzy, you are finished! You have seen Spera's path through. We must leave!" My guide's words barely register as I steel myself for what might happen when I touch him.

"Asher," I call out again and clamp my hand around his thick forearm. Shock passes through his eyes, and he spins toward the sensation of my touch. I reach my free hand back, ready to let it fly, when a grin spreads across his colorless face.

"He sees you! What have you done?" My guide gasps beside me and grabs my hand. I shove her to the ground, the instinct to fight back coursing unbridled through my body.

"Temper, temper, Spera," he says.

"I will find you and I will kill you!" I scream.

"Not if I find you first. Now I know you will return to me, and I know exactly what you will look like." His words force me back like a slap in the face.

"That's not what I meant to do," I whisper. He swaggers toward me.

"Yes, it is," he counters, his silvery white eyes rooting me to the spot. His hand whips around my head and his fingers tangle in my hair. With a low growl, he pulls my face to his and presses his lips hard against mine. Heat from his mouth takes over my body like a riptide. Spera's entire life flashes before my mind's eye as the current intensifies. I can't bear another moment. I shove my hands into his chest, gasping as he releases me.

A purple streak of lightning blazes down from the clear morning sky and crashes against the crystal ceiling, sending up a shower of sparks. The clear barrier begins to fracture in places as another bolt of lightning strikes the stone.

"I alone know your heart," he murmurs. His hand slides through my hair and claims my throat. He traces my pulse to the hollow above his mark. The red rings on my chest beg him closer. I can feel a warmth spreading along my collar. His eyes close with pleasure the moment the heat reaches his fingers. He flexes his palm above the brand, releasing me from his touch.

A splintering crescendo blows the heat away like wind to smoke. My hands instinctively lift to protect my head as a chunk of the crystal ceiling tumbles to the soft earth. The wall feeding into the pond collapses, and fire erupts from the rubble. My eyes dart back to Asher. Even though the world around us crumbles, his gaze on my face is steady and calm.

"I will always find you." His promise cuts through the deafening roar as the garden dissolves around us, and I am plunged into the deepest black I have ever known.

WIDE AWAKE

I can feel this new place before I can see it. It's bitter cold and thick. My skin feels like it's waking back up after being numb. All at once, my lungs begin to burn as they beg for oxygen.

Instinctively, I draw in a breath, but water shoots down my nose and floods into my open mouth. Frantic, I try to right myself but I can't tell which way is up. I kick out blindly. My toes scrape against a sandy bottom. I draw my legs underneath me, allowing myself to sink a little further, and then push off the floor hard, bursting through the surface.

The air is so cold, that each breath feels like swallowing a razor. Freezing rain pelts my face. Walls of earth and rock climb up each side of the river. Runoff pours over the high ledges, which tower at least forty feet above me. Dizzy and bewildered, I swim to the closest side and glance up. The hardwood trees, the reddish clay . . . I swear I smell manure. I'm back in the river at Wildwood

I begin to shake as a deep chill sets in. A scream of frustration escapes my clenched teeth. I have to find a way up.

"Think, Tanzy!" I berate myself.

Don't think. Just listen. Spera's raspy voice resonates within my reeling brain.

"Listen to what?" I call out. She doesn't respond. I will her to come back, but all I can hear is the steady hammer of my heart. *One-two, one-two, one-two.* I lock into the rhythm. Fear and indecision evaporate, leaving pure instinct.

Climb.

I move one hand at a time up the slippery cliff. Finally, my hand reaches forward instead of up. I dig my fingers into the solid ground and heave myself over the lip of the ravine. The rain pelting on my bare skin is an afterthought to the hard-won ascent. I am nearly delirious with exhaustion and relief. The prickly sensation of familiarity skitters across my skin like a spider. I'm alone on the ridge trail in the exact place where Dad and Teague fell to their deaths.

"Tanzy." Lucas's voice spins me around. He emerges from the trees a little way down the overgrown trail. I look back down the ravine and then to his beautiful, scarred face. I let out a grief-stricken sob and drop to my knees.

"Tanzy" he repeats, and sprints in my direction.

I close my eyes against the sight of him. I can't take any more. I want to go home. My heart weighs too much. What I've lost weighs too much.

Together, they blot out Lucas's face, and I collapse to the rain-soaked earth.

THE CALM BEFORE
THE STORM

S tale smoke taints the air. The smell triggers a memory like an electric shock. Suddenly Spera's face, twisted in agony, writhes in my groggy mind. I bolt upright. The soft something I'm sitting on shifts beneath my movement. A solid hand steadies my body and prevents me from toppling over, but the world around me keeps spinning. Where am I? Who's here with me? Why am I all wet?

My dimly lit surroundings come into focus a little at a time. Pressed pine walls. Rakes and pitchforks. Loose hay on the floor. A glowing safety lantern on a nail hook. Stacks of alfalfa in the far corner. I'm in the hay shed at Wildwood Farm.

"You're shaking, Spera," Lucas's smooth voice says from behind me. I jump at the sound and quickly scan the room for Spera. His eyes are on me.

"Is this real?" I whisper, wrapping my arms tightly around myself. The dress from my journey is soaked through with rain water and sticks to my skin.

"It is," he says and kneels beside the hay bales serving as my bed.

"Was that real? What I saw . . ." I drop my eyes and shudder. The memories are foggy and distant. Each time I reach for one it slides further back into the depths of darkness. The feeling of terrible loss lingers heavily in my chest. I press my palms onto either side of my head and grit my teeth against the onslaught of violence. The screams. The grief.

"Spera?" Lucas asks, his voice heavy with concern.

"I'm Tanzy. I'm not Spera."

"You are both," he offers.

"No, I'm not. She was brave and strong. She wasn't afraid of anything. I'm not any of those things."

"I think you are." Lucas sits beside me and offers the support of his arm. I lean into the warmth of him. The jagged scars that mar the side of his face are visible even in the dim light. "You're shaking." He shrugs out of his jacket and slips it around my shoulders. I rest against his chest. The sudden heat and the droning rain on the roof act as an elixir to my jumbled brain. I relax into his firm hold and slip a hand around his waist, startled that I have a memory of the curve of it. He presses his cheek against the top of my head. For the first time in a year, I fall asleep feeling like I'm right where I belong.

RED IN THE MORNING

I open my eyes. The hay shed is less magical in the gray light of dawn than it was overnight. Lucas is breathtaking as he stands guard at the slanted doorway. I silently push up from the bale of hay, reluctant to break the spell.

"You didn't sleep?" I ask softly, trying not to startle him. He turns to look at me, and a smile warms his tense face.

"No. I couldn't leave you unprotected."

His words are amazing and terrifying—amazing that he wants to protect me . . . terrifying that I need it. I climb to my feet and inspect myself. My dress is wrinkled but dry. So is my hair, which is coal black and as unruly as a yearling colt. I reach up to pluck a few strands of hay from the dark tangles. Vanessa's ring gleams on my finger. I'm glad to have it back, and to have her back. I can't wait to tell her what I saw.

My eyes move back to Lucas. Well, maybe I can wait a little while. I twist the ring upside down and push her from my mind. Vanessa, of all people, would understand.

"It's a beautiful morning. Come see," Lucas says. I tiptoe across the blanket of hay and take his hand in mine. Surprise softens the lines on his face.

"It's beautiful," I say. Above us, the early sky is streaked with burgundy. "Storm sky." I point to the horizon.

"Another one is coming," he muses.

"Is Asher?" The question slips out before I can stop it.

"I wish I knew. He's hard to predict and impossible to track. He's a man of many faces."

I shudder at the last memory of Spera's life.

"He saw me. He talked to me. It's my fault that he found me. If I hadn't been so stupid . . ."

Lucas lets out a little chuckle.

"That decision you made in the garden was Spera through and through," he says, his eyes softening at the memory. You showed your face to Asher, but you also showed me."

"You disappeared. How did you see what happened in the garden?" I ask.

"I traveled behind the veil so Asher would have a harder time killing me if he'd decided to try. The veil works like a one-sided mirror. We can see through, but mortals can't," he explains.

"I didn't learn much about the veil itself or how to open it."

"You are in good company there," Lucas starts. "No one is absolutely certain how to open it. We know opening it will bring the Vessel immortal life, and sealing it forever will kill the Vessel. Otherwise, it's a mystery. A handful of powerful Unseens hid parts of the ritual within six different riddles. They cast them all around the world. Asher and his advisor have been hunting for them for thousands of years."

"Raffin," I say, recalling the gray cloaked figure. Lucas nods.

"Asher still doesn't know everything about how to open the veil, but he may know enough by now. And if he does, he won't stop hunting you. I would give my own life if it meant you were spared this choice. That's why I tried to keep you hidden. I realize now that you were created to make this choice, in this lifetime or the next," Lucas says. "Asher will find you, and it will begin again. This choice will always lie in your hands. Asher will not stop until he has found the door in the veil and forced you to make a choice."

If Asher took me to the door this moment, what would I do? What if I'm not ready? What if . . . Vanessa's frantic voice splinters through the thoughts flooding my mind: *Don't! Please, David, don't do this.*

I gasp, clamping my hands on my ears as my head fills with her screams.

Tanzy, help me! If you can hear me. Something is wrong with David. He's lost his mind. He's coming after me. I think . . . I think he might be Unseen! Tanzy!

"It's Vanessa!" I cry out.

"Where?" Lucas asks, looking around.

"Something's happening. Something bad." I press my hands into my eyes to try to relieve the waves of pain. "I think Dr. Andrews . . . Asher is coming after her!"

"Where did you get this ring?" Lucas asks, snatching my hand. The dome swirls blood a fiery gold. I jerk it away from him, stunned by the roughness in his touch.

"Lucas, I have to go. I don't think I have much time."

"It's imperative you tell me who gave you that ring," he demands.

"Vanessa gave it to me, and now I have to get to her," I beg softly. I turn east toward the rising sun and Vanessa's home.

"Tanzy, please wait," Lucas says as he races to catch up with me.

"I'm sorry. I have to do this. She's in trouble. I've already watched her die once. I can't see it again. I know you understand that."

He stops in his tracks. His expression is like nothing I've ever seen before. It almost makes me wait, but I can't let anything happen to Vanessa. I'll never be able to forgive myself if I get there too late.

"Meet me there," I call over my shoulder, and start running as fast as I can.

LOVE AND LIES

My feet pound into the grass, propelling me forward in giant strides. Oxygen fills and exits my lungs to a rhythm I recognize—the same tempo that drummed against the dark of night when Asher's beasts chased down Harbor and me. Now Asher might have Vanessa cornered. He won't win this time. The black horse's blood that saved Spera now flows through my veins and feeds my muscles. His speed. His strength. His heart.

I'm coming for you, Asher.

I close my eyes and allow the strength to guide me in the right direction. The currents of air act like a road map. I shift a few degrees north and push myself faster. Wildwood's acreage is behind me in less than a minute.

Hang on, Vanessa.

She answers me immediately, calling out for me again in terror. I leap forward, demanding even more of my burning legs. Time and distance blur. The terrain becomes steeper as I finally reach Keswick. Rain falls and makes the ground slick. The wet stones give off a warm earthiness and I use the scent like a beacon to guide me the rest of the way. Vanessa? I call out to her. Nothing comes back.

I crest a near vertical hill and almost collide with a logging truck that makes its way down the road. I throw myself into the wet grass to keep from being struck. Around the bend, I spy the black truck still parked on the shoulder. *Vanessa's road.* Relief washes cool over my sweaty skin. The hardest part is still ahead. Am I strong enough to stop Asher? Am I willing to end a life again if I have no other choice?

My mind fills with Spera's brutal final moments. Lenya's suicide. The torture Lucas still carries in his eyes. A new resolve condenses my thoughts into one goal: changing history. I will do whatever it takes to keep Vanessa alive.

I leap across the street, glide over the black-board fencing and race blindly for the summit of Vanessa's property. The face of the gigantic house is completely still, covered in a thick curtain of rain. Neither life nor light peeks from its long windows. The statue in the fire fountain is whirling faster than I remember, liquid flames spilling over the edge and leaving trails of steam on the driveway.

The driver's side door of David's car hangs open. I swallow the dread climbing my throat, and silently move to the French doors. They're flung wide and reckless to each side. Tiny, sparkling shards of glass litter the foyer. They're under my feet too, but there's no pain. The only thing I can feel is a gut-wrenching need to get between Vanessa and David.

I step further into the hushed entryway, waiting for a sign. My breath echoes off each polished surface, and my mind creates silhouettes in every towering shadow. *Where are you, Vanessa?*

I close my eyes and let my other senses take over. The metallic scent of blood stains the air. I realize the scent is coming from upstairs. My bare feet meet the jade stairs without making a sound. I pause at the top and flatten my back against the marbled wall. An anguished moan shatters the thick quiet. I chase it down the hall and to a closed door it came through. I wrap my fingers around the curved handle and feel the hint of resistance by the engaged lock. I snap the handle from the door and shove the thick wood completely out of its frame. As it falls to the ground, I close my hands into ready fists and prepare to defend Vanessa.

David's eyes snap to the broken door. Tears streak his face. His hands shake, hovering over Vanessa's still form.

"What did you do?" I cry out, moving toward Vanessa. David rises and blocks her body from my view. "Vanessa!" I shout.

She lets out a low whimper and rolls onto her back, helpless and exposed. My pulse roars within me, drowning out the piercing silence in the dark room. Every movement slows down. This feeling is familiar—the adrenaline rush in the woods, my blood responding to the worst kind of threats. He opens his mouth to speak, but I've seen enough. I know exactly what it feels like to watch her die, and I refuse to watch it happen again.

He stiffens as I move toward him. His jaw tenses. I can hear the sound of his teeth grinding together nearly as loud as the thunder outside.

"I am going to give you one chance to get away from her," I order.

"Over my dead body," he snarls, and draws a fist back in warning. It's all the permission I need. I close the distance between us in a single stride and pause for a fraction of a second, letting his punch pass by the left side of my face. He stumbles forward, thrown off balance. My first strike lands squarely on his chin, throwing him backward. He slams against the wall, and air rushes from his lungs. Vanessa stirs on the floor, drawing my gaze. Her nose is bleeding. The side of her face is already darkening with bruises.

"One chance," I reiterate, my eyes moving from her to David as he staggers to his feet.

"I am not leaving here without her," he says.

"Then you're not leaving," I warn. He lets out a grunt of painful effort and charges again. I drop back as my leg coils at my hip, and then explodes forward. His sternum gives way under the force of my bare foot. He cries out in agony and drops to the ground, clutching his chest.

"Why are you doing this?" he asks through ragged breaths. "I only wanted to help you."

"You don't want to help me," I say, near tears. "She's my friend. More than that. A sister. You aren't going to hurt either one of us anymore."

His bewildered stare moves to Vanessa as he crawls toward her. He closes his fist around a piece of paper by her side. Before he can get any closer, I snatch the collar of his shirt and fling him away from her. He lands on his back in a heap.

"Last chance," I growl. He doesn't move for the door. A human would have run. A human should be dead.

"I found her like this," he mumbles, his eyes rolling in their sockets as he tries to focus.

"Liar!" The memories of Spera and Lenya's horrible deaths flood my mind. I grab his throat and pin him to the ground. "Show me! Show me your true face, Asher. I know you're in there," I demand.

Instead, he brings his hand to my face, still clenched around the piece of paper. I read the first sentence, and my world goes still.

Darling, Tanzy Hightower is very dangerous and I have reason to believe she wants me dead.

The rest of Vanessa's perfect script blurs on the page. My eyes move to Dr. Andrews's desperate face as my hands fly open. He tries to force a word out of his mouth, but blood trickles out instead. His wet fingers wrap around my forearm as the light fades from his frantic stare. His hand and his head drop back together as a weak, last breath leaves his lips.

A high-pitched hum fills my ears and tunnels into my brain. I step back on trembling legs. He's dead. Dr. David Andrews is dead. I killed him with my bare hands. He helped save my life, and I just ended his. Behind me, someone giggles. Vanessa sits up and wipes the blood from her face.

"Vanessa?" I whisper.

"Tanzy!" Lucas's voice spins me around again, but he's not there. The air crackles and distorts. A living shadow darkens the broken doorway and then solidifies, arms and legs materializing from the quivering mass. His scarred face finally emerges. My eyes follow his shocked gaze to the blood soaking my hands.

"What have you done?" he asks, his face the picture of panic. Neither my mind nor my mouth can form a response.

"Don't act so surprised, Brother," Asher answers, emerging from the shadows of the far corner. He brushes past Lucas and moves in my direction. "We made her for this, after all. She was born for this. My queen." He traces a perfect circle in the air between us, leaving a smoky ring in its wake. The middle circle scar on my chest erupts with heat, glowing in the dark room. I gasp with the shock of unexpected pain.

Asher smiles. "Two down. One to go."

SURROUNDED

I stand in the center of the room, panting and disbelieving, surrounded by Lucas, Asher, and Vanessa, who are all alive and well. Less than a foot from me lies Dr. Andrews. He isn't dissolving into the elemental beads of an Unseen. The blood leaking from his face has slowed to a trickle. His chest is still for too long. He's gone. *I killed him. I killed him.*

"Well, this is exciting," a familiar voice purrs from the doorway. I turn, and the world shifts in slow motion. Dana is standing in the open door. I blink. She's still there. What is she doing here? I hide my blood-soaked hands behind my back.

"Nice work, Tanzy," Dana says. "I told you she works best under pressure," she continues, winking at Asher. She walks past me, pulls Vanessa to her feet.

"Dana," I say, barely a whisper. "How could you?" Even though we're standing in a room, my entire being feels like it's underwater, weighted down below the surface, being pummeled from all sides by different currents, flipping end over end. I don't know which way is up. I'm scared to reach out for something solid for fear it will come loose and crush me.

Lucas makes a move toward me but Asher stops him with a hand and backs him against the wall. Lucas's voice is yelling words like "run" and "get out," but they blur into the buzzing noise that hasn't left my ears.

This can't be happening. This isn't real. Wake up, Tanzy. Wake up!

"Spera's efficiency is clearly transcendental. As is her surly temper. Turns out it can be put to good use though," Asher muses, smiling at the body of Vanessa's husband.

"Who knew?" Dana quips.

"I knew," Vanessa smirks. Her ivory face twists with such fierce resentment I hardly recognize her. I expect to feel another stab of pain inside, but there's nothing solid left to cut.

"You set me up," I cry out, trembling with shock and betrayal

"Duh," Vanessa says, smirking. "But as you can see, I had plenty of help." The room spins, and I catch myself on the wall.

"God, you're pathetic. This, Asher? This is what you've waited a thousand years for? You think she's your Vessel? You have to be kidding me," Vanessa sneers.

"Vanessa," I plead. "He's a monster. He's just using you."

"Right. I'm just the stand-in. The runner-up. Your substitute. Maybe the first time around, but not anymore," she says through her teeth.

"Listen to yourself! You don't even know what you're talking about. He killed Spera. He will kill me, and he'll kill you too," I shout.

Her eyes darken as they move to Asher. I follow her gaze, my throat constricting as I take in the sight of Lucas trapped in Asher's hand. His mouth is still, but his eyes beg me to run. To leave him behind. *That's not going to happen.*

"You made it so easy," Vanessa says, pacing. She stops and turns to face me. "Didn't anyone ever tell you not to ride alone?" she says, her voice dropping to a menacing note. She lets out a cackle, and then slides an arm around Dana's waist. "Have you put it together yet or do I get to tell you about the fun we had chasing you through the woods that night? Although I have to hand it to you, you put up one hell of a fight. That horse of yours has quite a kick to her. I found her, by the way. Don't worry. I'll take good care of her. I've always wanted a horse."

The memory the first time we met in the hospital is crystal clear in my mind. The bruises and wounds along her collar bone, the marks she'd denied were there. They made a perfect horseshoe.

"Don't you just love surprises?" Vanessa smirks as she brings a finger to her lips and turns to look at Lucas. "Has he told you how much he helped me?"

"He warned me about you from the beginning. He would never help you!" I cling to this truth, the only thing I know for sure. The only thing I have left. It's always been Lucas.

"Oh, yes he did," she says again. Vanessa reaches up and pets his scarred cheek twice before giving him a sharp slap.

"Why don't you see for yourself?" Vanessa taunts and grabs my hand. Instantly we are on the seldom-traveled trail at Wildwood Farm, moving along the lip of the ravine.

"You don't have to show me this. I relive it every day," I say. However, the girl who watched the river for hours waiting for her father to surface also wants to believe Vanessa might still be on my side. Was she tricking Asher by being so unkind just like Lenya had been? Was she trying to show me a way to save us all from him? I grip my fingers around hers and stare her in the face, watching closely for any sign.

"This is how I remember that day. The day everything began. See it through my eyes, Tanzy," she says. The view shifts down the trail forty or fifty feet, staring head on at Teague and my father as they lead the way down the Ridge trail. My eighteen-year-old self follows close behind on Harbor. She stares into the trees to her right, startled by the black apparition.

The view begins to zoom in as Vanessa slinks closer. The shapeless static jumps to the ground in front of Teague. He rears to his full height, and then bolts forward. The sound of Teague gathering a stride before the lip of the ravine makes me instinctively close my eyes, but the memory plays on. He jumps, straining for the other side that he'll never reach.

My younger self tumbles from Harbor's galloping retreat, and runs toward the place they went over. Vanessa's perspective lowers as she crouches lower in the underbrush. She's not watching my younger self. She's watching the quivering dark still visible on the trail. A human form begins to take shape in the shadow. Legs, arms, and a head emerge and solidify. The features sharpen and color fills in the void. As his face turns down the trail to Vanessa, my heart goes still. Lucas. He takes one more step toward my grieving, eighteen-year-old self before slipping back into the cover of the trees.

I stagger away from Vanessa and stare at Lucas, mouth agape. Lucas's eyes search my face as my knees surrender to the crushing weight of this betrayal.

"You killed my father." It comes out in a whisper, but the words echo in my brain, banging from side to side like a battering ram.

"He did," Vanessa says with a pout. "What are you going to do about it?"

"You can do whatever you want to him, Spera. I'll be happy to hold him for you. It would be so fitting for Lucas to serve as your third kill," Asher says.

There's no one, *no one*. I am alone in this crowded room. Maris was right. I'm on a chessboard, but I am the lone black pawn in a sea of white. The king is ahead of me. The queen within a single turn of knocking me off the board. I have no one left to lose. If only I could run to the door of the veil and seal it, so Asher and the Unseens will leave me and my world alone, forever. Prevent Lucas from tricking me into falling for him in another life—*my life*. Keep Vanessa from gaining my trust, only to thrust a knife into my heart. But I can't imagine taking a single step. The weight of these truths is too heavy. The sound of someone sobbing works its way through my thoughts and pulls me to the surface. It's me. I'm crying.

"Asher, we don't need her. I have enough of what we need from her. We have hundreds of horses to match. We even have Harbor. I think we should start with her. What do you think, Tanzy?" Vanessa pauses, no doubt anticipating a reaction.

Harbor. She has my horse. A spark of fight reignites within me, but I'm outnumbered. I have no idea how to find her. How can I save her when I may not leave this room alive? She's as good as dead, and it's my fault. I can't lift my eyes from the floor, each second heavier with deceit and failure than the last.

"Tanzy can't possibly be the true Vessel. The Vessel is a fighter, a warrior. She will have to guard your child against every attack. Do you see her defending your child any time soon? I am enough. We will find a way without her," Vanessa says, glaring. She's right. I have failed everything I've ever loved. I don't have anything left to fight for.

Yes, you do, a familiar voice skirts the farthest regions of my mind, drowning out whatever else Vanessa is saying.

Spera?

We are one.

It's too much. I don't know what to do.

You don't have to know. Today is not important. You must live to fight. You are the final piece. You are the only piece. This is all for you, because of you. You are enough to fight for.

Understanding swells within me. All of these lies and tricks and effort—they are for me. A thousand years of waiting and scheming. Incredible, impossible measures taken on both sides to keep me hidden and to draw me out. They need me. No matter the cost of the past. No matter the price of what lies ahead, I am the only piece.

Vanessa says something to Asher, her perfect face now little more than that of a stranger. I don't hear her words. I only hear the steady rhythm of her pulse, see it rising and falling along her neck. Blood courses through her veins like that of a mortal. I don't know if she is Seen or Unseen, but she's on my side of the veil . . . She can die.

I spring to my feet, snatch her by the throat, and slam her against the wall. Dana moves toward us, but I stop her with a look. Asher can't attack me as he still has Lucas captive in his hand. No one can help Vanessa now.

I bring my mouth so close to her ear that it feathers across her skin.

"You're wrong, Vanessa. Asher doesn't *need* you. He doesn't *want* you. He doesn't *think* about you. He thinks about *me*. Only me. Your blood won't open the veil. You are not the Vessel or the true queen. I am. We both know that. We've always known that. I am the one and only piece," I say as I stare into her fearful eyes. "I have only just begun to fight. What you will be, is my third kill. Not today. Maybe not tomorrow, but I am coming for you. Make no mistake of it."

I run a steady finger down her cheek and pull away. I keep my gaze locked on hers. Their jade centers are fractured with doubt and coated in glistening pain.

"Be seeing you," I murmur, menacingly. My eyes dart to Lucas for a moment. I see the pain and regret in his eyes, too. Without another word, I leap across the room and crash through the glass doors. The shattering glass announces the final break as I leave them all behind.

COLLIDE

Landing in a puddle of broken glass and rain water doesn't hurt. I want it to. I want to feel something I can identify. This overwhelming crushing numbness has no name, no limit, and it's pushing harder by the second.

Dana. Vanessa . . . God, Vanessa . . . and . . . I can't bring myself to think his name. I force thoughts of him aside and race across the open lawn to the cover of the trees. I glance back to the dark house only once, but no one has followed me out.

"You sure do know how to make one hell of an entrance. Well, exit, I guess," a girl's voice says from behind me. I whirl to face her, drawing my hands into a defensive position.

"Whoa, no need. You can put those fists away," the girl says and steps from a cloak of dark shadows. Her pale skin and white, blonde hair make her look like a ghost in the misty grey fog, despite the hot pink tinted tips of her hair. The weak light filtering through the canopy of limbs stripes her face. As she steps closer, she nervously tugs at a piece of her chin-length hair. Her other hand clutches the faded strap of a well-worn messenger bag slung across the front of her black sweatshirt.

"Who are you? And don't even think about answering me with some sort of question or riddle. I'm all done with that crap," I snap.

"My name is Jayce," she says, hands in the air. "I'm riddle-free and I'm on your side," she insists.

"I'm on no one's side," I say and pass her to move deeper into the forest.

"You do have a side, Tanzy, and we need you," she says, following close behind. "You think you're the only one? You're not. There are hundreds just like you, who have lost what you've lost. It's not just Asher you're up against. There's a war coming from two sides. You can't escape the squeeze on your own. There's a way out of this, but it starts with trusting me," she says.

"Where have I heard that before," I scoff with a shake of my head. I start to run ahead, wanting to leave all of this behind.

"Fine! Make a go of it on your own. They'll find you one way or another. If it were me, I'd want to bring just as many people to that fight as they will," she shouts after me.

I pause and glance at her over my shoulder. If I'm really going to try to take on Asher and Vanessa on my own, I'd be foolish not to see what Jayce knows before I leave.

"There are others like us? How many?" I ask, turning back to her.

"I live with six others, but there's no way to know a total number for sure." She jumps at a sound of something rustling in the trees.

"Where's Lucas? I saw him go in the house. Asher didn't kill him, did he?"

"No," I say and look down.

"He's still alive and you left him in there?" Her pale eyes widen. "I didn't see that coming."

"He's just as bad as Asher. Maybe worse. He killed my father," I practically shout angrily.

"Look, I'm not in Lucas's fan club. As far as the I'll-take-a-bullet-for-you types go, he's not great, but he's not a killer. Not anymore at least. So leave him if you want, it doesn't matter to me. But you might want to get your facts straight," she counters.

"The only fact I need to know is that he's the reason my dad is dead."

"That's only partly true," Jayce says, raising her brow. "You saw what happened between Spera and Lucas in Spera's life, right? He pledged his loyalty to the Vessel, to keep her safe, no matter the cost." She takes a few steps in my direction.

"That day on the trail, Vanessa was waiting for you. Lucas jumped onto the path to try to stop you guys from going any farther. I can't imagine he knew your dad would die because of it. It's not like he drove your dad's horse off the ledge. And dude, not to be cold, but your dad should've jumped off. If I'm on a horse and it's running out of ground, I bail. But I wouldn't get on a horse to begin with, so that's really neither here nor there," Jayce says, shrugging. Rage bursts inside of me, funneling heat to my limbs and hate to my heart.

"You don't get to talk about my father," I roar, storming toward her. Then I freeze in my tracks.

"How do you know about that?" I demand, tears rolling from my eyes.

"We all do. It was the beginning for all of us. Don't you get it yet? Lucas was trying to keep his world, this war, Asher, all of it . . . away from you. He wanted you to just go on being a regular girl. Even if it meant without him." Her words sink in like heavy stones. Lucas had been so desperate to prevent all of this from happening from the very beginning, no matter the cost.

"Maybe we can save him," I whisper, tugging gently at the braided grass bracelet he had tied around my wrist just a few hours ago.

"No way, Chica," Jayce says, and shakes her head. "Not now, anyway. We have to have the element of surprise on our side to get all of us in and out of there in one piece."

"What if they kill him?" I can barely get the words out.

"They won't. He's the perfect bait," she answers with a shrug. "They'll keep him alive as long as you're alive."

I can't stomach the idea of leaving Lucas with Asher, but Jayce is right. There's no way I could get him out right now.

"Let's roll, Tanz. We don't have time to waste," Jayce says.

"Don't call me that like you know me. You don't know me, and this is not a 'we,'" I snap, gesturing between us.

"Oh, I know you. I know the heart of you," she says. Her fingers shake as she reaches toward the middle circle of my mark. "You made it quick. You didn't have to." She lets her hand drop, and steps ahead of me.

With a start, I realize the faint stripes across her face and hands don't change with the light as she moves. I recognize the scratches from the girl Spera fought. Cavilla. Cavilla's soul and the tiger's blood, have found a new home in Jayce. This girl is the same girl I watched Spera kill. She's the girl Spera prayed for and now her new incarnation has come to help me. The humility and strength of her soul becomes immediately apparent.

"It's Tanzy," I say, and fall in step beside her. "Please don't call me anything else."

"You got it," she says with a shrug.

"How do you know all of this?" I ask, suspicious. She levels her blue eyes at mine.

"Because I know what it is to be Asher's queen. I know the power, and I know the price."

"How were you his queen? You died." I almost regret asking the question, but the time for tact has long since passed.

"Don't you mean you killed me?" She delivers the correction like a punch line. "Spera's life wasn't my first rodeo and it wasn't Vanessa's either. We had been through Asher's process countless times before Spera's generation. When you're a queen, you have access to the oracles, and they can show you any previous life."

"Vanessa said she had never seen her past life," I mutter.

"Haven't you figured it out yet, Tanzy? Vanessa talks a lot, and most of it is a load of crap," Jayce quips. "Lenya played Spera like a fiddle. From the sounds of it, Vanessa played you too, big time."

"What's to say you're not playing me now?" I ask bluntly.

"I guess you're just going to have to trust me. The way I see it, you're running low on options and information. I can give you both," she offers.

"What else do you know then?" I press.

"That no one is strong enough to stop Asher on her own," she says. "Not even you."

"And you really think the two of us are enough?" Agitation snips the end from each word.

"It's not just us. We have Hope on our side."

"That's beautiful. Really. Maybe if the world doesn't end you can go into business making warm and fuzzy cards for warm and fuzzy people," I snap.

"I'm not talking about warm and fuzzy feelings of hope, Tanzy. I'm talking about the name Hope. That doesn't ring a bell for you?"

"I only know one person by that name and trust me, there's no way you're talking about the same person." I slam the door closed on the subject of my mother as fast as I can. I'm barely holding it together as it is. All that's left of me is bound together by rage, and fueled with the guilt of leaving Lucas behind.

"You really don't know anything, do you?" she says with a growl and balls her fists at her sides. Part of me wishes she'd throw a punch already, and give me a place to release the adrenaline pouring unchecked into my veins. A bigger part of me wants to leave her behind. I turn away from her and start down the hillside.

"No, she doesn't Jayce. I never wanted her to have to know about any of this. I had to give her a chance at a normal life," a new, haunting voice answers Jayce, and stops me in my tracks. That can't possibly be who it sounds like. As she steps out of the trees, there's no denying it. Her features are the same. I could still trace them with my eyes closed. But she's not the same. Not at all. Her eyes are clear and bright. The lines of grief are gone, her pale skin as smooth as marble.

It takes everything I have left to summon the courage to speak a single word.

"Mom?"

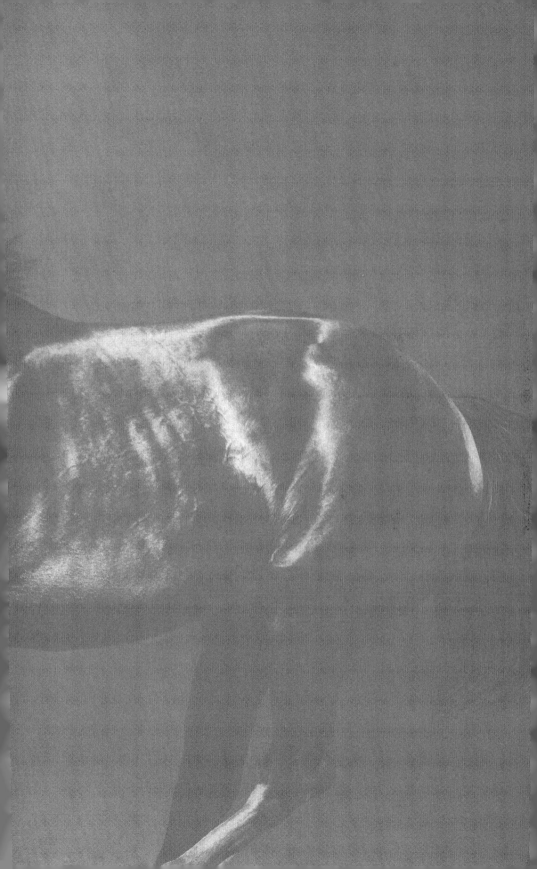

ABOUT THE AUTHOR

Young-adult author. Equine professional. Southern gal. Especially fond of family, sunlight, and cookie dough.

I wrote my first book in seventh grade, filling one hundred and four pages of a black and white Mead notebook. Back then I lived for two things: horses and R.L. Stine books. Fast forward nearly twenty years, and I still work with horses, and hoard books like most women my age collect shoes. Its amazing how much changes... and how much stays the same.

Tanzy Needs You!

Did you enjoy Wildwood? Reviews keep books alive . . .
The Unseen world will collapse unless you leave your review
on either GoodReads or the digital storefront of your
choosing.

Tanzy and Lucas thank you. . .

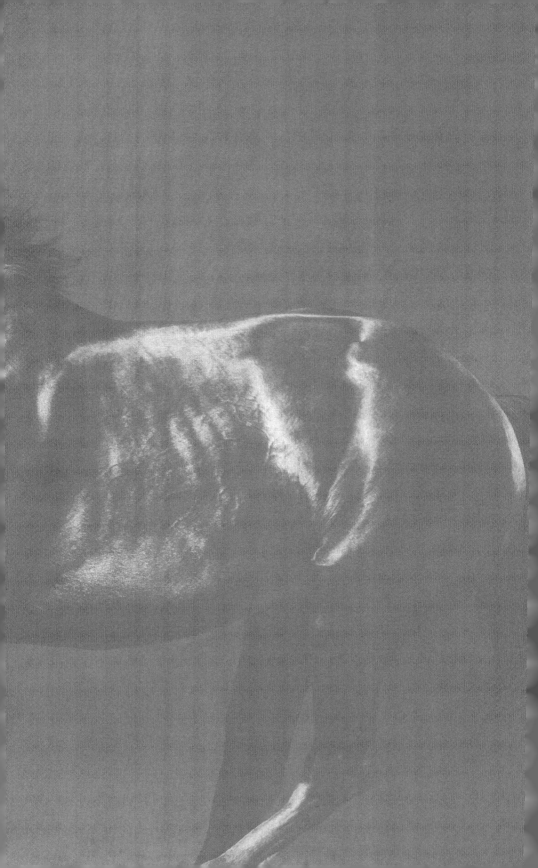

Made in the USA
Columbia, SC
26 December 2017